HOL

THE DEVIL'S GAME

ALSO BY DAVID HOLLAND

The Devil's Acre
The Devil in Bellminster
Murcheston: The Wolf's Tale

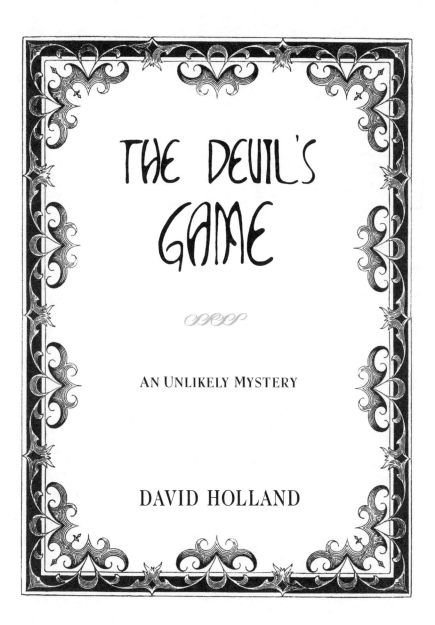

THE DEVIL'S GAME

AN UNLIKELY MYSTERY

DAVID HOLLAND

THOMAS DUNNE BOOKS
ST. MARTIN'S MINOTAUR ✹ NEW YORK

THOMAS DUNNE BOOKS.
An imprint of St. Martin's Press.

www.minotaurbooks.com

ISBN 0-312-34077-X
EAN 978-0-312-34077-3

First Edition: December 2005

10 9 8 7 6 5 4 3 2 1

To Jeff and Donna and Jeffrey,
our country friends

THE DEVIL'S GAME

CHAPTER I
SMOKE AND ASH

Simon Curdle, MP, gurgled and chuffed and roused himself to near consciousness, raising his head an inch above the cluttered desktop. He passed a probing finger into the corner of his lips, stopping a thin stream of spittle, and blinked through a virulent haze that made his eyes burn. Surveying the landscape about him like a general inspecting his troops after the carnage of battle, he eyed through squinting lids the wads of crushed paper and dripping pens, the splattered globs of ink from the crusty inkwell and the empty brandy bottle lying on its side like a field cannon.

Clutching at the sheet nearest at hand, he read in a thick, mumbling voice, "Here in the hallowed halls of Westminster." Simon Curdle chuckled and blinked some more and rubbed his smarting eyes. "Haloed walls of Blestminster," he tried, and, finding the sound amusing, he chuckled again.

It was October. Parliament was long recessed, but as a Member of many years' standing Simon Curdle enjoyed the liberty of the Commons, and he often used the dark studies and dusty library in the transaction of his personal business, thus saving himself the expense of offices and clerks, paper and ink and coals. Curdle's business, when Parliament was not in session, consisted of drafting letters. With the determined display of conscientious vigor peculiar to politicians, he would study all the latest reports published by the various ministries, hold close conference with whichever of his honorable colleagues was willing to speak to him, decide for himself which bills were likely to come before Commons in the next session, and then write lengthy letters to all the moneyed interests involved, soliciting "emoluments to stem the pernicious tide of reform." That, or "emoluments to undam the nurturing waters of reform." Either way, he preferred the word *emoluments* to *contributions.* It sounded noble, he thought.

He sat up and coughed, rubbed his eyes and coughed again, a wet, rattling hack. Simon Curdle was a spare, lean, hungry-looking man, eager and anxious to please, with a domed forehead circled by a laurel of gray hair. His skin was pale, though mottled with crimson flecks that centered about the red of his nose like punctuation on a page. He passed a sweaty palm over his face to dispel the haze that seemed to gather there, yet his blurred vision persisted. He waved his hand in the air, but seemed only to swirl the fog before him. "Ah well," he considered diplomatically, and repeated one of his favorite apothegms: Any inconvenience that cannot be got around, can certainly be ignored.

Curdle returned his eye to the letter. Should this be a conservative or a liberal appeal? he wondered. Not that it mattered materially. A quid knows no party. Yet Curdle was wise enough to recognize (as who would not?) that the liberal tide was ebbing. It's true, he recalled, the Tories took a ferocious drubbing in the general election of '32, the Year of the Great Reform. All those eager hands raised for the first time, ready to vote the Whig ballot from sheer gratitude. But reform stumbled on its own success. The liberal cause had faltered, and the Tories were readying a call for new elections.

What a lively dance, Simon Curdle laughed to himself. Still, while a wise man saw that reform had reached its furthest boundaries, hope for reform lived on. All those liberal pounds ready now, two years later, to spur on the great cause. Yes, he nodded silently, smoothing the page across the desk and taking up a pen, a liberal appeal. Liberality is a liberal virtue, after all, and he laughed again at his own drollery.

Of course, when Simon Curdle's vote was tallied, notched by the recording secretary onto one of the tens of thousands of wooden planks that had been used to measure the people's will in Parliament these centuries past, it could be counted on to fall squarely with the Tories. His was a conservative borough, an ancient and reliable borough where things rarely changed and never easily. Yet, despite his voting record, Simon Curdle prided himself on being open-minded. Every farthing won a hearing with him. Each shilling he received was paid for with a knowing word whispered into an appropriate ear, Whig or Tory. In the end, why should his opinion dictate his vote, he reasoned, or his vote move his opinion? What was a man's vote, really? A hand raised in assembly, an "aye" or "nay" breathed in a moment, a mark scratched on a wooden plank.

Simon Curdle coughed again, rubbed his stinging eyes again, and glared menacingly at the coals smoldering in the hearth. "Miserable old pile of stone," he grumbled in the silence, his spirits suddenly turning morbid. The chimneys always smoked in Westminster Palace. And today the furnaces below were bellowing like rapacious dragons, incinerating the old wooden tallies at long last, mountains of votes allowed to pile up over centuries, the physical embodiment of laws long forgotten turned now to smoke and ash. He rose and tottered toward the hearth to rattle a poker up the flue, but the cloud that hung in the room had grown so thick that he could only grope blindly about, coughing and gasping with every breath.

Finding his way to the wall, he bent down and traced a path along the outskirts of the study. He was looking for the door, to open it and air the place out. He wandered far enough on his way that he suspected the door had gone missing, was put aside to await the coming session, and for some reason this fanciful notion caught hold of his imagination until a very real terror crept through him. With one hand brushing feverishly across the wainscoting ahead, he reached up with the other to his throat, loosened with fumbling fingers the already loose cravat as he coughed and rasped some more. At last, his hand fell upon the metal latch of the door, but instantly recoiled. The handle was hot!

"Damn chimneys," he muttered, and not pausing to wonder further at this, frantic now and desperate for air, Simon Curdle took a kerchief from his pocket, wrapped it hurriedly about his palm, and took hold of the latch.

The door would not give! Someone was holding it closed on the other side! He could feel the other fellow tugging! Not one man, either, but a party of men! They roared to one another, he heard them, the hoarse confusion of many voices. Simon Curdle gripped the latch again, with both hands now, determined to make his way out of his stifling prison, and leaning back with all his weight, gave a furious pull.

The world exploded in flame. The air was flame. The walls were lapped in writhing tides of heat. The floor was swept by tongues, a field of flame. Simon Curdle gasped and the breath he sucked into his lungs was fire. He shrieked and fire left his lips. His clothing wrapped about him in tattered shreds of agony as he sank to his knees, and before his head crashed to the floor Simon Curdle was dead.

Outside was night. An orange river crept under an orange sky. Black columns and towers of flame twisted and whorled out of the city's heart, knitting earth to heaven. The thick of midnight lay at bay like a dark army surrounding a fiery host, and London was alive as only London lived. Boats, skiffs, and wherries pocked the golden surface of the Thames, shadowy arms working idly to hold place against the current, to keep in sight these showy wonders of hell. Gawkers crowded the lanes and streets, the riverbanks and the great Westminster bridge, while whores and cutpurses strolled among the crowd, earning their day's breath the only way they knew. Perched atop a light post on the bridge, teetering above the common throng with one leg wrapped about the iron form to free both arms, both hands, a man in coarse trousers and a nightshirt held a sketch pad and pencil in his fingers, feverishly traced the swirling lines, captured the shape of shapelessness, the form of what was formless, to fire his imagination later into art.

Parliament was burning, the Palace of Westminster, the world of Pitt and Cromwell and Thomas More, the heart of government, if not its soul. The wooden tallies that had been set to burn after centuries of collecting in closets and cellars now burned too well, and the furnaces had given way, fire escaping up and out and through the palace, engulfing Commons and Lords together on the banks of the great river Thames. And as men and women stood by now and watched, and while many wondered what such a catastrophe might mean in these troubled times, and while many more whispered to themselves and to their neighbors and cast their eyes up to the dark sheet of heaven, not a single thought was spared for Simon Curdle. Not a soul knew to mourn the Member for Bellminster.

CHAPTER II
CONTESTED FIELDS

*H*e's dead? . . . Dead?"

The word stumbled over the mayor's lips and was ignored, and Tuckworth felt a quick pang of sympathy for the poor, befuddled man. This was not the first such meeting the dean had attended in Bellminster, important gentlemen gathered in an important place to discuss a death. He breathed deeply and tried another calming sip of tea. Were such calamities truly more prevalent these days, he wondered, or did the advancing years make him sensitive to every mention of the word *death*? He sighed and returned his attention to the stammering figure of Mayor Padgett, sitting across from him in the oiled opulence of Lord Granby's drawing room.

The mayor managed only to stammer a bit more and look about the room helplessly. "You mean he's . . . he's quite dead?"

Lord Granby took a second slice of spiced cake from the silver caddy, its display of exquisite china rising amid the dozen eminent worthies scattered about the room like chessmen, before sitting back down in the warm comfort of his easy chair. "I'm entirely too fond of cake, you know, but what can I do?" he confided, turning to Tuckworth, who chuckled in spite of himself. "Yes, Winston," his lordship answered after nibbling for a moment like a gleeful schoolboy. "I'm not certain what degree of 'dead' will satisfy you, but Curdle is certainly as dead as a man can be."

"But . . . but, if . . . but . . ."

Bates leaned forward from behind the mayor's chair. "If no body was identified, can the authorities be certain?" the young man intervened, relieving the mayor of the need to finish his question.

"I don't know how they were supposed to locate a body in that smoldering heap," Granby observed. "I understand the palace blazed away through the night and most of the next day."

"Is there any *reason* to believe that he might *not* be dead?" asked Wilfred Cade, Bellminster's wealthiest and most outrageously corpulent lawyer, owner of his own modest estate and a stable of horses.

The mayor sputtered unintelligibly for a moment in reply.

"Yes, of course," Cade responded, fairly glowing with prosperous authority, "we're all aware, I believe, of the *rumors* surrounding Mr. Curdle's activities in his character as a *private* individual. *Rumors,* I must remind you, gentlemen," he added, his words sharply clipped so as to carry no meaning beyond that which was intended. "Of course, he garnered *no* remuneration from his position, and what little he could earn *beyond* that post hardly covered his living expenses, let alone his gambling debts. At least, that is the *common* story about the man, which is more than I could attest to *personally.*"

"Well," interjected Granby, "the common story isn't far wrong. Curdle was always short. I've a stack of letters from the man this thick," and his lordship held up the piece of cake between his fingers, "all of them begging funds. Still, that's no reason to think he's done something as ludicrous as run off into obscurity once he had the chance. You're just being romantic now, Winston."

The mayor pulled himself up rather proudly, and Bates behind him adopted a shocked expression at this subtle slight. Bick, the mayor's other assistant, stood off some few yards and appeared impassive.

Lord Granby cleared his throat. He had called this meeting himself, had assembled Bellminster's most prominent figures with only a few hours' notice, sent out his coach and barouche and even a pony cart to bring them all to his estate as quickly as he could. It would not do to proceed with injured feelings, especially from the mayor. His lordship turned to the plump, disinterested cleric sitting at his elbow.

"What's Tuckworth say, eh?" he asked, sounding too light-hearted to be truly easy. "I daresay mysterious disappearances are bread and butter to our vicar."

All eyes turned toward the dean. Just more than a year had passed since he was promoted from his position as vicar to this loftier station, keeper and protector of Bellminster Cathedral, responsible now for the reconstruction of that ruined masterpiece, and still people found it difficult to call Tuckworth *dean*. Such forms never concerned him in the least, however. He actually preferred the quaint familiarity embraced by the lesser title. No, what concerned him was this persistent belief that he was some sort of oracle to be petitioned whenever anything dire and sinister foreboded. People were lining up to see him these days with their grave suspicions and dark secrets, and always these portents amounted to nothing, or as good as nothing. Such notoriety rankled him, made him feel like something out of a three-volume novel.

"Tell me," he inquired after a brief pause to collect his thoughts, to remove his spectacles and to rub the bridge of his nose as he spoke, "in what state were Mr. Curdle's closets?"

"His closets?" Granby echoed.

Tuckworth replaced his spectacles, wincing when they pinched his nose. "Yes, his closets. Was anything conspicuously absent? Clothing or bags? A portmanteau, perhaps? A man wouldn't escape from his debts with only a single suit of clothes to his name.

And what of his study? Were any papers lying about or books left open? Any unfinished correspondence? Then there's the question of his silver."

"Silver?" muttered Sir Anthony Heald, retired colonel of the Grenadiers and director of the textile mill. The great wings of his side whiskers trembled in the air as he spoke. "You mean knives and forks?"

"Yes. Did Curdle leave behind any personal articles of value, things that might readily have been turned into cash? Not just silver. Cuff links and watches. I should imagine that dropping off the earth, fooling your creditors into believing you're dead without actually depriving yourself of a life worth living, must take tremendous forethought. Hidden stores and reliable preparations. A secret room let somewhere. I can't imagine one could do it, at least do it successfully, on a whim." A short silence ensued, and Tuckworth became suddenly aware of the company's attention upon him. "Anyway," he hurriedly concluded, "a letter to his landlady should be sufficient to set your minds at rest in that quarter, not that I think it matters to us one way or the other. If the man's gone, he's gone."

For a moment, every face turned from Tuckworth to the mayor, who seemed more than usually uncomfortable. The mayor's discomfiture was relieved by Reverend Mortimer, the young and severe rector of Bellminster, who cleared his throat in remonstration. "You speak, Mr. Tuckworth, rather cavalierly of the departed soul, I must say," he intoned, his sharp nose raised toward the ceiling. "I cannot share your easy attitude, however. No, I find I cannot. The death of this man, the passing of a fellow creature, it is a matter of some moment to us all, and I believe a brief period of silent reflection is in order." Mortimer bowed his head reverentially, forcing the others to do the same by his example.

Tuckworth spoke up first, and perhaps too quickly. "I meant no disrespect."

"Of course not," Granby confirmed, grinning at the dean with a quick, thoughtless grin. Still, Tuckworth could not help but feel that his remarks *had* been more casual than was right. Perhaps death was becoming too easy a topic for him, after all.

"We none of us mean any disrespect," his lordship continued. "But we've got to face facts, eh? Curdle's dead, or gone or what-have-you, and that means one thing."

"A by-election," Cade declared.

"A by-election," confirmed Granby, nodding at the flurry of excited glances striving to catch his eye about the room. "There's little doubt that the party will force a general election upon the government next session, and we'll need our man in the thick of the fray. Got to cause a stir if we're to win back some of what was lost two years ago."

At the mention of that political debacle, when the Whigs were swept into Commons in unprecedented numbers, leaving scores of Tory Members wandering the provinces without seats or the prospects of seats, every head nodded darkly. Every head except Tuckworth's, that is. Politics was not a game he favored, and while he voted his conscience truly enough, he always managed to do so quietly and rarely voiced his opinion in company.

Reverend Mortimer coughed a very dry and spartan cough. "And whom will the Tories send us for the election?" he asked. "With so many fine names eager to return to the next session, I presume we will have some prominent figure to represent us at last."

The others muttered their agreement at this, and more than one recognized the opportunity these events promised for Bell-minster. Curdle had been a reliable Member these many years, always backing the party with his vote. But he had also been a distant Member, born in Rochester and raised in London and almost never leaving the City since that time in his youth when he won his first seat, a convenient borough in East Cornwall. Indeed, he had not been to Bellminster in over eight years, and many believed he would have been hard put to locate the town on a map of the Midlands.

So all eyes turned to Lord Granby expectantly, eagerly, ready to hear what great name would be written on the parliamentary rolls as the new Member for Bellminster. Granby appeared less than eager to meet their gazes, however, and directed his words to Tuckworth.

"Well, now," he began, not very enthusiastically, "it appears the party have given a great deal of thought to our situation. A great deal. You see, we delivered so handsomely last time, sending Curdle back with a strong majority, as always, that they've really come to think of Bellminster as a done thing."

"As well they should," Sir Anthony insisted with a tug at his whiskers.

"Yes," Granby continued, speaking very quickly and staring at the dean. "So, you see, they've settled on us as a certainty, as I said, and so, you see, they're leaving it up to us to decide. Letting us select our own Member."

Several heads leaned forward in astonishment. Greedy glints sparkled in greedy eyes. "You mean," Cade half-whispered, "we have the pick of the available men?" And each heart leaped at the remarkable honor.

Granby hemmed and waved his hand irritably in the air. "No, no, that's not quite it. What I mean to say is, we're to select our Member from among ourselves. A local man, you see."

The room crackled with a tense silence, tense not with crestfallen hopes or unstated fears, not with disappointment and dismay, but tense with calculation, tense with a dozen minds reworking their worlds, their dreams, their fortunes.

"A local man," murmured Bates.

"Yes," Granby went on more slowly now, having gotten over the bump along his way. "You see what an extraordinary confidence the party place in us. They know that Bellminster will deliver as Bellminster has always delivered. So their reasoning is, why waste a name where none is needed." He leaned forward and took another slice of cake. "Tuckworth?" he asked, offering the plate.

The dean shook his head thoughtfully.

Granby shrugged and sat back again. "Anyway, that's how the party see it. An honor, is what it is." And for a moment, the room seemed enveloped in calm repose.

Then it lurched like a ship at sea as eleven mouths opened to speak at once, and eleven hands shot forward for attention.

"Indeed, a great and most singular honor," Mortimer asserted more forcefully than the rest in the stentorian tones he reserved for the pulpit. "Your lordship is quite correct. Clearly the warriors of the party must fight the battle in contested fields, not in Bellminster. And what a rare opportunity for one of our own to shine his light afar. A very great and very singular honor, Lord Granby. We are all to be congratulated, most particularly Lord Granby for having deftly steered the champing team of circumstance to our benefit, and also that unknown he who will be blessed with his countrymen's benediction of service. Congratulations to him as well, whoever he may be." And the rector bowed from where he sat in homage to his lordship.

They'll be tearing at each other's throats by evening, Tuckworth thought to himself.

"Yes," Cade replied to Mortimer's sermon, "but who *will* it be, eh?"

"Who, indeed?" Granby exclaimed, in sole command of the room once again and more than a bit grateful to the rector for his intervention. "That's what we have two weeks to decide. Who will it be?"

"Two weeks . . . weeks?"

"Two," Granby said, raising a pair of knobby fingers into the air. "Two weeks to name a candidate. And then three for the election and the man can be off to London after that. Quite the game for someone, eh?"

Indeed it was, quite a remarkable game. Less than six weeks to be thrown from the provincial obscurity of Bellminster into the great roar and hubbub of London, from the faded distance of fen and field to the halls of Parliament itself (or what was left of it after the fire). To be styled an MP by Christmas, it was more than most of them had dared to hope for in a lifetime of hopes. Even those who were too humble or wise to seek such ambition for themselves felt the tempting lure of the game, the chance to make another man's fortune and hold his gratitude as a prize, the indebted ear of a Member, and as they trooped from the room at last, splitting into little packs of whispering souls, huddling into Granby's rich array of vehicles for the ride home, every man of them nurtured two confidences, the one to share with his neighbors and the other to hold dear for his heart alone.

Only two men failed to feel the great allure of the game, and those two were left together after the rest had gone. Granby had wanted to try the dean's opinion of these developments so he had detained him, and Tuckworth preferred to go home in solitude and even meant to walk the whole way, the countryside was so lovely in late October.

"Well," Granby began as he led his guest from the drawing room to the more private realm of his study, "what do you think of my little bit of news?"

"It's dreadful about Curdle," the dean said, trying to make amends with himself.

"Yes, yes. I know that. But what of the chance we've been thrown, eh? What of that? One of them is going to be a different man come Christmas." He pointed out to the retreating throng.

"To be honest, I don't think much of it one way or the other," Tuckworth replied, following his lordship into the study and resting in the luscious comfort of a perfect chair.

Such an answer failed to satisfy Lord Granby, though, and he waggled a finger at the dean. "Now, don't you go contrary on me. This is the greatest news to come to Bellminster in many years, and will be the greatest of a lifetime for some one of our young wags."

"For one of our young Tories, you mean."

"Well, why not? Bellminster is Tory."

"Even if the nation is not."

Granby looked put out at this, and it was not always advisable to put his lordship out. But he had come to hold a remarkable respect for Tuckworth and his opinion. Indeed, in two instances in the past year, the dean had proven himself a truly singular man, wise and observant, daring and honest to a degree rarely found in anyone, and certainly not in one so unprepossessing as a country parson. Granby was willing to indulge the dean in his contrary temper.

"All right, then," he conceded. "The news is not so momentous for everyone as for one in particular. But which one? That's what I want to know from you. Which man would you back, if you were in the mood?"

Tuckworth considered for quite a while, although his mind was not dwelling on the question Lord Granby had put to him. At last, he leaned forward in his chair and looked deeply at his companion. "Why did you set them on each other like this?"

Now it was his lordship's chance to turn contrary. "I don't understand you at all, Tuckworth," he said petulantly. "I ask you a civil question—"

"I'll tell you why I think you did it," Tuckworth went on, leaning back again. "I think you already know your man."

Granby appeared startled for a moment, before expressing a vigorous denial. "That's nonsense! As though I'd waste my time and everyone else's—"

"And more than that. I think now that you've made your decision, you're stirring up a hornet's nest simply for your own amusement."

"*That's* where you're wrong!" Granby insisted.

"Which is to say on the other point I'm right. You *have* selected your man. And you've hosted this little party so that in the next two weeks you can discover who might be opposed to you even before you announce your choice."

Lord Granby spluttered for a moment like a simmering kettle, then erupted, pounding his knee with his fist in frustration. "Dammit! Dammit! There's such a thing as too clever, you know, vicar." And his lordship stewed and fretted for a full minute in silence, angry that his game was spoiled and rubbing his knee where he had bruised it. Tuckworth waited patiently.

"Well?" Granby asked at last, but the dean maintained his calm, easy silence. His lordship huffed. "Don't you want to know who?"

Tuckworth shook his head. "No," he answered, and Granby threw his hands vainly to the ceiling. "What will be gained if I know?" the dean continued.

"I'll have the benefit of your advice, for one thing."

"What advice will you listen to after your mind is made up? What can I tell you that would matter? It's not my advice you want but my approval."

"And what if I do?" Granby confessed, sounding almost hurt now, thwarted and defensive. "I value your approval, Tuckworth. It means something to me to know you fall in with my ideas."

"But what if I don't fall in with your ideas? Where does that leave either of us?"

Granby considered this very seriously for a moment. "But he's so clearly the best man."

"Good. As long as you're satisfied, that's all that matters." Tuckworth rose to depart.

"You won't entertain my little secret, then? You don't have to tell me what you think of it. Just hear me out."

Tuckworth shook his head. "I've too many secrets now, from too many people," he muttered, suddenly looking very sad and very old. He knew Lord Granby well, knew him to be an incorrigible gossip, knew that he had to unload his secret on some sympathetic bosom if only to show what a clever choice he had made. He'd never be able to keep his secret for two weeks. But Tuckworth was determined not to be sympathetic, at least in this instance. "The less I know," he told his lordship, "the less trouble I can get myself into." He rose and moved toward the door. "Thanks for the tea."

With that, the Dean of Bellminster left Lord Granby sitting petulant and unsatisfied in his study. He left his lordship's manor, his footsteps echoing against the ancient flagstones. He left the drive and set out on foot to walk the clear, crisp miles back to Bellminster, to walk and to enjoy the color of the leaves and the chill in the air and the gold of the sunlight. Tuckworth breathed deeply as he walked, filled his lungs with autumn's tang, the acrid scent of decay oddly sweet on the westerly breeze. He walked and breathed and tried to empty his mind and not to think. No, not to think at all. Or, if he did think, to try to forget that, in spite of himself, he had very likely guessed Lord Granby's choice already.

CHAPTER III
FIGURES SEEN AT A DISTANCE

L ucy looked down from where she sat among the wind-tossed grasses, brown and brittle after a dry summer and a wet harvest, watching the carriages crawl along the dusty road from Lord Granby's estate to the outskirts of Bellminster. From her vantage atop Cadogan Tor, little more than a rocky barrow capped with a sparse copse of poplars, she could only just make out the shadows of men huddled close together within the darkness of the coach. She recognized the figures in the barouche, however, the mayor and his pair of cronies, and she could not easily miss the vastness of Wilfred Cade squeezing poor Reverend Mortimer to one side in the pony cart.

"I wonder what they've been up to?" she asked aloud, and then louder: "Father said something about going to see Lord Granby, but he never mentioned—"

"Can you not keep still for two minutes together!" Raphael snapped at her, stepping away from the canvas before him and casting his paintbrush testily to the ground.

Lucy's eyes shot fire at the utterance, and it was evident even to a casual observer that her afternoon had been spent in open contention with the young painter. In a moment the heat within her fell back to something chill and icy, however, and she affected a look of superior disaffection, tossing back the raven curls from her white brow and patting her hands into the billowing folds of her dress where it spread about in the grass. "I'm certain I haven't moved a muscle in three quarters of an hour. You're just being pettish."

"Pettish," Raphael muttered, stooping and taking up the brush again, trying to clean the dirt from its few stiff bristles with hard, smudged fingers. His blond hair tousled in the light breeze, and the limp corners of his collar flapped up and down against his throat. "Pettish," he repeated dismally, and gave up the brush for lost, casting it aside into the grass. "The light's almost gone. We might as well quit."

Lucy looked about at the brilliance that surrounded them and felt her heart turn, if not softer, at least more malleable. She tried to smother her injured pride in a woman's care. "Raphael," she asked from where she sat, "what's troubling you? It's not just your painting, I know that."

"It *is* my painting," he answered curtly and began to cram his oils and brushes into the wooden box he always carried about with him.

Lucy rose to her feet, somewhat less gracefully than she might have wished to do. Her joints ached from resting in the same posture for so long, and with a forced and unmannerly grunt she limped over to Raphael's easel, coming around to peek at what his hours of labor had produced. The painter paused in his packing but did not turn to face her as she studied the canvas.

Lucy twisted her head this way and that. Her brow creased in consternation. "But you've hardly painted me at all," she observed, her voice rising with indignation. "I'm just a little yellow blot in the middle distance."

Raphael went on with his packing. "I painted the landscape, not you," he told her as he worked. "You provide a human—"

"I've been sitting here since luncheon so I can be a yellow blot?" Lucy turned upon him. "You might have used a cow as well as me!"

"I needed a human figure there, something to draw the observer into the landscape and balance the poplars." He stood and grabbed the canvas off the easel, wrapping it roughly in oilcloth. "I really don't have time to explain the elements of composition to you," he remarked.

"Oh, don't you? But I have time to sit out here all day for no reason, I suppose."

"Dammit, Lucy!" He spun about sharply, knocking the easel over into a heap on the ground.

For one awful moment they stood there, glaring at each other, Lucy Tuckworth and Raphael Amaldi, their eyes burning with resentment and confusion, the smoldering betrayal that grows when the one you care for most deeply causes you the deepest pain. They struggled not to say dreadful, hurtful things to each other, things they longed and feared to say, and their hearts burrowed within their two breasts, cowering in love and despair.

The moment withered away, and Raphael seemed to wither with it. "Go home, Lucy," he muttered. "I'll see you tomorrow."

Lucy's eyes narrowed as she sought for some way, some means to forgive him, a path back to that glowing, friendly time when they were all to each other. It had been weeks since they had shared more than a few empty pleasantries. No way showed itself to her, however. That path lay hidden.

"I have work to do tomorrow for Father," she said, gathering her skirts about her. "I don't think I'll be able to get away at all until evening."

"All right. Tomorrow evening."

"Is that almost done then?" she asked, nodding toward the cloth-covered canvas on the ground.

"It's done now," he stated, not stopping from his packing. "As done as it will ever be."

They stood there on the hillside. For an instant the conversation froze to something like finality, not exactly ended but no longer alive. The knowledge of things unsaid, things perhaps unsayable, festered within them both. Lucy turned one second later and walked off down the hill.

Why can't I make him tell me what's troubling him? she thought as the distance widened between them.

What am I doing, making her suffer so? he thought, reviling himself and his heartlessness. What sort of monster am I? All she needs is a word, a touch from me. Why can't I give her what she needs?

What does he need from me? she wondered as she reached the road. She remembered how things had been a year ago, Raphael painting the cathedral at all hours of the day and in all weather, learning its every corner and crevice by dusk and by dawn, within and without. He had been happy doing it, and she had been happy watching him do it, and together they had grown close as friends, and then close as something more.

But the cathedral had burned down. He had gone back to London at last, ventured to make a name for himself, to paint his way into the galleries and shows, one of so many young painters struggling for a well-lit square of space on a wall. Why had he gone, when things were so much better before?

I'm a failure, Raphael thought at last, the same thing he had told himself every evening as he shouldered his pack and easel and set out for Bellminster once more. Paint landscapes, he had been advised. By John Constable, too, one of the greatest painters of the age. Paint the face of God in nature. It was true, Raphael had no gift for portraits. He recoiled at seeing something so unreal as men and women sitting placidly upon the canvas, captured though not alive. But a landscape made the world appear even more vital, more vibrant and thrilling, the pulse of nature rendered real through art. Yet no one wanted landscapes today. Or if they did,

THE DEVIL'S GAME

they wanted pretty pictures of rustic groves peopled with sylphlike youths, arcadian fantasies, no real vision. What good was John Constable's advice if Constable himself was part of a dead school? And why must he take out his frustration on poor Lucy? What had she ever done but love him? And what could he offer her in return? A home? A life? Security? Or sacrifice his hopes on the altar of her love, kill his dream that he might live in hers, a fine domestic limbo?

How can I heal his hurt? she asked herself again as she walked on to Bellminster.

And as she walked, a pair of loving eyes followed her in the distance, and then looked up at the solitary figure of Raphael on the hill, and Tuckworth sighed and shook his head. Well, he thought, it's for them to work out between them. I only hope they work it out soon. Dreadful to see love smothering like this.

An image leaped to his mind's eye, the final moments of his dear Eleanor's life, the racked breaths of his lovely wife as the cancer ate at her, the sweated brow that turned to him, alone there in the night, in their bedchamber, the gasping prayer to be released from an anguish that even God ignored. He had released her himself, when God refused, hoping that the pain would end. It did not end, however. It was only made over to him, passed to his heart with her final breath as he had kissed her cracked lips and lowered the pillow to her face. Love smothered. God had abandoned him in that instant, or he God. When love was lost, it hardly mattered later who had let it die.

Tuckworth walked on, not even slowing as these dreadful memories lashed mercilessly at him. He was used to them by now, the dark secrets of his soul. Every man has his dark secrets, he had learned. And if his were darker than most, what of that? It was too late for him to rail against fate. *Fate* itself was an empty word to him.

He shook his head to clear his mind of the pain. He found it easier all the time to release himself from the past's malevolent spell. Too easy, perhaps.

The dean cast his eyes about, searching for some occupation that might relieve his thoughts from this incessant exercise of reflection and regret. He found his relief in Bellminster. The town spread wide before him, settled comfortably on the near bank of the Medwin Ford, the wood and wattle of the houses crammed in labyrinthine disarray, in sharp contrast to the neat brick grid of the New Town, on the far bank, houses trooped about the squat millworks with its trio of smokestacks (only one burning this day) like an army encampment, the two sides of the town, old and new, yet both withering now that the mill had no rightful owner, just the vague stewardship of directors. Bellminster and New Town. They were growing into two communities, two worlds. And crowning them both, the toppled towers of the cathedral, his cathedral, gutted and bleak, looking pure and golden nonetheless in the last splendor of the dying day. Off to his right, in the rolling distance of the hills, he could just make out the red-orange expanse of the Estwold, burnished in its autumn dress, aglow as if from an inner light that owed nothing to the sun, and his thoughts dwelled upon nothing but light and color and beauty.

His heart eased at these sights, for they were home to him, and the pain within was forgotten for a time.

Tuckworth was not an especially old man, as old men judge age, but he felt old, and that amounted to the same thing. At a time when life should be closing gently for him, settling into a soft round of familiar routine, the comings and goings of family and cherished friends, he felt that he was being forced into a second adolescence. Not a childhood, with its selfish ignorance of consequence and cares, but another approach to maturity, another try at awkwardly growing into himself. The past year had thrown him into a world of event and, yes, even adventure, and now here he was, called upon at every chance to state his opinion, welcomed into the privacy of Lord Granby's study to voice his thoughts. Who had ever cared much for his thoughts before? Granby was a friend, true, but not an equal one. They were separated by wealth and station, and rightly so. But now there was almost a timidity in the way the old fellow treated him, a wish to be thought well of by the dean that had never been there before. "It's only me," the dean had wanted to say to everyone. "It's just Tuckworth." But they held him now in a kind of esteem he found immodest. Why couldn't things be like they were, before the cathedral had burned down, before he had traveled to London, before so much had changed?

The thought of London and the cathedral forced his mind back to the present. His recent adventure in the City had brought much-needed money to the Cathedral Fund, and as money always followed money, work on the restoration was progressing quickly now. Already the crypt had been saved and laborers were busy repairing the floor. The crushed flagstones of the nave were being removed daily, and those that might be stolen from the dark corners of the apse and side chapels, and made to fit, were being moved to new homes after centuries of lying secure in the shadows. Abraham Semple, builder and foreman, had wanted to replace the entire floor, but Raphael had devised a scheme by which a great deal of cost might be spared with a little judicious repositioning. So the ancient stones of the cathedral were given a new life. Later, fresh-cut stones would be brought in to those out-of-the-way corners where they would be needed, and only a practiced eye could tell the difference, or so Raphael had assured them all.

Even Semple had grudgingly admitted the likelihood of the plan, though all of this was vastly mysterious to Tuckworth, who understood little of it but trusted the young painter's judgment. The dean possessed only the vaguest understanding of the cathedral's finances, as well. That was Lucy's affair, her quick, textbook mind grasping easily the columns and figures that he found unbearably dense and dull. Were he a younger man, certainly he could have worked his way through that maze of numbers, he assured himself. But he was not a younger man, and his patience seemed to have withered with age. It was good to have young people about him at his time of life, he thought. Age must give way, after all.

He looked again at the town in the distance, the two halves, old and new, locked together in a shared future, and he thought of Lord Granby's choice. A new man for Bellminster, and that would mean a young man. "One of our young Tories," Granby had said.

Tuckworth found himself speculating again, drawing almost certain conclusions from what he had seen at Lord Granby's, and what had been said, and who had said it. And who had said little. Yes, his lordship's choice was a fair one, a likely one. But unlikely events often sprang from likely beginnings, Tuckworth knew. Granby must be aware that his selection would not sit well in some quarters and that certain hopes would be forever dashed, or else he would not have allowed himself these two weeks to prepare the way, to feel out those who might oppose his choice.

And yet.

And yet, how important was it really, this man or that man? Granby held the reins that drove the town. The dean was wrong to think that age would gladly relinquish its preeminence to youth, not if he knew Granby as he thought he did. Tuckworth chuckled to himself and kicked at the dust of the road, raising a brown cloud to his knees. Well, he considered, it was going to be a grand game, and well worth the watching. And he was gratified to recall that he would not be getting involved in it. Yes, he thought, he had avoided that entanglement rather deftly. So, feeling pleased and more than a little impressed with himself, he walked on to Bellminster, into the spreading shadows of evening.

Those who follow closely the ways of nature teach that the life span of a fruit fly extends only from sunrise to sunrise. From dawn to dusk it is given every opportunity to make its way in the world, encompassing the vigor of youth in a morning, adulthood in an afternoon, middle age about teatime, and the sage wisdom of advanced years through the evening hours. So does a fly make real what in man is merely metaphor. And yet, as brief as that spark of life may appear to men, it might be a biblical term of three score years and ten compared to the span that a good juicy bit of news could remain unknown in Bellminster. By the time Tuckworth's easy stride had carried him home, word of the election was already buzzing about the town from one corner to the other, from the farthest end of New Town to the oldest gable of the oldest wing of the Granby Arms, that sprawling, tumbledown inn that never seemed quite finished, or else not half begun.

As the dean walked through the streets, rarely meeting a face that he had not known these thirty and more years, smiling at sturdy men and stout matrons whose lessons he had heard when they were children, nodding to gray heads that had been dark and thick in his memory, the first words to greet him were not the usual cares for his peace, but the overheated inquiry, "Have you heard?"

"Have you heard the news, vicar?"

"Great doings! Have you heard?"

He smiled as he passed house and shop, watching the merchants untie their aprons, bring in their wares from the street, and shutter their windows while contented shoppers rushed home with their parcels and late buyers bustled about, begging to be let in for just one small purchase. This was Bellminster as he loved most to see it, alive and active, rustling to the sound of the first fallen leaves of autumn tripping on the wind, colored by a roseate sky as the sun flamed its last life beyond the farthest hills. Already he could see the glow of candles in the windows and feel the chill of October drape the town in night.

"What news, eh, vicar?"

"Do you know the news?"

And to every eager eye and enthusiastic query he merely nodded and said, "Yes, yes," and smiled. Something in the air as he walked, some flavor on the quickening breeze that blew up from Medwin Ford, some magic cast by these dying days of the year made him think of youthful days gone by, made Tuckworth feel almost young again himself so that he strode with a jauntiness quite unlike him. Even the sudden view of the scorched towers of Bellminster Cathedral, the roofless nave, and the gaping, colorless windows could not dim his spirits this evening. Tuckworth walked across Cathedral Square, waving to the day's last stragglers as they ran off to their suppers, glancing at the hale and ruddy glow from the tavern at the Granby Arms across the way, and entered the humble vicarage that had been his home so many years now, nestled against the towering wall of the cathedral like a kitten nuzzling its mother.

"And it's about time, too!" Mrs. Cutler scolded from the kitchen, as though they had been in close conversation already. "Out about the countryside all day! Like as catch a cold, not even a scarf about your neck or mittens to your hands."

"Now, now, it wasn't as cold as that," Tuckworth assured her, and he looked about for Lucy.

She was in the parlor, stirring up the fire in the grate, squatting before the hearth in an attitude that was far from genteel but that added to the sense of contentment swelling Tuckworth's heart.

"Hello, my dear."

"Hello, Father," she said, not looking up from her work, not coming to him for a hug or to lead him to his chair. He knew her sadness as clearly as though it were his own, knew her cares and her fears though she had never spoken openly about them. He could not tell if she was trying to keep her pain from him, or if she trusted him to know what made her heart ache. He had always been the one to hide his suffering from her, despite her longing to help, and it caused him grief now to think that she might have learned such dreadful silence from his example.

"Are you well, Lucy?" he asked.

She rose with a weary sigh, then turned a sallow face to him with a smile that seemed to arrive just a moment too late. "Of course I am, dear," she said, crossing over and leading him into the room, to his chair.

He sat down and looked at her back as she turned away to worry over the fire again. For an instant he was about to say something, he was not certain what.

Young Bit came bursting through the kitchen door, followed closely by Mrs. Cutler. The child, rescued just a few months before from the worst abuses, ran to the dean and stopped suddenly, standing before him with a serious expression. She was always so serious with him, he thought, and so easy with the others.

Bit's blond curls bobbed as she gave a quick curtsy. "G'd evening, Mr. Tuckworth," she said.

"Good evening, Bit."

"Well, and did you hear the news?" Mrs. Cutler asked excitedly, coming up behind the child, her hands covered with flour.

"News?" Tuckworth repeated, casting a last worried look at Lucy. "What news?"

CHAPTER IV

A GOOD DEED

October was ending, and Guy Fawkes Day drew near with its bonfires and children's games, its pennies and pranks, a sad holiday
for Tuckworth. It would be a year to the day (or near enough)
that fire had consumed his cathedral. Still, only he appeared to
mark the anniversary. Elsewhere in Bellminster all talk was about
the election. Factions had sprung up overnight, grown, wavered,
and flickered out. Names flew upon the autumn wind like leaves
and were as quickly swept away. Wilfred Cade made himself conspicuous about the town, which was not so very hard to do. Horace
Hardesty, an officer of the bank and a prominent director at the
millworks, attended Reverend Mortimer's Sunday service at
Bellminster's fashionable St. Matthew's Chapel, stopping afterward
on the pavement to speak in a casual and friendly manner with the
wealthy, well-propertied congregation. Even Ian Fellowes, a tough,
prosperous farmer with the rents of three other farms, came to
town himself on Market Day and extended more than his usual al-
lowance of credit to the public. All while a strong, sturdy band of
carriages marched up to and back from Lord Granby's estate from
dawn to well past midnight.

In just three days the temper of the town had gone from drowsy inattention to the bustle and buzz of a hive of fractious hornets. And nowhere was that buzz so incessant, so busy, and so brilliant as in the tavern of the Granby Arms. Bellminster knew its share of pubs and alehouses, scores of tiny holes and affable chambers, sorry hovels serving out lemons and gin, hearty British breweries where men and women might find light amusement to fill the empty darkness, but there was only one Granby Arms, and there always had been only one.

This evening, a Monday, the Arms was alive with debate and dissension, smiles and sulks as the men tried their hands at fortune-telling, squinting like gypsies into the future to see where and at whom fate might nod, or sitting idly back and judging the predictions sent flying fast about the room, or merely sinking into the oracle of the beer. Laughing loudest of all, stirring up adversaries and setting faction against faction, grinning like a death's-head through the swirling smoke of twenty pipes and sweating like a fiend, was John Taggart, the short, stout innkeeper and Master of the Revels, drawing pint after pint at the bar. There were good times and bad times in Bellminster, Taggart knew, and few times as bad as these they were in, but no time was as good for the Arms as an election, and he glowed amid the spirits of his company, good spirits or bad but thirsty.

"Hello, Taggart," Tuckworth called over the din, loosening his scarf and settling in at the bar as the innkeeper rushed past with four tankards clutched in his fists.

"Vicar!" Taggart cried, nodding with a smile that said his happiness was now complete.

"Sherry, Taggart. It's cold outside," the dean ordered, sounding almost rough and rollicking, before turning his back to the bar so that he might take in the crowd thrumming about him. Here was the place for him to renew his spirits, he thought, the day had felt so dismal. It had been his habit in years past to peer into the Granby Arms occasionally, to chat with the laborers of Bellminster and learn from them how best to be their minister. He had always felt himself welcome at the bar or nestled into a close corner, and if the voluble flow of talk was somewhat checked by his clerical presence, he had never noticed. Now that he was retired from active ministry, the habit lived on by its own momentum, with a single alteration in its performance. Tuckworth still watched over the cares and concerns of the men about him. Only lately, as he sat and listened, he sometimes drank a little more than he used to do. Just a little.

"Next game, vicar?" Waters, a pock-faced greengrocer's man, crowed from a chessboard in the corner, holding up a bishop to tempt the dean. There was always a game of something going on at the Arms, with the next round of drinks usually the forfeit.

Tuckworth smiled and waved, but shook his head. "So, Taggart," he said as the innkeeper set an amber glass upon the bar, "are you getting good odds on the election?" The dean knew that, as few of the men in the tavern could vote, not owning property, their only interest in the election was sure to be a gaming one.

"Odds?" the barman repeated innocently. "Now, vicar. No need for me to be acceptin' wagers to make my fortune on this election. I've enough to do keepin' them taps goin'."

"Yes," Tuckworth chuckled. "I daresay you have."

"Asides," Taggart added with a leering wink, "it's too soon to place odds. Hardly know who's in the race as yet."

"Well, you're very wise not to get involved too early." The dean raised the glass to his lips and took a noisy sip. This was a world Tuckworth loved, the true life of Bellminster. He knew every man about the place, and they all knew him and welcomed him, too, in their fashion. Not that his continued habit had gone unnoticed in certain quarters. Reverend Mortimer, for one, found cause to remonstrate with the dean, but that only made Tuckworth think better of the practice.

A sharp wind shot through the tavern as a boisterous mob came tumbling into the Arms, large, noisy, well-appointed figures wrapped in thick coats and silk mufflers. "Taggart! Taggart!" a faltering voice shouted, and Winston Padgett's face emerged, red and shining, from the folds of a bushy collar. "Is your back room free . . . free?"

"Free and open to your honors," Taggart beamed, looking more inexpressibly delighted than ever to see such fine gentlemen hungry for his hospitality. "Fire's goin' and room's dry and warm. Step in, gen'lemen, and I'll send the girl to you directly."

"With a bowl of rum punch, eh . . . eh? Hot rum punch! Best Jamaican! Why, bless me, look at this, Bates!" The mayor raised a fat finger and pointed it at the dean. "Who were we speaking of just a moment before in the street . . . in the street, and who do we find? Dean Tuckworth, you'll join us, certainly."

The dean was certainly not inclined to join the mayor and his roistering party, but before he could utter anything more than a short cough in reply, Bates had a grip on his lapel, and they all swept through the tavern and into the back room. Once there, the company unwrapped themselves to reveal some eight or ten men, all prosperous, all respected, and all drunk. They fell rather closely about a scarred old slab of an oak table, all except Tuckworth, who took a seat in a corner by the fire.

"Now, where were we . . . were we?" Padgett began.

"The fat one," declared Bates, and everyone laughed at this as though it were the sum of wit.

"The way he waddles about the town," a voice called from the middle of the table, "chasing votes like they was ripe sugared plums."

"I daresay he'd chase a sugared plum with greater enthusiasm," another jester called, and all broke again into wet brays of laughter as pipes came out and a pair of smoldering dips passed around.

Tuckworth sighed.

Before long the girl arrived, sloshing a large, simmering bowl of punch into their midst, and the assembly were ordered to fill their glasses for the toasts, a ceremony that Mr. Bates presided over with fawning adroitness. They drank first to His Majesty, as was only proper, "the father of his people and terror of his enemies, that lion, that Solon, that king." Next they drank to Lord Granby, "that he might always judge the merits of his fellow men with that same perspicacity for which he was so well and justly famous." This they followed up with a toast to the united healths of the voters of Bellminster, "that sage and Athenian body who wield the greatest power historical man has ever devised." So they continued to charge and recharge their tumblers, and screamed for more punch when the bottom of the bowl peeked up at them, honoring the wives of the voters of Bellminster ("very Beatrices of wisdom and guidance"), the shopkeepers of Bellminster ("heart and soul of the town"), the farmers ("stout yeomen and true Britons, all"), the navy ("unscalable wall of defense"), the army ("fierce Myrmidons"), and on and on.

Through this robust parade of healths and honors Tuckworth managed to sit quietly, sipping at his one glass of punch, and then at his second but stopping there, unwilling to join in with his whole heart this affecting celebration. His reluctance had nothing to do with his mood, which had tended toward sullenness all day, nor was it from any qualms over the oppressively political nature of the meeting. Though his presence might be construed as support for the mayor, he was ready enough to deny the charge as politely as he could. No, there was something else in the proceedings that disturbed him, something mean and willful. The dean kept an eye on Padgett as the toasts progressed, each one more lavish and spirited than the last, and he detected what he thought was a nervousness in the man, a profusion of goodwill more forced than natural, a discomfiting air of desperation that led the mayor to drink more deeply than the others, to fill his glass more frequently, and to stammer and to stutter more markedly. And as bowl succeeded bowl, as the party grew more boisterous and loud, Tuckworth began to suspect that at least two or three of these men were urging the mayor to his excesses, taking their drunken amusement from his greater drunkenness. A shared glance, a subtle nudge, a sly grin behind a shadowing palm, small signs played about the edges of the crowd, signs that Tuckworth caught and worried at.

"To that unnamed someone," Bates shouted now, dipping his glass into the bowl and lifting it dripping before him. "To that man whose name Dame Future holds upon her rolls, who will be asked to represent his fellows in the coming Parliament. That unknown personage—"

"Though some might know him, eh?" joked a voice from the throng, to the winks and nods of the rest.

"—That mysterious gentleman—"

"Not so mysterious," chimed another voice.

"—That light of the world soon to be unbusheled—"

"Here, here!"

"—To the next Member for Bellminster!" Bates finished and turned to Mayor Padgett and raised his glass overhead.

"The next Member for Bellminster!" half the company echoed, following Bates's example, while the rest laughed and poked their neighbors.

"What do you think of that for a toast, Mr. Tuckworth?" Bates asked, turning suddenly to smile upon the dean, who was taken quite by surprise and looked momentarily as dull as the mayor himself.

"I think it's a very well-spoken toast," Tuckworth managed, couching his words carefully through the haze of smoke and steaming punch.

"Yes, but what of the matter of the toast?"

Mayor Padgett's flushed face looked around, suddenly bullish and aggressive. "What's . . . what's the matter with . . . with the toast?" he demanded.

"Nothing, your honor," Bates asserted with a knowing glance around the table, evoking a gulp of stifled laughter. "I meant only the subject of the toast, and I was asking our dean what he thought of it, that's all."

The mayor seemed unsettled for a moment, as though he suspected he was being made the butt of some jest, but his eyes soon lost any trace whatever of suspicion that lay behind them, and he dived once more into his glass.

Tuckworth saw all of this in an instant, and in an instant a whole tale was unfolded to him, so that he wanted nothing more than to separate himself from this heartless revelry. "If you'll excuse me," he said, rising and squeezing awkwardly to the door.

"Will you leave us, then?" Bates called after him as hands groped ineffectually at the dean's coat.

"I must," Tuckworth answered, sidling along the wall, evading the importunate clutches that tore at his arms and wrists. "I'm afraid, yes." He unclasped the last finger from his coattail and emerged from the room into the freer air of the tavern. He looked about. No one noticed him. No pair of eyes turned his way, squinting at him as he reentered the room. The same thoughtless debates, the same wet councils harangued the smoke as it circled and circled the rafters. And yet the Arms appeared oddly different now, less inviting and murkier, so that he suddenly felt out of place there. Tossing a coin onto the bar in payment for his sherry, the dean stepped back out into the night, unseen and alone.

Tuckworth took four bold strides across the yard and stopped. He stood in the coach yard of the Arms, staring down at the dust swirling about his feet. Overhead, a few bold stars blinked silently in the autumn sky as a stern sliver of moon cut through the clouds. Around him leaves danced and gibed on the breeze, rattling past his ears, but still the dean stood motionless, stolid, numb to the world about him, with only the fingers of one hand, his left hand, slowly clenching and unclenching as though grappling with some rod.

Tuckworth took a quick step on his way and stopped again. He paused for a heartbeat, then spun around and went back into the tavern. Catching the eye of the serving girl, he called her over and whispered into her ear. She nodded, disappeared into the back room, and emerged shortly after with a nod to the dean and Mayor Padgett at her heels.

Tuckworth approached the mayor, grasped him by the arm, and pulled him aside to a shadowy corner.

"A very festive group, your party," the dean began awkwardly, uncertain now how best to say what he had to say, a thing he would much rather have avoided saying, especially to a man who had never shared his confidence before.

Padgett only looked back dimly, passing his palms down his trembling jowls.

"I hope you won't take offense at what I'm about to tell you," the dean tried. He paused. "But I feel it's only in your best interests that you should know my suspicions."

"Susp . . . spicions?"

"My thoughts. I just don't think you ought to be so overt in your efforts to . . . well, to curry favor with these men."

The mayor's slack face melted into a look of sublime condescension. "My dean dear." He stopped, momentarily confused, before continuing in a more conspiratorial voice. "Politics," he whispered loudly, wagging his head and placing a heavy arm across Tuckworth's shoulder. "Elections. How it's done . . . done."

Tuckworth began to question within himself the wisdom of the advice he was about to offer, but it was too late now to turn from the course he was set to pursue. "Yes, I know. I only think you might wait until Lord Granby has announced his choice, the man he plans to put forward. You might save yourself some embarrassment, that's all. Good evening," and the dean turned to leave.

A hand detained him. Tuckworth turned back to confront the mayor's dark eyes, pained eyes, questioning, masking an ill-formed hurt. "Wha . . . what do you know?"

The dean hemmed self-consciously. "I don't know anything. Nothing at all."

"You s'spect?"

Tuckworth recalled that meeting with Lord Granby, just a few days ago, the schemes and plots simmering behind all those faces, the startled questions and demands for news. And he recalled that one face, placid, implacable, knowing.

The dean sighed. "Where is Mr. Bick this evening?" he asked.

The mayor looked confused for an instant, then shrugged his shoulders. "Head cold . . . cold," he muttered. "'S been poorly lately, but . . ." and his voice trailed off. His eyes narrowed.

"Yes, well," Tuckworth said, "I'd best be getting back—"

"Bick? Bick?"

"It's just a presentiment I have."

The mayor suddenly looked angry. "Not possible . . . not . . . !"

"No, probably not," Tuckworth replied, suddenly feeling that his better instincts had led him into a snare.

"Bick?" the mayor repeated, his anger turned insipid, the very real chance of the thing slowly materializing for him from out of the fog of his dull senses.

"I tell you it's only a suspicion, but best to be guarded, eh? Best to be ready for anything."

The mayor looked into the smoke-filled air, his eyes vague and unfocused, his mind fallen into a sort of standing stupor.

Tuckworth waited a moment, wondering if Padgett would say anything further. He tilted his head slightly in an effort to reach the mayor's attention, but the man was battling demons now, demons that always had some grip on his fears and hopes, a very private war. Tuckworth backed away and once more left the tavern behind.

Alone again, walking against the frosty wind as it upset autumn's flotsam and sent tattered scraps of night tumbling across Cathedral Square, the dean was forced to face fears of his own. Somewhere, between the idea and the act, his right intentions had turned to guilt. Was it right to have said anything? Was it enough that he meant to do something good for a man he had never properly considered before? The mayor was fully able to direct his own course. Was it proper to interfere? Was the dean even right in his suspicions?

Yes, he was right. Tuckworth knew it. As well as he knew Lord Granby, as well as he knew Bellminster and what lay ahead of him in the wan moonlight, he knew that Bick was the chosen man.

So really, what harm had he done in divulging his suspicion to Mayor Padgett? The man would discover the truth eventually, and by then embarrassment might have turned to humiliation. What harm had he done in trying to do the mayor some good? Better to have the truth now, like a rotten tooth pulled quickly, before infection set in. Besides, what harm could he possibly have done?

CHAPTER V
MEDDLING

ou've upended the applecart, that's all you've done!" Lord
Granby fretted, pacing back and forth in the dean's study. The
tick-tick of his cane punctuated his irritation with each step.
Tuckworth watched as Granby aired his dusty wrath, nor could he
help considering that as terrible as it was to have a powerful enemy, it was more dangerous perhaps to have a powerful friend.

His lordship had cracked with his cane upon the vicarage door
with the dawn, looking white and patriarchal in the rosy half-light,
fierce and glowering and biblical. His knocking had roused Mrs.
Cutler, who had roused the dean and the entire family, so that
Tuckworth now sat before Granby in his study while the women
huddled about the door and Bit remained calm and unmoved in
the parlor, clutching loosely at her limp rag of a doll.

"I've had Winston Padgett at my throat all night long," fumed
his lordship. "All night! Sounding for all creation like a jilted lover,
like a schoolgirl. Ludicrous! Tried to get the man to see reason and
hold his tongue, but you can lay a penny to a pound he'll have his
revenge on me before breakfast this morning. Nose it about that
the game's up and Bick's the man and has been all along. Make me

look like a proper devil to half the gentry and a great old fool to the rest. I've got two positions open to me now, you see that, of course." Granby darted a scornful nod in the dean's direction. "Of course you see it, such a clever man. I've either got to toss off Bick as a bad investment, which he is *not,* or confess myself the most tiresome old schemer in the county."

Which, thought Tuckworth to himself, you are. "Certainly the reaction won't be so great as you imagine," the dean tried, hoping not to extinguish Granby's ire so much as to poke and to prod it, letting it rage until it burned itself out.

"You've no idea about such things, Mr. Tuckworth! No idea!" he stated, bumping into the dean's chess table and upsetting the problem Tuckworth had arranged for himself. "This is politics and no idle game. I daresay even with your great cleverness you can't see into so many hearts at once. You said one word to the mayor! One meddling word! And you've snuffed the aspirations of a dozen powerful men and turned their energies against me."

"But they'd never stand against you, your lordship. You *are* the party, after all."

"Dammit, Tuckworth, you've no idea! The delicacy!" Granby stopped his pacing and turned to confront the dean, his pale, unshaven cheeks puffing as anger colored them a mottled, sickly hue. He struggled to find a word, some smarting blow to hurl, but only huffed incoherently for a moment before resuming his walk about the study.

Tuckworth was startled. He had been the target of Granby's emotion before, had crossed his lordship in subtle ways now and again and suffered the old man's haranguing lectures. This was something else, however, something more than common anger. There was frustration here, and fear, a sense of stumbling at the finish line, coming up lame at the last only to see the world rush by, and the dean suddenly understood what this all might mean to a man of Granby's years. A tiny seedling of guilt began to root in Tuckworth's heart. Had he overstepped himself?

Granby stopped again and pointed his walking stick at the dean. "Your meddling—" he began, but before he could utter another deprecation a soft knock cut him off. The door opened a crack, and Mrs. Cutler's disembodied voice floated into the room.

"Mr. Mortimer here, sir, to see his lordship at his convenience."

"Mortimer?" Granby repeated, irritated at the thought of just one more querulous fool come to devour his patience. A moment's reflection, however, and his lordship looked mildly assuaged. "Mortimer, good man," he told the door. "Tell him I'll be right out. And *you.* I'll thank you to keep out of these matters in the future. Politics is not a game for you, clever as you are, and I've no time to . . . to . . ." Unable to say exactly what he had no time for, his lordship merely huffed again and stormed out.

Tuckworth emerged some five minutes after, meeting Lucy's searching glance and Mrs. Cutler's sharp and silent accusation with a studied, indifferent air.

"Well, Lord Granby certainly seemed energetic this morning," he commented, his remark falling with an unnatural weight to the floor.

"Father," Lucy began.

"Good morning, Bit," the dean tried again, greeting the child with a theatrical pat on her tousled head. She never could keep her golden locks combed properly, for all Mrs. Cutler's tugging and pulling at them.

The child ducked under the gentle weight of his hand and made a sort of curtsy where she sat, but said nothing.

"Father," Lucy repeated, and this time Tuckworth sighed and looked up.

"It seems," he confessed, "that I thwarted some particular plan his lordship has set his heart to. An offhand comment to the mayor, nothing more."

"More than enough," sniffed Mrs. Cutler, nodding her head severely as she charged out of the room and into her kitchen.

"How serious is it?" Lucy asked.

Tuckworth stepped over to his daughter and took her hand. "You heard how serious, I think. At least it's no more serious than it is."

Lucy looked deep into her father's face, searching for some sign. He would never be able to hide anything from her, she thought, nothing important. Yet all she found was a calm resignation, the woeful certainty of cloudy times ahead, but nothing dire or dreadful.

"All right," she said at last, patting him gently on the arm and placing a kiss on his cheek. "Only do try not to meddle in all this election nonsense. You know how delicate our finances are. The Cathedral Fund is just starting to shape up. And I know Lord Granby's contribution isn't much, not really, but if he withdraws his support—"

"Don't worry, Lucy," Tuckworth assured her, pleased to have caused no more bother than this, and he was soon away on his morning walk about Bellminster.

The day was chill and stinging, with a flinty sky and the dank of impending ice on the breeze. The town seemed muffled by the wind as by a damp scarf, and men and women scurried through the cold, clasping tightly to their collars, nodding their cheerless, stiff "good mornings" to one another through clenched teeth while children ran coatless and wild on their ways to school. It was just the sort of cold to startle a warm autumn into thoughts of winter, and Tuckworth liked it. He liked the threat of frost upon the windowpanes, the subtle smoke that hung upon each man's lips, the huddled bodies staying just a moment longer in the glow of the shops before bursting out once more into the crackling air. A month from now, he knew, such weather would hardly cause comment, would be a welcome relief from more bitter winds to blow, but now it was a healthy, tingling slap in the face, and he liked it.

There was something on the breeze he did not like, however, something just beyond the reach of his senses that grew within him as he walked. At first it was the vaguest sense of unease, as every eye glanced at him and every head nodded, and then every eye and head turned back again to give him a second notice. And soon the words would catch upon the wind and swirl about him, like a dying echo just at the edge of his hearing, as though he were catching thoughts, not voices.

". . . Mayor . . ."

". . . Bick . . ."

". . . Granby . . ."

". . . Vicar . . ."

That seedling of guilt began to spread its roots through his heart, gnawing and biting at him, scratching into the fissures of his weary soul. Had he been wrong to confide his suspicions to the mayor? Had he been meddling in things he had no business with? Politics, after all, was not a pursuit he had ever cared for, ever much gossiped over or brooded on as others did. When men asked about politics, he had learned, they sought only agreement, never insight, and so he avoided the talk of it, kept his peace when the topic arose or, when pressed, tried always to obscure his views in a polite fog.

"H'lo, vicar!"

Tuckworth nodded to a plump merchant taking down the shutters from his storefront windows. "Late to be opening," he observed, but received only a vacant smile in reply, and walked on.

Still, he considered, what was it but the way of men in the world, this politics. Who was to say it was no business of his? He had acted out of charity, with no design or thought of advantage. He had wanted only to save the mayor from humiliation. What reason was there in that for such guilty foreboding?

A bobbing, green-bonneted head stole before his path, whispered, "Morning, vicar," and bobbed off again.

"Good morning, Mrs. Seaton."

And yet there it was, that cloying, wheedling seed of guilt, a guilt bred of uncertainty, of doubt, the dean's old disease. No thought he ever carried, no opinion or reasonable act he might venture upon, could escape that festering question, Yes, but what if . . . ? His mind lived in a middle world, a place between this and that, though not that gray place bordering the black and white of right and wrong. Rather, it was a world of hue and shade, of tint, of tone, a world where black and white had no place at all, like his old cathedral when the setting sun pierced the stained glass windows to dye the very air he breathed, to fill his soul with color. Doubt was the light illuminating his sphere, doubt and uncertainty the sparks that threw all in relief, giving form and shape to color. How could a man not doubt in such a world?

"Vicar!" The word struck at him from somewhere on his right. He glanced and saw two smiling faces, a pair of burly carters lifting boxes down from their wagon. Tuckworth nodded.

Still his guilt grew inside him, the harvest of another man's planting. But no, he would not have it. He would not allow Lord Granby's anger to bear its fruit in his heart. No, nor Lucy's cares, either. Meddling? How had he meddled? The election was as much his business as it was that of any Englishman, at least of those privileged to vote. This guilt was a chimera, groundless and senseless, a waste of time even to think on it.

He brushed against a well-muffled body passing along the pavement.

"Watch your damn . . . Oh, dean . . . g'morning."

The man was gone before Tuckworth could rightly recognize him. One of the mill directors, perhaps? Someone important, anyway.

Well, the dean thought, rounding out his inner debate, so this election is my business after all, and I have no cause to feel guilty. Good for me. Well done, Mr. Tuckworth. A bold resolve, he asserted to himself with a sardonic nod, a brave position to take considering my only involvement lies in casting my vote.

He smiled at this firm resolution, his reasonable conviction that he had no cause to feel guilty, married now to the nagging sense that he was going to feel guilty regardless, and the certainty, the absolute certainty, that it mattered not a whit. He smiled, and he felt sad and strangely empty, and he walked on with guilt still gripping at his heart.

Behind the dean, in the distance now and fading into the crowd, the important figure who had brushed so quickly past him turned a corner and trudged on through the cold. Mr. Bates had not slept that night, not since the mayor had returned to the back room of the Granby Arms and told him of Tuckworth's caution, the sour knowledge that Bick had been chosen by Lord Granby himself. The mayor had blurted it out in front of all those drunken faces, those eager ears ready to ridicule. Bates had broken up the party as quickly as he could without seeming concerned, though word doubtless spread about the tavern after they departed, the mayor still stammering in wounded dignity and confusion.

By the time they had reached Lord Granby the whole story was likely bounding about in the darkness like a rugby football, knocked this way and that for the general sport of the town. (Even now Bates could hear the snickers as he passed, or thought he could.) That meeting with Granby had been a fruitless exercise, an awkward round of accusations and denials until at last a confession was wrenched from his lordship. And what good was a confession when you had no power to punish?

Bates pulled his collar more tightly about his throat and plodded along. This wet cold seeps in everywhere, he thought, and sniffled.

Then, after Lord Granby's, Bates had gone back to the mayor's parlor, that jungle of extravagant greenery and polish, crammed with lustrous, costly furniture and merchant gimcracks, where he had been forced to play nursemaid to Padgett's hurt pride.

"But it's not fair, Bates," the fat fool had muttered like a child's refrain in the flickering of the firelight. "It's not . . . not fair."

"It's politics, sir. That's all." Bates had grinned a soft, knowing grin, trying to ease some confidence back into that quivering mass. "It's only politics. All we need is a way around this little bump in our road."

Padgett looked surprised, almost frightened. "You don't mean to openly defy Lord Granby? You . . . you can't mean that we should run against Bick . . . Bick? Run against my own assistant?"

Bates shrugged. "I mean only that this is politics, and so the game isn't up until the votes are cast. And as for Bick being against us, I don't see that it counts for anything. It certainly won't count with him." Bates picked up a little porcelain thing, an ill-glazed terrier with an oriental face, and ran his finger along the smooth cool of its back. "I've had some thoughts on how we might proceed. Made some inquiries already, in preparation. I'd not defy his lordship openly, of course, but these things are never done openly. We must continue to work, but only just out of sight, below Granby's notice for a time, until we're strong enough."

Padgett's eyes narrowed. "Strong enough? Enough for what?"

A snorting laugh emerged from the shadows of the room, and a tall, stout figure rose from a hard chair and stepped into the light. "Strong enough for a man," a woman's clear voice urged. "Strong enough to take your own, or what's rightfully yours. Strong enough to stand on your feet and not totter about like some new-weaned babe."

Bates grimaced inwardly, though his smile showed no mark of his thought. "Listen to Mrs. Padgett, sir," he said. "Let her good sense guide you."

"My good sense." Mrs. Padgett snorted again. She was a formidable woman just beginning to pass beyond the middle of her middle years, fashionably clad in a lavish dressing gown, her dark hair streaked with gray light. She was more handsome than attractive, not warm but matronly, a well-intentioned woman, perhaps, though hard, with a hardness her husband lacked. She had a panther's rough way with her cub, prodding him to a predatory sense of himself in the world, shaming him into pride. The mayor had Bates's allegiance, and needfully so, but the mayor's wife had Bates's respect, and even a bit of his fear.

"My good sense says you've got to fight for this, if you want it," she admonished her husband, who looked furtively between Bates and her, seeking sympathy somewhere. "So Granby doesn't want you. So toadying little Bick is the man. Well, I'm sorry. Nobody wanted you to open a warehouse by the river, but you did."

"Now, Nell . . ."

His wife strode up to him, planting herself before his chair and looking down. Her eyes were black, but something not unlike concern shone out from their depths. "And no one asked for a second and a third warehouse when the barges started coming regular. And who asked you to be assemblyman, eh? Or justice of the peace? Who took notice of you then? Did Granby seek you out? I don't recall his lordship giving a rat's fart for you 'til he couldn't help it, 'til we'd bought up enough votes with food and liquor and lost loans that he had to take you on for something."

Padgett glanced up at his wife, his eyes suffering, his brow creased and damp. He looked struck by these words, not the less painful for the truth behind them. "You're hard, Ellen," he muttered.

Ellen Padgett sighed. "Life's hard," she replied, not without a hint of softness now, a tenderness that spoke of some real affection, some remnant of kindness in an unkind world. The woman bent down and placed her hands over her husband's where they rested on the arms of the easy chair. "Nobody wants you, it seems, nor ever did. The question isn't what they want, Padgett. It's never what they want. It's what *we* want."

A remarkable creature, Bates considered as he walked homeward through the chill of a Bellminster morning. Yes, it would serve a man quite nicely to have such a wife. In the end, her flint and steel had hammered some spark of ambition back into the man, had made him see that forward was the only way now, even if that way lay in shadows and shade for a time.

His wandering had brought him through the markets and shops of Bellminster into the more rundown lanes of the Old Town, dirty streets and ancient homes with greater character than comfort, so quaint as to be just barely livable, the sort of neighborhood that was either a way station to better things or a trap impossible to escape. Bates turned into one of the less miserable buildings, a grand old palace once, now cut up into modern flats so that each suite of rooms was a labyrinth of elegance and pasteboard, fine moldings and flat plaster, slipshod angles and old-fashioned workmanship. In Bates's position, assistant to the mayor, politics held more fame than money. He climbed the stairs, three flights up, and entered the cool darkness of his rooms.

His young wife looked up from the breakfast table, which was crammed into an alcove that had once been a pantry. He spared a glance for her that said he did not want to be bothered, then threw himself into the one plush chair in the sitting room and nodded instantly off.

Mrs. Bates, blond and slender, little more than a girl, rose quietly. She had heard the talk in the hallways last night, knew what her husband had been working at even without his telling her. With a step as silent as a mouse's, she moved to Bates's side, looked down lovingly, nervously, anxiously at his troubled face, disturbed as it always was by worries, even in sleep. One gentle hand, delicate and white, settled on his shoulder, but he shrugged and the hand fell aside. She knelt down then, resting her head upon the arm of the chair, careful not to trouble him, not to touch his elbow or stroke his fingers with her moist cheek, not to invade his slumber with even so much as the soft caress of her hair. She sat there, silent, loyal, waiting.

CHAPTER VI

THE BLUE COCKADE

erhaps it was the cold that numbed all fellow feeling to a leaden dross. Or as some wizened heads contended (with a surety born of that which is indefensible and therefore unassailable), it might have been the full moon that infected the town, or that part that was infected, with a fever of unrest. Or still the blame lay in the very revelry of Guy Fawkes Day, that impish season when more mature reflection was suspended and all license unleashed. To be a child again would be a marvelous thing, or so some think who have forgotten what childhood is.

Afterward, everyone had devised some explanation for what came to be known as The Riot, or more properly, The First Riot. Lunacy or fairies or just the wickedness of a sinful nature, every cause found a voice. All had their reasons for the riot, all except Tuckworth. It struck him as particularly inexplicable, and ominous.

The bonfire was set ablaze just past sunset, but Guy Fawkes was a fiery celebration, and all the town, it seemed, had turned out in Cathedral Square to dance around the flames. Not Reverend Mortimer, naturally, or some few others who thought the festival a pagan sacrilege, but Tuckworth was there, with Lucy watching after Bit, and Bick and Lord Granby smiling upon everyone blithely, benevolently, and the mayor and his party, and Adam Black, too, who had the honor as sexton of the cathedral to light the bonfire, that tower of garden refuse and crack-legged chairs, spokes and broken wagon wheels, of bracken and dead, rotten timbers. The pile lit quickly, and soon the flames were tossing up to the stars, ash white and brown and gray rising on the hot wind to settle back down upon the crowd. Children pranced and old women smiled and clucked and pretty young girls scampered about the edge of that shifting circle of light as strong young lads scampered after them.

Granby and Bick strode through the crowd together, arm in arm, the stooped old man white and lean, the young man lean as well and straight, both looking as pleased with the world as though they had set the universe in motion themselves and were only now strolling out to enjoy their handiwork. They smiled with confidence and jested with whomever they met, and after they had passed, their agents passed behind, saying, "Isn't that man Bick a fine fellow?" "There's that about him what makes a chap just feel right about things." "He's a goer, that Mr. Bick is. Goin' right to the top."

Tuckworth was almost amused by it all, the transparency of it, so like a mummers' play at Christmastime, when everyone in the gallery knows the lines as well as the actors do themselves, familiarity adding to the fun. And yet he knew that this is how it was done, quietly, backwardly, always working from beneath and behind, never up front. This courting of the people—the property-less, voteless people—still had its purpose, for even the voteless had a voice. Yes, and that voice might sway the mighty. Tuckworth smiled and shook his head to see Wilfred Cade rising from his camp stool, draping an enveloping, magnanimous arm about young Bick, placing his benediction on the Member-to-be in front of all the town. So every feeling must be kept submerged, every desire smothered, and all hope—save one—left now to wither on the mountainside like an infant Oedipus, seducer and betrayer of its parent.

Tuckworth glanced at the mayor and his small party, Bates and Mrs. Padgett, huddled together, talking among themselves. That was the mayor's trouble. The man seemed always to want it too badly, advancement or position or whatever it was he chased after. For small offices ambition might serve, might even be laudatory, might goad a man on to worthy deeds. But ambition was rather like a coachman's whip. Its flicking tongue spurred a sluggish team forward, but the better the animal, the less need there was for its sting. For so grand an office as Parliament, ambition must be kept in check, must be denied or at least masked. God help the man who wants too much, Tuckworth considered, or too openly.

The dean looked up at his cathedral, spare and skeletal in the brilliant moonlight, stark and bleached and long, long dead, and he noted a solitary figure at the farthest height of the steps, crouched in the gaping hole of the doorway beneath the tympanum's apocalyptic vision. The dean squinted into the hazy half-light that swirled about that high corner, so far removed from the bonfire. It was Raphael, staring down upon the massing throng, huddled over his sketchbook and crayons. Here was an ambitious man, too, Tuckworth thought. He gave a look down below toward Lucy. She was mercifully occupied with Bit, coaxing her into games with other children.

Raphael did not see him approach at first, so rapt was he in his work. Tuckworth was able to walk right up to him and to stare for a fleeting instant over his shoulder, watching the artist's feverish hand dart and strike at the paper under the moon's bright eye, limning in charcoal the pagan festival, making all seem dark and unholy, a writhing beast below, the teeming, hundred-headed Gorgon with its heart of fire. The dean himself looked down at the sight, so homely and benign to his eye, and thought, Is that quite right? It wasn't the Gorgon with so many heads, was it?

Raphael slammed his sketchbook shut with a leafy clap and turned suddenly away, surprised and unsettled, leaping to his feet in embarrassment.

"It's all right," the dean reassured him. "It's only me."

The painter glanced sideways at Tuckworth, a piercing look from the corner of his eye, and he appeared to relax a bit, but only a bit. "Yes," was all he said.

"I've been wondering all day where you were," Tuckworth told him, settling against the columns of the doorway and looking down again on the square.

"I've been out in the fields, sketching."

"So Lucy informed me." The dean tried to keep this from sounding like an accusation. "I'm glad to have found you at last. I have greetings for you from Leigh Hunt."

Raphael's interest piqued at once, eager for news of the famous critic and poet whose acquaintance he had first made with Tuckworth in London. But he said nothing.

"Yes," Tuckworth continued, as though Raphael had spoken. "Just a friendly note, you understand. The fellow's the most curious correspondent." The dean pulled a letter from his pocket and, opening it, tilted the sheet heavenward to catch the moonlight. "Rambles on about this and that. He makes particular inquiries into your progress here."

Raphael snorted derisively at the thought of his making any progress. In three months' time he had produced not one piece worthy of the word, neither landscape nor portrait, nothing but a few halfhearted attempts and sketches, endless sketches.

Tuckworth read Raphael's anguish, read it in the stiff set of his jaw and the line of his shoulders, and he coughed. "Well, of course it's difficult to judge such things, and Hunt, good man that he is, wants to pass along his encouragement to you. Naturally he does.

But he has something else to offer, something more tangible. He asks if you might be interested in a commission."

Raphael caught his breath and jumped, turning now to face Tuckworth with eyes lit by a volatile hope. "A commission?"

"Blue for Bick!" The shout went up from some anonymous voice among the crowd below, a daring call, loud and earnest. Tuckworth glanced down, startled that Granby should approve of something so open.

"Yes," he replied at last, looking back to Raphael and handing over the letter to the young artist's thirsty fingers. "A paragraph Hunt's inserted just there about a collection of poetry some young man is publishing, and he needs—"

"Illustrations?" Raphael's disappointment was utter and profound. He gave the letter back to the dean in disgust.

"Blue for Bick!"

"Illustrations," Tuckworth said again, trying to sound encouraging. "That's right, illustrations. It seems you gave Hunt a study of the cathedral at dusk. Just something you tossed off, or so he says, and he's been showing it among his friends and acquaintances."

"It was nothing. It *is* nothing."

"Hunt was charmed by it."

"I don't do sketches. Not seriously."

"It's a commission, isn't it? It's money."

"A pittance."

"Work, my boy, it's *work.*"

"But not my work!" declared Raphael, brandishing his sketchbook before him like a shield. "These are studies, not art, small steps to something greater, something grander."

"No one says you have to stop painting," Tuckworth insisted. "No one wants you to give up your art. But you might try something a bit more . . . well, popular, just to make money while you go on."

"I'd be robbing myself of time. Time's precious to me."

"But, Raphael—"

"I'm no illustrator!"

A figure, small and swift and shadowy, ran up the steps two at a time, accosting them with drunken bravado. "Blue for Bick!" he shouted, and roughly pushed a blue cockade into Raphael's hand, then stuck another onto the dean's collar with a great shove, jabbing the pin through to prick the skin, before bolting off again.

Tuckworth stumbled backward and Raphael reached out instinctively to steady him. The dean removed the blue feather with a wince and stared at it, then looked at Raphael in amazement. Raphael only stared back, equally mystified, and both men turned to survey the scene below them. The cry was going up now—"Blue for Bick!"—from every corner of the square. The dean looked about and spied Lord Granby, his white head craning to see who made this immoderate row. Some disturbance in the shadow of the Arms attracted Tuckworth's attention, a small band of fellows racing through the crowd, rudely handling those about them, though it was impossible to make out why or to what end.

"Blue for Bick!"

Several scuffles erupted now, here and there, and one daring soul darted up to the bonfire and emerged again with a flaming brand, running about the square, waving it like a makeshift torch in the air and scattering people about him. The cry of "Blue for Bick" carried on the wind, echoed off the cathedral walls, was being hailed by the very bricks of the pavement. Tuckworth and Raphael looked at each other once more, their quarrel forgotten in this sudden disturbance.

The shock of alarm overspread Raphael's face, and he pushed his sketchbook into the dean's arms with a frantic glance. "Lucy!" he cried and went flying down into the throng.

Tuckworth bounded halfway down the steps after him, stopping as he saw Raphael dash headlong through the square, straight to the place where Lucy and Bit had been playing, to where the artist had been watching them, watching her all night. But Lucy was no longer there. From his vantage above the square Tuckworth scanned the crowd, back and forth. The pockets of disturbance were spreading, running together into a single vast melee, but also contracting within the square, centering about the fire. Saner souls were already hurrying to the outskirts, and now Tuckworth saw her, Lucy clutching Bit in her arms and moving resolutely toward the vicarage, away from all trouble.

The dean turned back to where Raphael was still searching feverishly. Some small fellow had leaped at the young painter, was trying to smash a blue cockade to his coat, but Raphael shrugged him off easily. Raphael looked up, back to the cathedral, back to Tuckworth. The dean pointed in Lucy's direction. "That way," he said stupidly, helplessly, for no one was by to hear him.

Raphael nodded and started off, but the man he had cast to the ground clapped him about the knees and he stumbled and fell. Tuckworth lost sight of him and, panicking, descended another half-dozen steps before stopping once more. What could he do? He looked about and down into the crowd, taking another three or four anxious steps. Some plan, he needed some definite . . . There! Constable Wiley was running along the edge of the crowd, coming in his direction.

"Wiley!" the dean cried. "Wiley!"

The constable slowed and looked about in confusion, like a baby called out of a restless slumber, then started off again.

"Wiley!"

This time the man saw Tuckworth waving his arms. He quickened his pace and was soon at the dean's side.

"Madness!" Wiley sputtered, grasping the dean's sleeve like a drowning man. "It just started, like *that*! Just started!" The situation was clearly too much for Bellminster's small constabulary, and the poor fellow was frozen with desperation, at sea in a flood of mayhem.

"Wiley," Tuckworth said, his voice sharp and commanding. "Raphael is trapped in there!"

The constable shook his head. "It's bedlam!"

"He's being attacked!"

Wiley hesitated and Tuckworth gripped his arm tighter. Then, like a man lost in the dark who catches sight of the light beyond, Wiley's eyes filled with a sudden purpose. Yes, here was work he might do. "Where is he?"

Tuckworth pointed uselessly, then took a sharp, steeling breath. "Follow me." Together they plunged into the fray.

Their journey was a lunatic's daydream, a wild progress through arms and backs and shoulders as they pushed their way through. The dean's only impressions were of forms, not faces, shapes of men buffeting and bruising, a general brawl that seemed to have no aim, no sides, pitting each against all. And yet, despite Tuckworth's earlier fears, he soon discovered how little danger there actually was in the square. Men ran about, shouting and jostling, and sometimes pummeling one another, and blood flowed here and there from noses and knuckles amid the flutter of a thousand blue cockades on the breeze, but there appeared to be more noise than violence to it all, and as often as anyone bumped into the dean and his escort on their journey the two men were greeted with a doffed cap, or at worst a hasty shove, in deference to Tuckworth's age and position. Only once were they offered any serious threat of violence, colliding with a frightened young man in their path who blustered at them incoherently, but Wiley clapped him about the collar and sent him on his way with two slaps to the head.

They arrived at last at the spot where Raphael had fallen, or as near to it as they could come, but Raphael was gone. Tuckworth and Wiley stood back-to-back, looking desperately for the painter until, above the general roar of "Blue for Bick!" the dean heard his own name.

"Dean Tuckworth!"

He turned and saw Raphael, bloodied but strong, his jacket torn, standing guard before the bonfire, Adam Black at his side. Tuckworth grasped Wiley's sleeve, pointing, and soon all four stood together.

"Raphael!" the dean began, alarmed at his friend's wild appearance.

"They're trying to get at the bonfire!" Raphael explained briefly, and Tuckworth saw at once the danger, rioters raging through the town with flaming torches in their fists. Raphael had formed a small company, just a half-dozen sensible men who now encircled the pyre, keeping everyone else at bay. The dean took his place with the rest. At first they were outmanned, and one or two ruffians managed to force a way through and carry off their burning prizes, but soon, with Raphael and Wiley ordering the defense and Adam Black ready to hurl aside anyone daft enough to come near his bonfire, the high spirits of the crowd subsided. As abruptly as it had all begun, so it ended. Tempers cooled. The fiercest rowdies abandoned Cathedral Square, making their ways through the streets for a time, small bands of four or five men loudly flaunting their bravery in the darkness. Some few windows were shattered and some few heads bloodied and one small fire was set and quickly extinguished.

When all was done, when they all had a chance to collapse in the vicarage parlor at last, when the only disturbances left were Lucy's tears as she tended Raphael's cut lip and the breathy outbursts of indignation from Mrs. Cutler, only then did the dean have a chance to consider what had transpired. And the more he thought of it, so immediate, so volatile and quick to spread, the more worried he became.

This couldn't be Bellminster? he said to himself. This couldn't be my home? And the more he thought that it could not be so, the more surely he realized that it was.

CHAPTER VII
JO

A in't the place," the foreman said with a knowing wipe of his red, pockmarked nose. "It's the times."

"I know what you mean, Semple," replied Tuckworth, his face tinged with the gray of resigned dejection. "I do. I just never thought times like these would come to Bellminster."

"Ill times is like rain, vicar. Come to all places 'fore long, will-ee or nill-ee."

The two men stood looking down from the ruined clerestory, that naked gallery circling the top of the cathedral walls, exposed to heaven and the clouds, and they surveyed the work of Semple's crew on the floor below. From that height, with no roof intervening, they could spy the remains of the bonfire, black and still smoldering. In the corners and crevices of the square bluish tufts of cockades clogged the pavement, driven by a chill November breeze, but except for the lonely figure of Adam Black, busy spreading and shoveling load after load of charred refuse into a cart to be hauled away later, the square was empty, the entire town giving it a guilty berth this morning.

The dean sighed. "Are things so bad as that, Semple? Are the people so desperate?"

"Desperate enough, with no work nor hope for none."

"But I thought I knew these men. I thought they were incapable of such an outrage."

"Well, what you knows of the men is what you knows, vicar. I imagine you're as well thought on as any man alive in Bellminster, but don't put more store in such affection as it'll allow. You're a vicar, and these men are men. *That's* a difference." Tuckworth winced at the distinction, true though it was. "You look to their souls, and that's fine," Semple observed, leaning over the lip of the clerestory and staring down at his laborers busy beneath, "but they've got their children's bellies to look to, and their wives nagging for more in the cupboard, more in the larder, or a better place or a better life, more things and nicer things. A man feels that worse than he feels his soul's sickness, 'scuse me for sayin' it."

Tuckworth leaned over as far as he dared and peered down. "Do they all feel this way?"

"Oh, not them lot. They're happy with the work, though it might not pay as much as it would've done two years ago." Semple cast a doleful eye at the dean. "Enough feel it, though. Most. Half the town ain't workin', and the half that is, is scared for the future. But don't lay the blame of all this on every one of 'em. Only a few had a hand in that," he insisted with a jerk of his head toward the square.

"It seemed like more than a handful last night."

Semple nodded. "Like puttin' a match to gunpowder. Just a few wild ones sets the others off and makes a great display."

The conversation died. There was nothing to add. Tuckworth knew he could trust Semple's observations, colored though they might be by the man's politics. Few in Bellminster understood human nature as well as Abraham Semple did. Satisfied with their inspection, and the progress of Raphael's scheme for the cathedral floor, they descended a stony, spiral staircase inside the wall and emerged once more into the daylight. The men were all at work, some fourteen strong and fortunate backs lifting cracked flag-stones and paving stones and laying in new marble, and Tuckworth could not help but notice the black eyes and fresh bruises and the day-old scars that adorned them as they sweated, and he questioned once again what he really knew about Bellminster.

"Here," Semple said, taking the dean by the arm and leading him away from the worksite. "Here's the chap I want you to meet." Approaching them through the door of the cathedral was a remarkable-looking gentleman. He was a gentleman indeed, that was obvious, with a beaver hat and a gold-handled walking stick, shiny boots and a bottle-green coat with a bright yellow waistcoat. But he was a gentleman in miniature, a dwarfish hunchback who hobbled along awkwardly, though hurriedly, busily, with the help of his cane. "Greetin's, Abraham!" he called when he drew near, far louder than was necessary.

"Jo," Semple said, reaching down to shake the man's hand. "This here's that Reverend Mr. Tuckworth I was talkin' on. Vicar, Jo Smalley."

Smalley smiled a pearly smile and extended a hand to the dean, who took it gently. Smalley's grip was firm, though, and amazingly strong as he pumped Tuckworth's arm up and down.

"Pleasure, Mr. Tuckworth," Smalley declared. "Pleasure, indeed. Abraham tells me a good deal that's laudatory about you. Pleasure to make your acquaintance."

"Mr. Smalley," Tuckworth replied with a sort of bow.

"Now, you must call me Jo. Jo's my name, and all my friends is free of it. It don't wear from use. And as every man I meet's a friend, every man calls me Jo, and so must you." He flashed another smile and pumped Tuckworth's arm one last time before releasing it.

"Jo," repeated the dean, trying the name and finding it fit. "I'm afraid Semple has told me little about you, except that you wished to meet me."

"There's little of me to tell," Smalley joked with a wink and an explosive laugh. "My name tells you all about me. Smalley. Aye, he's a close one, our Abraham. Only gives out what he needs to and no more. Good chap. Indeed, I did want to meet you, Mr. Tuckworth, and havin' done so, I'd like to know you. Come, let's walk." And with no more introduction than this, and while Semple went on with his duties wearing a self-satisfied grin, the dean found himself strolling with his new acquaintance as though they were old and tested friends.

"Quite the business last night," Smalley began as they came out of the cathedral and started down to the square, the dwarf taking Tuckworth's arm in a steely grip. "Quite the bit of business."

"Ugly business," Tuckworth said with more regret than reproach in his voice.

"You think so?"

"I don't know how else to characterize it. It was a riot, and that's something I hoped never to see in Bellminster."

"Nor never hope to see again, I daresay."

Tuckworth glanced down at his companion, but he said nothing. They reached the bottom step and wandered off across the square.

Smalley chuckled. "You're a close one too, eh? Like our friend Abraham? I respect it in you, Mr. Tuckworth. Does you credit."

The dean only glanced down again, uncertain what to make of Jo Smalley, though in no particular rush to make anything of him at all. "You wished to meet with me for some purpose?"

"Indeed, indeed. Abraham recommended I speak with you. Says you're a man of profound insights and notable discretion."

Tuckworth reflected that his discretion had been called into doubt lately by Lord Granby, but he only nodded noncommittally, encouraging his companion to explain himself.

"Well," Smalley went on, "I can see you're not a man who lets his curiosity run off with his good sense. I only want to pick at your brain, to get to know Bellminster through her vicar."

"Why should you want that?"

"I'm thinking to start up a business venture in your town, but I need to know it's the right sort of place, a place where I might meet success."

"And what sort of business are you in?"

Smalley squeezed the dean's arm. "Well, you're a right question-and-answer sort. That's a rare type of fellow. Most leaps on to their conclusions straight off, like they're in a passion to get away with 'em. But not you, eh?"

The dean smiled. "Your business?"

Smalley looked up into the dean's face, slid a finger beside his nose, nodded and winked, as though he were initiating Tuckworth into some great conspiracy. But he said nothing.

"Are you stopping at the Granby Arms, Mr. Smalley?" the dean asked, apropos of nothing as it seemed.

"That I am."

"Then I suggest you pass an evening in the pub and speak with Taggart, the innkeeper. He'll tell you all you want to know about Bellminster from a business perspective and a good deal more besides."

"Now, you've got to promise to call me Jo, right? I'll tell you, vicar, I've spoken with John Taggart. Innkeepers and tavern keepers, always the best ones to start with. But I'm in want of . . . oh, let's say I need sager counsel."

"It's advice you're seeking?" Tuckworth shook his head and clucked his tongue. "Then you'll want the mayor, or Lord Granby. I'm afraid I'm about the last man in Bellminster you should be talking to. I have no great interest in business matters."

"Which makes you the perfect man for me. Now," Smalley plucked at the dean's sleeve and brought him to a stop outside a coffeehouse, "let's rest in here for a bit and I'll explain myself open and honest, and you decide whether I'm a man to be trusted. For it's clear you don't trust me, and I like you better for it."

They sat at a table near the front window, and while Smalley drank cup after cup of strong coffee and Tuckworth indulged himself in a single pot of chocolate, they spoke for most of an hour on a parade of topics: on the weather and the crops; on the mill and the cathedral; on John Taggart and his trade; on Abraham Semple and his; on the price of corn and the cost of bread and on the new locomotives starting to spew and steam about London. On a score of different topics they spoke, and not once on the topic of the election. And yet, as Tuckworth realized from the moment they had sat down and as each passing second confirmed him in the opinion, they were talking about the election all the time.

"Dreadful about your man Curdle," Smalley offered at last, draining his cup and pouring again. "A fine member, or so I'm told. Still, Lord Granby's got another fine man in that Bick. He looks to have things all his way."

"It's always been so, certainly," the dean answered.

Smalley's eyes brightened slightly and he leaned forward, his brilliant teeth peeking between full lips. "You think he won't have things all his way this time, though? Is that what you mean?"

"I mean only what I say."

The dwarf stared into Tuckworth's eyes, a deep, intelligent look, and the dean stared back unflinchingly.

Smalley brought his hand down upon the tabletop with a sudden slap. "You've decided me," he exclaimed. "It's taken me some time to decide, but you've done it. Mr. Tuckworth, may I speak to you in the strictest candor and confidence?"

"No, I don't think you had better."

For a moment, Smalley sat frozen, with no hint of surprise, no shock or dismay registering on his face, only a great, calm stillness. Then he sat upright in his chair, shot up like a clockwork man, though the serene look never left him.

Tuckworth grinned slyly. "Mr. Sma—"

A tic in Smalley's eyebrow stopped the dean short.

"Jo, before you confide anything in me, before you decide to take me into your confidence, I want to ask you something. How long have you been in Bellminster?"

"Five days." He spoke flatly, and it was clear to Tuckworth that the man's pronounced curiosity was manifesting itself in a marked absence of curiosity.

"Five days?" the dean repeated. "In five days you've learned a great deal about the town. A great deal. Names and places and positions. Who wields power and who only thinks they do. You seem to know us inside and out. Only five days? Don't you find it curious that in five days' time I haven't seen you in the streets once? Not once? Forgive me for noting, but you're hardly a man to be seen and forgotten."

Smalley bowed his head slightly, conceding the point.

"I wouldn't count Lord Granby a close friend," Tuckworth went on, "but he is a very old and respected acquaintance. I won't hold a confidence from him, not if I could help it."

"Is there some reason why my confidence should exclude his lordship in particular?"

Tuckworth weighed his next utterance carefully before committing himself. "The government have their own man to run for the seat. *You* have your own man. That's what you mean to tell me."

By no twitch or tremor did Jo Smalley betray his thoughts. "Why would you think your election matters to me?" was all he asked.

"Because it's the last thing you wanted to know about, but it's the first thing a man entering on a business venture would have asked. Because I know Abraham Semple, know his mind, know his views. Because there's no better time for the government to make a go of it, with the Tories leaving the field open to a local man. Because you've been acting the spy for five days, keeping out of sight though you've managed to gather a remarkable amount of information. Because, as you say, I am a question-and-answer man, and so I know when I'm being canvassed. Because every topic you've raised involves a political question, a populist question, except perhaps for the weather, though I'm sure you find cause for assurance in that as well. Because of any number of little things that add up to it."

Smalley hesitated. For a long minute he sat unmoving, his eyes fixed on the dean, his mind churning, working to salvage the moment. And then, to Tuckworth's astonishment, and with a slow and easy grace, something melted away from the man, something false though fair, a brightness that was more theatrical than sincere. It seemed to seep out of Jo Smalley, this pleasant façade, to reveal something more human that lay just beneath. It was as though Jo took his polite leave and left Smalley behind in his place.

"You must forgive me, Mr. Tuckworth," Smalley confessed in a voice much different from what he had been using. It was more mellow, less manic and flamboyant, and it pleased Tuckworth rather well to hear it. "I misjudged you, it seems."

"How so?"

Jo Smalley shook his head. "I won't insult you nor embarrass myself by sayin'. But misjudged you've been. So, you know why I'm here, and you have the information without exchanging a promise of confidence for it. Where does that leave me? I wonder. Will you take the news to Lord Granby straightaway?"

"I told you, Lord Granby is a very old acquaintance."

"You told me that he's not a friend."

"I said he's not a *close* friend." The dean considered, speaking his thoughts aloud. "I think his lordship deserves to know the seat is being contested. Doubtless I'm not the first man you've canvassed in this way, secretly, but it's only right that these things be performed in the open."

"For his lordship's sake?"

"For the sake of the people."

"By the people, I expect you mean the franchise."

"I mean all the people, Jo."

"And not just them as votes?"

The dean shook his head.

Smalley settled back in his chair, looking quite comfortable for the first time. "Well, I've been sent up to the provinces that I might smooth our man's way, and here I've stumbled out of the gate and made a mess."

"And who is your man?" the dean inquired.

Now it was Smalley's turn to shake his head, showing his teeth once more, and Tuckworth could not help smiling back at him. "I've given away enough this morning," the man said. "I need *something* to surprise your Lord Granby with."

"Doubtless it's some national figure I've never heard of. I don't take much interest in politics."

"*That* is a shame, Mr. Tuckworth. You've a gift for it."

"I hope not. Why do you say so?"

"Because the only trick in politics is to see through what a man shows and get at what he is. That's what you've a gift for, seein' through a man."

The dean made a sour face, demurring from such unwanted flattery. "I'll keep my light firmly under a bushel, then," he said, rising. "Could you tell me one thing, Jo?"

"Maybe I could. What is it?"

"That trouble last night. Was that your doing?"

Smalley jumped down from his chair. "And why would I want to promote Bick? Isn't that Granby's task?"

"It might have been Lord Granby's doing, and it all just got away from him. That's one possibility. But it was a carefully planned disturbance, and the final effect was to harm his lordship's cause, so it's possible that it was planned for that very purpose, planned by someone else."

"And if I told you I had nothing to do with it, would you believe me?"

"I'd believe you if you told me you did."

Smalley chuckled. "I'm afraid I didn't arrange that little demonstration, which leaves you doubting whether I'm to be trusted still."

Now Tuckworth chuckled, and the two men went back out onto the street together. Before they parted, the dean took a last look down at his companion. "Will I be seeing you about town now, Jo?" he asked.

Once more in public view, Smalley's manic character rose up within him, like a great coat he put on against the wind of popular scrutiny. "Great foolishness trying to hide myself now you've flushed me, vicar. I think me and my fellows might just move things along a mite ahead of schedule. Yes, I think things is going to move pretty rapid here on out."

Tuckworth watched as the little man bustled away to lose himself in the crowd, and he felt strangely gratified, pleased with himself somehow, though for his life he could not say why. Turning, he made his way, not in the direction of Lord Granby's, but toward the Great Hall, to the office of the mayor.

CHAPTER VIII
AMBITION

D ean Tuckworth passed into the fusty shadows of the Town
Hall, navigating its labyrinth of corridors and passageways,
halls and anterooms, where the official heart of Bellminster
beat its quick, official pulse. Perhaps twenty men made up the machinery of the town, that grinding bureaucracy that tied Bellminster to the larger world, yet those twenty toiled away like fifty, like
a hundred. Petty administrators and aged secretaries, youthful
clerks and officeholders biding their pensions, sage idlers and energetic boys in love with the dust of authority moved forms about
all day long, from one desk to another, one moldy corner to the
next, passing sheaths and reams and files about from hand to hand
until all had gone the full circuit of the building to rest at last in
some lightless, lifeless cabinet, a paper mausoleum. Titles and
wills, certificates and permits, applications, bills, records, reports,
affidavits, minutes, proceedings, contracts, proclamations, and
claims were stamped, sealed, and stuffed tight into the drawers of
the Town Hall, stuffed and forgotten.

Such a hive of busyness, Tuckworth considered as he delved
deeper into its secret ways, into the very heart of the building, to
the office of the mayor. There he found young Danny Trees, the

eldest Trees lad, who sang in the cathedral choir not four winters past, whose nose he had wiped and whose scraped knees he had cleaned with spit, huddled over a writing desk, scratching feverishly at some document with its ranks and files of figures.

"Hello, Danny," Tuckworth said, happy to see a face he knew so well, scarred though it was of late by pimples and the sparse seedlings of a nascent beard. "How long have you been working here?"

"H'lo, vicar!" declared the lad, before remembering himself and his place. He coughed, and a severe indifference cast itself over his eye. "May I inquire into what business you got with hizzoner?"

"No business in particular, Danny. I just want to ask him a few questions about that disturbance last night."

The boy lowered his face to his writing. "You'll need to make a 'pointment," he informed the list of numbers before him.

"Will I?" the dean asked, amused at Danny's officious manner, the art of a boy playacting the role of an adult. "Well, I'm sure it's all right. I'll only use up a moment of his time," he promised, taking a step to knock on the office door.

Danny spun about in his chair and clutched at the dean's coattails. "Here now, you can't do that!"

Tuckworth came up sharply and turned about, startled. "I only—"

"Hizzoner ain't to be . . . I mean, he ain't in. You'll need 'pointment!"

The dean stared closely at Danny now, squinting in the yellow-gray half-light of the sputtering oil lamp. "Danny, is that a black eye?"

Danny Trees did not answer, but only looked for a moment at the dean with the frightened defiance of a third-rate official. Then, turning back to his desk, he flipped open an appointment ledger. "Hizzoner can see you tomorrow at ten."

"Tomorrow at ten?"

The lad jotted Tuckworth's name in the book and clapped it shut. "Tomorrow at ten," he repeated, with an air of finality that the dean found almost dismissive. And, in fact, the dean *was* dismissed, for at that moment an ancient clerk came limping up to the desk to drop a stack of yellowing pages on it, and Tuckworth was to all appearances forgotten. He started his journey back up into the sunlight.

Danny Trees gave a guilty glance at the dean's retreating back, and then a furtive glance at the mayor's door. A moment of unwonted introspection, and he returned to his work.

On the other side of the door, the mayor and Bates were huddled in close council. "It . . . it . . . it," Padgett stammered from behind his desk, while his aide sat in an old leather chair with straw bursting from the seams, his eyes closed to reinforce his patience. "Dangerous, Bates! It was damn . . . damn dangerous!"

Bates opened his eyes, a strained smile traipsing across his lips. "It was only a simple demonstration," he said reassuringly. "Merely testing the waters. And if it all went off somewhat better than anticipated?" He leaned back, deep into his chair. "Well, at least we know how volatile the situation is."

"Yes, yes! But so does Granby!"

"His lordship must have had some inkling that things are not quite as they've been in the past. We have a Whig government now, after all. The party are in opposition."

"Not here."

"No, not here. Bellminster is still firmly Tory," Bates conceded with a magnanimous sweep of his hands. "But that's not to say Bick should be left to waltz his way into Parliament. Granby must have expected a contest. Why else would he have played out his little charade? He needed to bring each man's ambitions into the light, so he would know where to lay his favors in paving Bick's way."

"Favors? Favors?"

Bates caught the glint of avarice lighting the mayor's eye from within, and his heart winced at it. He loathed all petty greed himself. Only a great greed, like a great ambition, would suit Mr. Bates. "I wouldn't be surprised to hear that Cade is named a director of the mill sometime just after the New Year," he went on. "And I imagine Ian Fellowes can proceed with his plan to enclose his pastures without any interference from the Town Assembly." Padgett nodded, slowly appreciating what Bates had seen from the start. "This will be an expensive election for Granby, and he wants to know at the outset what the cost will be. I'm sure he has it calculated to the smallest farthing by now, has every man's price in his book."

"And our price?"

The younger man shook his head.

"We . . . we won't . . . ?"

Bates leaned forward, his closeness adding urgency to his counsel. "Last night settled it. And it should have unsettled Granby. Bellminster is ripe for an election, a *real* election."

"I . . . I still don't see it. How can we run against Granby? He's already bought . . . bought the votes he needs. You said so."

"We aren't going to run against him. The Whigs will run."

As simple as it was to shock the mayor with even the breath of a well-planned strategy, Bates was still gratified by the dumbfounded look on the man's face.

"Whigs?" Padgett whispered. "Whigs?"

"Whigs," Bates insisted.

The mayor begged to know how it was possible. Of course, the Whigs had long been a presence in Bellminster, at the fringes, never a power, more popular among the disenfranchised rabble than with the voters. Like mice in a church, they were always underfoot, there but not there. How could Bates be certain they would run? What did he know? With whom had he spoken?

But Bates would not say. Indeed, he became markedly quiet, almost morose. The truth was, he felt suddenly disaffected. Why should he take any pleasure in proving his acuity and proving the mayor a fool in the process? It was too easy and too far beneath his talents to bother to explain himself so often to such a man. So he fended off the mayor's entreaties with talk of a hunch, and "We'll see" and "I might be wrong, but it's the only chance we've got."

Only it was no hunch, and he was not wrong.

Bates left presently, telling Padgett that they must be prepared, that they must remain superior to circumstances, that matters were about to develop quickly and they would need all their wits to hold their heads above the coming tide. He told the mayor anything that would keep the man pacified and alert. Taking his hat and coat, he withdrew, stopping briefly in the outer office to spare a soft, needful word with young Trees. He had to get away from the mayor if he was to plan their course properly.

Out on the street, Bates bundled his collar up about his ears, moving in his usual fashion, head lowered, hat pulled low, staying to the inside of the pavement. He knew about the inquiries being made by someone unseen, someone curious and subtle. He had his ears out in the town listening, his eyes watching, noting everything. He knew how to play the game the way it was played in London, below the surface, mining beneath his adversaries, sticking to the shadows and planning in darkness. That's how he had settled the mayor into his office. It's how he would move him along to greater things. He chuckled as he strode through the thin Bellminster crowd. It all seemed so sinister at times, with plots and counterplots to be devised, traps laid, secrets and lies to be guarded or meted out in delicious tidbits of strategy.

He came up against a large fellow walking the other way, stopped short to force the man around him. Last night had been little more than a feint, though it had gotten rather out of hand. Still, a successful feint. Granby would recognize his vulnerability now, would be forced to play the game in earnest. But against whom? The old man would be tearing his white hairs out to know.

The Whigs, Bates thought. The Whigs. Once they stir up the pot, there's no telling who might float to the surface.

London, that's where the game must end, where all men of talent found their path to lead. London! And who cared if his wagon was pulled behind that fat fool Padgett? One team was as good as another to get you where you're going. At least the man had a worthy woman to help him. She understood what they were about, even if her husband couldn't. He conjured the image of Mrs. Padgett. There was a woman to make your fortune. Bold as a hussar. Ready for what-have-you. A clear eye, her mind focused on her ambition with a clarity not one man in a hundred could claim. Even a fool like Padgett must advance with such a woman urging him along.

Church bells chimed the three-quarters. The dinner hour was approaching. He set his feet in the direction of home, a feeling of dejection upon him from what cause he knew only too well. He would have preferred to stop for a meal at some eatery, a coffeehouse or even a pub. He usually took his meals away from home. Home, he thought. There was an odd word for a man such as he. But just now he needed quiet, solitude. Home was good for that, if for nothing else.

Bates arrived at his modest flat, and his wife's heart jumped when she heard the key in the lock at that hour. "Is everything all right, Charley?" she asked, running up to him in alarm as he entered, her plain dress flouncing about her slim, girlish figure, almost unripe it was so delicate.

"Of course everything's all right," he answered irritably. "How should everything be but all right?" He saw the wounded look on her face, the wide, watery eyes always too ready to take offense, to shed a tear. He sighed. "It's all going well. I just came home for dinner and to get away from Padgett. I've got to find a little space to think." He moved toward the back of the flat, toward a curtained alcove he kept as a study where his wife knew never to disturb him. "Bring me my dinner, Susannah," he told her. "I need a few good hours by myself to plan things."

She reached out to him, her hand wavering in the air between them, hanging there. "Charley," she said, in a voice nervous with feigned ease. "Charley, Mother paid a visit this morning."

Bates continued a few steps as though he had not heard, then stopped abruptly. He said nothing.

"She thanks you again for what you've done for Danny. The boy's that beside himself with pride—"

"What does she want?" he demanded, not bothering to turn around.

"Nothing. Nothing really. Only, she mentioned how much Dad's been drinking with all the time on his hands. He still ain't found work, though he looks every day, or almost."

"Hasn't."

"What?"

"He *hasn't* found work, Susannah. Not *ain't.*"

She hesitated, confused. "No, he hasn't found any work." The words came out carefully, with a precision that lurched across her tongue.

Bates turned slowly about. "How much?"

"She didn't ask for anything, not outright."

"How much, Susannah?"

"Just, if something else came up at the Town Hall."

"How *much!*"

"Five." She said it as a child speaks a forbidden word.

"We haven't got five to spare. You know that."

"Which is what I told Mum, but if some work came up for Dad, then he'd be able to earn it himself."

"There's nothing at the hall." And he turned again to leave her.

"Danny—"

"Danny can be of some use!" he shouted, spinning about once more, his anger and frustration surging suddenly within him. He paused, though his eyes spoke fire, and she took an involuntary step back away from her husband. "There isn't anything," he explained as calmly as he was able. "Not at the hall. Not anywhere." He saw her nostrils flare as she tried to control the tears, she who was mistress of nothing trying to master her own emotions, and he suddenly felt for her, pitied her, pitied his wife the husband she had. "We can maybe let them have three," he offered, trying to sound soft, understanding, stretching a hand out to her, to touch her arm. But there was no love in his hand, only pity, and she turned and ran from the room, the tears mastering her at last.

Bates muttered a curse under his breath. What did she expect of him? Why was her family always reaching out their empty fingers to grasp at *his* purse? She had other sisters with other husbands, common, laboring men. Why did they have to snatch at *his* coattails?

He glanced at the alcove, but he could still hear her sobs in the far room.

"I'm going out to dinner," he announced to the air. "I'll be home for supper. Danny's coming by after he leaves the office." He considered for a moment. "He'll sup with us."

At least he could spare her mother the cost of feeding that lad for one night, he thought. Pausing for a moment longer, Bates turned and went out again, not sure where he was going, certain only that he would not be dining with an easy heart. Behind him, the room was left empty and quiet, save for the sound of his wife's distant sobs.

CHAPTER IX
SECRET SOCIETY

D avey Rose! Davey Rose!" The cry cut across the room's dreadful din like a ship's bell in a fog. "Davey Rose!"

Danny grinned at this reminder of his cleverness, the name he had concocted for himself with such careful forethought, and hurried over to the corner table, a scarred maple slab on trestle legs. "Shut up, yer bunch o' louts!" He blew out the solitary candle with a sharp puff. "Shadow's enough light fer our business." He squeezed himself onto the cracked bench.

Six or eight figures circled the table, with perhaps another half-dozen standing about closely. They huddled in this unnamable hole in the New Town, a front apartment of rooms turned into a gin house. Most of those waiting for Davey Rose, as they knew him, clutched pints of ale in their fists, though some few drank hot gin. They all clenched pipes tightly between their teeth, the waxing and waning of each breath casting a devilish aura over their faces.

"That were a good business last night, eh, Davey?" wagged one wit.

"A bit too good for my master's thinkin'," the young spy chided.

"His lordship go squeamish?" another voice asked laughing from the shadows. "Ol' Granny 'spect nothin' come o' nothin'?"

"Hsst!" Danny hurled a half-empty tankard at the fellow's head, missing by a whisker's short end, though leaving a pockmark in the wall beyond. The suddenness of the attack caught the attention of all, and Danny eased regally back and surveyed the crowd about him.

Their features emerged slowly from the unlit corner, faces joining with the shadows, eyes and teeth bright in the red glow of their pipes, hair long and matted or shorn near to the scalp, noses bent and cheeks sunken and sullen and more than one marked by a wicked blow. They were all hungry, all dirty, and all children. If they each could have told their ages, there likely was not one over fifteen years. Danny had picked them all especially for their task, taken them right off the streets, angry idlers he could bully, none too clever, yet not too dim, souls eager to take orders, ready to break out or break up without caring why or for whom. Days ago Charley had given him a very certain idea of what was needed, and Danny was sure he had built the gang to do it.

Only they had started too well.

"You were brave last night, bucks. No doubt. But don't never forget. This here's a secret society, right? And no man can say who or what moves our hand. Nor no man better, d'ya hear me?"

He leaned forward, his eyes fierce with menace, and glowered directly at the target of his late anger. The boy grinned a chip-toothed grin and nodded with the arrogant servility of youth.

"Good. It's good we should understan' each other." He leaned back again. "I ain't never spoke my master's name in this company, and them as is sharp enough to guess at it might keep their mouths shut. Someone fetch me a pint and a light," he ordered, reaching inside his waistcoat and bringing forth a pipe and a leather pouch. They all stood by while the youngest of their band, a boy no more than ten, though tall and gangly, raced to get his commander's drink while a second ran to the fire and returned with a smoldering dip. Danny held the glowing end to the bowl of his pipe, sucked in three deep gasps of smoke and blew them out again in blissful repose. Then, cooling the fire in his throat with a long draft of foaming ale, he got to his business.

"You're too good, lads," he said. "But that means you're good enough. Well done."

"When can we do some more?" a young voice asked, the smallest of their lot.

"Listen at 'im!" the boy next to him said as he nudged the poor child into the wall, jarring his head against the boards.

Danny laughed through his clenched teeth, sending up a merry whorl of smoke. "I knew you was brave lads! Ready to go it again so soon? Well then, who of you can read?"

Two wary hands went slowly up into the air.

"So many scholars as that? You're a regular liter'ry society, boys." Danny produced a slip of paper, folded neatly, from his pocket. "This," he said, handing it over to one of the readers, "is a list of business establishments. Names and addresses. They're great supporters of my master's aims. Or will be by tomorrow mornin'." Danny chuckled at his joke, and most of the rest chuckled with him, casting uncertain glances at one another. "You go to the alley back of Millgate Lane. There you'll find buckets of blue paint and brushes. Tools of the trade, right? You take them brushes, and you take that paint, and you go to them addresses there and you paint the name Bick right on the fronts of them shops."

"On the shutters, Davey?" someone asked.

Danny Trees sneered. "Now why would a fool paint it on the shutters, as can be took down in the mornin' with no harm? Take down the shutters first, quietlike, and paint it on the windows, right across the casements. Paint it on the doors, too, if you've a mind and enough paint. But mainly on the windows. Big letters. B-I-C-K. You as can read, show the others how. Got me?"

Heads began to bob up and down in the shadows.

"Is that all?" Their nods were checked. The question came from the back corner, out of the farthest reach of the shadows, from a slender, whiplike figure. The voice was dour and disgruntled, filled with all the icy contempt a young heart can feel, yet the tone was strangely soft as well. "What are we, then? Housepainters? Is that all you've got?"

Danny eyed this rebellious angel darkly, a troublemaker among troublemakers and his gravest concern. Even last night there had been too many questions from that one. "And what is it you think you are?"

"I ain't yer prankster, that I ain't," the figure shot back from beneath the shadow of a dirty cap. "That were a good bust-up last night, and I got to scrape my knuckles on a few heads as I've been lookin' to bruise. But I ain't no court jester to be paintin' up winders." Thin lips spat on the floor. "Where's the profit, eh?"

"Don't gin make a youth talk brave, then," Danny laughed. "Where's the profit in that glass your holdin' on to so tight? Where's the profit in your scraped knuckles and them bruised heads you got to lay out last night? Profit, lads? Are you wage laborers then, to line up for your day's shillin' once the job's done?" Danny looked back and forth among the shifting crowd of faces about him, eyeing his young Lucifer closest of all. "Are you no better men than your dads, to measure out your days by the paymaster's ledger, a tick mark in a column of figures? Is that how you sell yourselves, boys?"

Young Lucifer shrank deeper into the shadows. "I sell myself for a profit, that's all. And profit I ain't seen."

"No, you ain't," Danny admitted, his face open as he glanced about at the others, his voice free and inviting. "Tell me, d'you think my master makes his wage by the week? Or by the month, even? D'you think he steps up to the paymaster, his hand held out like some beggar?" Heads shook slowly, though Lucifer held back. "Do you?" Danny asked again, his eyes boring through the dark to find Lucifer's own. The rebel shook a smooth-cheeked, shaggy head and was still. "No, he don't. This here business, lads, is in the way of a speculation. Like money built on the great 'Change in London, a speculation. You lays up your 'vestment now, in the early goin'—"

"My what?"

"Your 'vestment! You lays it up now, and when profit comes in later it rains down on you like manna from heaven. And in the meantime, you takes your profit where you finds it." Danny lifted his pint high before them all in illustration and drained it dry. *Quod erat demonstrandum.*

Every brow furrowed. Every mind churned to grasp Danny's meaning, to understand the nature of their speculation, the cut and color of their mysterious vestment.

At last, a young voice chimed. "It's a wager, then?"

Danny smiled. "It's a wager, my bucks. You're backin' my master's horse. And the payoff comes after the race is run and not afore."

Even in the thick darkness of the gin house, a light seemed to gleam as every face, save one, grinned in dumb comprehension. Young Lucifer only nodded a grudging awareness.

The hour being late and the job ahead holding the promise of at least a modicum of mischief, the party broke up soon and re-assembled (all save Danny) at Millgate Lane. There, in a corner of the alley that skirted the millworks, they found a small reserve of buckets and coarse brushes covered by a stiff oilskin. These they meted out quickly, splitting their gang into four teams, the faster to work their night's work. Two or three boys would raid a shop, leave their mark, and reassemble with the others at a fixed location. Then the gang split up once more and moved on to the next four targets. It was an operation of supreme delicacy and clockwork precision, carried out with a strict discipline that His Majesty's own Grenadiers would have found admirable. One team especially, that under the leadership of young Lucifer, took to the labor with heart and a daring spirit. Indeed, it was not long before these three began to outstrip their brothers, improvising on their theme, marking every available space that came to their hands so that the face of Bellminster began to break out in blue BICKs like pimples.

As the night progressed and these rowdies moved through streets and shadows unmolested and unseen, this same team grew braver, louder, less cautious. Even such mild mayhem as their prank afforded was a welcome change from the nether life they lived, too old for their mothers' knees, too young for their fathers' notice, the grandest of children and the least of men. They capered down deserted lanes splashing their contempt on every door front and storefront, painting BICK in brash blue letters wherever it might fit, caring nothing any longer for the paper they had been given, the official list of official windows. The town itself became the canvas for their anger and its release, the cause of their unspoken hurt and the night's recourse from its sting.

None grew bolder than young Lucifer, though that dark angel took neither brush nor pail to hand, but like a general urged on the other two. Lucifer was quick to point out any likely space that might hold their mark, shoving the younger ones ahead and carousing loudly all the way, possessed of a genius for deviltry, the acknowledged judge of all their art, from whom the others sought a word of praise, a friendly nudge, a wink.

"That's fine, boys!" the rebel called to them, in a voice far louder than the night allowed. "Get them shutters down lively and splash it on thick!"

They obeyed with a recklessness that belied secrecy. They had to. It was beyond their power to do otherwise. Their very nature was to take an order with the same glee, the same violence, the same temper as that with which it was given, so long as their commander was one of their own. They laughed as Lucifer laughed, ran as their leader ran, breathed an air and worked by a light that emanated from those dark, sullen eyes. And like a bitch cur marshaling her pups, Lucifer fired these charges to wilder and more desperate frenzies.

"Here now! What's all this?"

A nightcapped head peered out from a doorway, a shivering candle aglow in a hard-knuckled fist. "What's this?"

All activity froze. The very blackness of the night congealed as the two boys, brushes in hand, their work dripping before them, stopped their hearts from beating. The man came out from his shop—his home—a faded nightshirt dangling to his bony knees, and turned about to look at his shutters cast upon the pavement, a bright blue BI splashing down his windows. The two lads backed slowly out into the street.

The man stood, dumbfounded, trying to make some sense out of the letters before him. "Bi?" he muttered, not angrily, merely confused. "Bi? What the—"

He fell to the dust of the pavement, a line of red cut into the back of his scalp. Lucifer stood above him, inserting a thick, squat bat back into a trouser pocket. All merriment had vanished from that face. The manic glee had melted away to be replaced by a raw and feral hatred. Lucifer stared now with the chilling eye of a grim purpose and brought a thick-soled boot down upon the man's face. This was followed by a savage kick into the hollow of his back. Lucifer kicked him once more, in the same spot, then moved farther up toward his nape, kicked him again and again, eyes glowing fiercely, spitting and hissing between attacks, setting on the fallen victim like the marble cutter approaches the stone, kicked his head and his face, his stomach, his ass, kicked the man until, livid and panting, Lucifer was weary from kicking.

Stopping at last, breathing long, deep breaths of tired satisfaction, the youth turned about to eye the other two, partners in the night's sport. But they had fled at the first blow, leaving Lucifer alone in the street to enjoy the rewards of such labor.

Left in solitude, that dark angel leaned against the doorpost of the shop and brought out the stubby end of a cigar, lit it, and puffed gently. Languid now, relaxed for a time, Lucifer pulled off her cap and raised a dirty face to the stars. The moon, goddess of all the night's mischief, stared kindly down, her milky light softening all terror, bathing all, good and evil alike, in the same alabaster glow. She clenched the cigar in sharp, white teeth, ran a slender hand through thick, matted hair, and passed the other over sweat-stained, hairless cheeks. In such a light, at ease now and calm, the features of that face changed their aspect, seemed translated from some foreign language to a more natural tongue, honest and native. All emotion gone now, Lucifer could at last lay aside those defenses, that brashness and ferocity that held the world at bay, the anger that was her armor. Though she would not hide what she was, she would not advertise it, either. She had seen what became of her sisters in the street that way.

With one last puff on her cigar, she looked down at the hapless shape in the dust at her feet, and went back to work upon him.

CHAPTER X
VOICES AND VOTES

Tuckworth stayed upon the pavement, one in a crowd of twenty at least, a crowd that grew with each man or woman who tried to pass. He stood and stared woefully at the window in front of him with its two blue letters, dried and cracked, B and I. Through the glass he could see Granby and Bick inside the shop, Mortimer and Chief Constable Hopgood huddled together, trading their secrets, waiting for word from Dr. Warrick of the Municipal Hospital. Granby had insisted that Warrick attend the poor man. His name was Evan McAllister, and he was as mild and congenial a coffin maker as any coffin maker was like to be, a man who never had a cross word for anyone in his life, nor ever had one spoken of him. A farmer bringing his cart of vegetables to market had found him lying under the window, blood seeping into the dust of the street in black threads, a stray dog licking at the wound in his scalp.

Why have they brought me here? the dean wondered, glancing down at the pavement, noting the drops and dribbles of paint, the smudged blue print of a thin, bare foot, a thick brush still lying, stiff and dead, where it had been discarded. He saw these things, and his mind set to work on them. What did they mean? How did they fit into the puzzle? Who would run about at night engaged in such a mindless act, barefoot and wild? And who would compound their prankish flight with such brutality, turning an innocent jest into something dire, something awful? Who?

Tuckworth would have stopped, would have left off such scrutiny had he been more aware of himself. This was not his business, after all. What did it matter to him? This was politics, wasn't it? And yet, he could not stop, not even if he would. He might as readily cause his heart to leave off beating or his faith to revive itself. And he knew just as certainly that this was why he had been sent for, this relentless probing and prying that he could not control, his eyes seeing things that were invisible to others. Only they were not invisible. Any man might see them, so why couldn't they? He watched the four figures within, shadowy amid the dreadful wares of the shop. They needed him, or thought they did, which was just as bad. But this was politics. It did not concern him. Somewhere in his soul, however, in that part of him that acted on its own, he began to doubt. There was something else in this, something beyond politics. Or beneath it.

Tuckworth heaved a sigh and resigned himself to where he was, doing what he was doing, knowing what he knew.

Hopgood stepped outside to stand by the dean and the crowd folded him into itself. "What d'you make o' that?" the chief constable asked, nodding his head toward the window.

Tuckworth shrugged.

"Reckon he was spellin' out Mr. Bick's name," Hopgood surmised, and twenty-five faces nodded to one another around him.

"Yes," Tuckworth replied. "I imagine he was. That name appears to have cropped up all over town."

"Aye, it's true." The chief constable seemed to want to say something more, shuffling his feet and glancing up and down at nothing, but he held back, and the dean was not sufficiently interested to ask him what his shuffling meant.

Tuckworth noted the flurry of activity within as Warrick emerged from the back, and both men returned into the shop. Boards and boxes and sarcophagal lids stood sentry about the room, mute guards that had failed their master. Already the doctor was telling Granby the worst of it.

"The man's covered in contusions, cuts, and scrapes. Skin almost gone from one hand, like someone ground his heel into it. He's senseless, and probably was during most of the attack."

"You mean," asked Tuckworth, "that he was beaten *while* he was unconscious?"

Warrick nodded. "Likely the best thing that might have happened to him. Fortunate, you know. His skull is cracked, face beaten raw, both arms and an ankle broken, one arm twice, and two ribs. And that's just what I can feel and see. No telling how much damage has occurred inside. A man would rather be insensible to that." Tuckworth had been led briefly in to see McAllister, and he could well believe the doctor's report. He had never seen a man so thoroughly beaten in his life.

"When will he be able to talk?" the chief constable asked.

"Talk?" Warrick shook his head. "*If* he comes out of it, he'll need laudanum to deal with the pain. Won't be very coherent for a long time. And that's *if.*"

"A nurse," Granby said. "He'll have a nurse. Around the clock. Warrick, you arrange it."

"I know a good woman," the doctor replied, and he retired soon after to attend to his patient and continue washing and dressing his wounds.

Mortimer hemmed delicately. "A fine act of charity, your lordship, providing for this poor man in his moment of need. Especially as you are not materially connected with his tragedy."

"What?" Granby asked irritably, but his eyes followed Mortimer's to the smeared window and his anger was subsumed to more practical considerations. "Oh, of course. Only, I like McAllister. Solid man, no wife, no family. He deserves it."

"Naturally he does," agreed Mortimer. "It is only Christian charity, after all." He smiled wanly at Bick, who smiled weakly back.

Hopgood coughed. "Pardon, your lordship, but don't it seem as though Mr. Bick *is* involved in this? Not materially, no sir," he interjected at once, seeing Mortimer's darting glance, "but immaterially, as it were."

Mortimer looked reprovingly at the chief constable. "I am surprised at you, Mr. Hopgood. What evidence can you present to implicate our friend here? Come, you must have some cause for such a malicious accusation."

"Now, now, I ain't accusin' no one o' nothin'. Only, well . . . his name is slapped up all over the town."

"Mr. Bick is a public figure, Hopgood," Mortimer pursued, placing a hand on the shoulder of the wounded man, who appeared shocked and innocent by turns. "Anyone with a paintbrush might have done this. The work of common vandals and barbarians. Yet you mean to imply . . . no, to assert openly that an honest fellow like our Mr. Bick, a fine fellow, a respectable and, yes, I might say it, a noble fellow like Mr. Bick had a hand in this outrageous assault?"

"Now, now, now," Hopgood repeated, waving his hands in the air as though he would wipe away the writing on the window himself.

"Or perhaps you suspect Mr. Bick of setting his lieutenants to work against that poor man within? Perhaps you think of some dire conspiracy raised against poor Mr. McAllister? Would you like to rouse him from his sickbed to interrogate him?"

"Stop browbeating the man, Mortimer." Tuckworth spoke softly, sadly. "Hopgood doesn't suspect Bick of having any hand in this, any more than he suspects you."

Mortimer smirked. "I am gratified to have escaped suspicion."

Tuckworth ignored the acid edge to the rector's voice. "All

Hopgood means, I'm sure, is that this crime might be politically motivated."

Hopgood pointed at the dean, afraid to voice his confirmation openly lest it be taken for something else again.

"So you adhere to the absurd belief that there is a conspiracy involved in this?"

"I believe nothing yet. I only state what's possible. I'm not even certain that it's likely, just possible." The dean walked to the window and looked at the letters from the inside. "Whoever did this was interrupted in his work by McAllister, that's clear. What's less so is why he beat the man that mercilessly instead of just running off into the darkness."

"Maybe he knows the coffin maker and don't want to be identified," observed Hopgood. "Maybe he was tryin' to intimidate him to keep quiet."

"Maybe. But it takes a good deal less to intimidate a man, and a good deal more to silence him completely. Besides, there's something vicious in this that goes beyond simple necessity."

"A man might panic."

Tuckworth shook his head. "Panic isn't aggressive, Hopgood. It tries to escape peril, not confront it. Besides, there was more than one hand in this."

"How can you be certain of that?" Mortimer asked.

"I counted nine Bicks on my way here, and from the sound of the street gossip, there are as many more in every direction, along every line of the compass, Bicks spread out across Bellminster everywhere. Clearly some gang were involved in this."

"Street ruffians," Granby grumbled.

"If we are to take what they've done here at face value, then they're strangely political street ruffians," Tuckworth pointed out. "Street ruffians who share your lordship's interest in the election? It seems unlikely."

"And why should it seem unlikely?" Mortimer inquired. "May not even the unlearned take an interest in politics?"

"Men with no vote rarely raise their voices in support of anyone."

Mortimer chuckled indulgently. "Well, you sound the proper Tory now, Mr. Tuckworth, although perhaps a bit behind the spirit of the age. Would you deny the common man his right to hold an opinion? Would you deny him his chance to enter the debate where and how he might?"

Tuckworth breathed deeply. "For God's sake, Mortimer, you know I meant nothing of the kind."

"In all honesty, Mr. Tuckworth, I never know what you mean, nor what your political views are. I confess, they are a mystery to all of us." And the rector looked meaningfully at Lord Granby.

The old man glared about him, uncertain how he should feel in such a remarkable circumstance. "It's injudicious," he declared finally with a dismissive wave at the window. "First a riot. Now this. You never saw this sort of thing in my day. The mood of the town is getting out of hand."

"It is, perhaps, reckless," Mortimer conceded. "This violence is truly regrettable, even repugnant. We must see to the bottom of it, naturally. But as to this," he motioned toward the window, "is it so unwarrantable? Could not our Mr. Bick have inspired—inadvertently inspired, you understand—an unfortunate and yet spontaneous outburst of sympathy among our less sophisticated brethren? It is the expression of such emotion we must decry, not its strength. Its result only, and not its cause. Clearly, your lordship has made an estimable choice in Mr. Bick, one that calls out the deepest feelings of support in our townsfolk. The streets are abuzz with talk of his gifts."

"Well, the storefronts are eloquent, at least," Tuckworth managed to jest, though no one laughed.

Mortimer eyed him narrowly. "Your humor is ill-conceived."

The dean shrugged by way of apology, embarrassed and guilty at his own levity, and he continued to stare at the window. "I still say the hands that did this have no interest themselves in the election," he asserted, trying to feel disinterested and yet sensing a stubborn pride rising within him, a desire to prove his point. Only a man like Mortimer could goad his anger so thoroughly.

"Come, Mr. Tuckworth," the rector continued. "What Bellminster man does not have an interest in this? Even among the commonality, even among those with a voice but no vote, as you glibly phrase it, the talk is all of the election."

"Hopgood," the dean replied, ignoring the rector. "Come here." The chief constable stepped over to the window and stood beside Tuckworth, staring at the backward letters. "Take a glance across the road there." Tuckworth did not point, but only nodded his head in the direction he wanted the chief constable to look. "Do you see them?"

"See what?" Hopgood answered, confused. "The people? There's a dashed many of 'em, that's certain." The mob had grown to fifty, and was growing still.

"Standing out front, just off the curb in the street over the way. Those boys."

Two young lads, not quite children, fidgeted from foot to foot in the dust and filth of the roadway. Hopgood stared at them, squinted at them, blinked at them, but he could see nothing unusual at all about them. They were only two lads.

"Do you see it?" Tuckworth asked again, and by now the others had assembled behind them to look out as well.

"Boys," Granby said.

"Their clothes. They're splattered with blue."

For half an instant Hopgood noted the flecks and splotches before dashing to the doorway. The boys were gone before he set a foot out of the shop, however, vanished into the crowd like a pair of mongrels into a milling flock. Hopgood went back inside.

"Boys?" Granby was saying in disbelief.

"Who has less of a voice, less of a care for the world than these?"

"But why would—"

"Notice the letters," Tuckworth said, pointing to the window. "That I a good half a foot lower than the other, just waist-high to a grown man. And outside on the pavement you'll find a blue footprint, a boy's footprint."

"Boys," Mortimer scoffed.

"And why not boys? It's a boyish prank, isn't it? Running about in the dark, taking down all those shutters, slathering on the paint. A whole night's work devoted to that?"

"But if this is boys' work," Hopgood asked, "why would they want Mr. Bick's name to throw about town? I mean, if this ain't politics, why wouldn't they write somethin' more . . . well, more provokin'?"

All eyes turned to the dean, and once more Tuckworth was made to feel that annoying sense that he was some sort of oracle, that they had all come to him for the truth. "I don't know," he said, sounding more proudly defensive than he intended.

"You don't?" responded Hopgood, nearly heartbroken.

"So all this conjecture of yours is merely that?" Mortimer derided. "I must say, Mr. Tuckworth, your swings of logic are quite dizzying. First the cause of all this is political, then it's not, and now it is again. I wonder where all your guesswork will take us next?"

The word stung. "It's not guesswork," Tuckworth insisted, "and you're not listening. We know boys had a hand in this. They provided the sweat. We can assume they have no interest in politics, that it was all a lark for them, yet we know that politics is behind it after all, or Bick's name wouldn't enter into it."

"So where are we left?" Granby asked.

"The boys might have been in someone's employ." For a moment the conversation stumbled into silence as each man considered the implications of the dean's statement. "It might even be possible to tie the riot in to all of this," he went on.

"I knew it!" crowed Mortimer triumphantly. "A conspiracy!"

Bick arched his back like a cat in a corner. "Are you saying that I—"

"No, no, no," Tuckworth reassured him quickly. "I'm saying *someone* did it, *might* have done it, but I don't know who."

"But you think it was me."

"Well, naturally it *might* be you, but it's not very likely. These acts, the riot and the vandalism this morning, they're not helping your cause much, are they?"

Bick looked confused for a moment. It had never occurred to him that such signs of support might act against him.

"Well, who's it like to be, then?" Hopgood asked.

Tuckworth opened his mouth to reply, but another voice answered for him.

"It's like to be me," Jo Smalley said from the doorway. "Only it ain't."

Smalley hobbled quickly into the room, sticking out his hand to Lord Granby and giving it that firm, sharp shake that Tuckworth had already suffered.

"Name's Jo Smalley, your lordship. Friends call me Jo, and as every man I meet's a friend, I wish you'd make yourself free of it. Jo. Only I daresay you'll call me a few other things before our acquaintance is over. Harsher things. Ain't that right, Tuckworth?"

Granby, his hand still trapped by Jo Smalley's grip, looked helplessly about him.

The dean sighed. "Jo is an advance agent for the Whig Party," he stated as flatly as he could. "He is here to prepare the way for his own candidate."

Granby looked down at the odd man, and Jo smiled back up at

him, an open, unafraid, alarming smile. "Jo?" he repeated, unsure what else to say.

"That's it!" Jo said. "Just 'cause we're set up in opposin' camps, it don't mean we can't be friends afore we rip each other to juicy pieces."

Granby jerked his hand away suddenly as though stung by a hornet. "Whigs?" he cried, realizing at last what was happening and who this man was. "What business do Whigs have in Bellminster? Who invited you? Who's your sponsor? Who's your candidate? Name the man!"

"Now as to all o' that," Jo answered, "you'll find out as soon as we announce, and not one minute afore. Can't go divulgin' my secrets t'other side ahead o' schedule, now can I?" And he turned and gave a pronounced wink in the dean's general direction.

Instantly, all care for McAllister and his shop, for boys and ruffians, for voices and votes dissipated in the prevailing wind of contention.

"Mr. Tuckworth," Granby said, his voice thick with injury and dudgeon, his flailing anger finally finding a target, "just how did you become acquainted with this . . . this man and his business?"

"I only met him yesterday. We spoke briefly and—"

"And when did you plan on telling me of his presence in Bellminster? When did you think it fit to inform the party of this . . . this invasion?"

"I hadn't—"

"No, I think you hadn't. I think not." Granby paused for a moment and stared at the dean, looked at him with a look so tender and betrayed, so full of confused and smarting pride that Tuckworth was forced to glance away. To defend himself would have been too painful for them both. "Hopgood," his lordship declared, "find out about those boys. Don't be too hard on them. Except for the young scoundrels who thrashed McAllister, of course. But the rest, just boys having their bit of mischief. Gentlemen, it seems that there's much to do, *now*." And with that last, lingering *now* hanging in the room above Tuckworth's head, Bick, Mortimer, and Granby left, marching out like a regiment on patrol.

Hopgood turned in desperation to the dean, his eyes imploring, begging some question he had not the courage or self-possession to ask. Of course, Tuckworth thought, he wants my assistance. Unable to make the request openly, or perhaps from some doubt created by Granby's sudden wrath aimed at the dean, Hopgood merely gave that look, so pitiful, so helpless, before trotting dutifully behind the others.

Tuckworth turned, glowering down at the little man before him.

Jo grinned. "Introductions is always such delicate things, ain't they?"

CHAPTER XI
THE DEAN ASKS QUESTIONS

hat on earth brought you there in the first place?" Tuckworth barked, his agitated pace checked by Jo's firm grip on his arm.

"The whole town was talking of it. I just thought I'd poke in my head."

"That's not what I meant. Why did you confront Granby that way?"

"Now, a fellow's got a right to defend his name when it's to be muddied by lies and accusations," the dwarf insisted. His more flamboyant nature had once again melted away, and he spoke with an ease and friendly lassitude that seemed to make him another man entirely and placed him in sharp contrast to the flustered dean.

"Were you that certain the blame for this would fall to you?"

Jo gave Tuckworth a reproachful gaze, rather like a schoolmaster disappointed with a star pupil. "Any fool who's been in the trade through a single campaign can see that this is a put-up job. These demonstrations ain't supposed to do your Mr. Bick any good, I can tell you. English voters take a dim view of mayhem and disorder in the streets."

"Very well," the dean conceded. "All right, you're the likeliest man. You've got a right to defend yourself, true. But did you have to burst in like that? It doesn't seem to me that you did your own cause much good back there."

"And how much good could I have done under more propitious circumstances?"

Tuckworth shrugged. "Little. Granby won't be convinced of your innocence, no matter what you say."

"O' course not, nor no man should. I don't expect anyone to believe a word I say in this town, not without proof."

The dean shook his head. "I don't understand you. If your guilt is a foregone conclusion, then what's to be gained by presenting yourself that way? Whom were you trying to convince? The chief constable?"

Jo shook his head and cast another reproachful eye upon the dean.

"Me?"

"And who else?"

"But why me? What makes me so deserving of your confidence? Why try to convince me you're innocent? Granby, Mortimer, Bick, they matter in all of this. It doesn't affect me one way or . . ." Tuckworth's voice trailed off into the soft rustle of the crowd as the reality of his situation slowly presented itself to him. He became aware of just how detached he was from the election. He saw again the look of fierce injury in Granby's eyes, the hurt and betrayal there, and he realized how he was exiled now from Granby and Mortimer and the rest, how separate and alone he was, and why that made him the perfect object for Jo's appeal.

The dwarf gave his arm another squeeze. "That's right. If not you, you who's more disinterested than anyone here, you who's respected and admired and known for your quick wits and sound council—"

"But I don't *want* to be involved in this," Tuckworth said, half pleading with himself. "I don't care who wins the election. I don't care who's undermining whose chances. I don't care about anything but my own peace and quiet."

Jo Smalley clucked his tongue. "That a man so smart should know himself so ill," he sighed. "Just human nature, I suppose."

Tuckworth stopped and pulled Jo into a side alley. "All right," he confessed. "I care about these people." His eyes darted toward the crowd before them on the pavement, hurrying through their separate days, the patchwork of Bellminster's life. "I care for their peace and their quiet, maybe even above my own."

"And now this violence is just starting to simmer and might boil over anywhere, at any time, already has done for one poor chap, boiled right up over that peace and quiet."

Tuckworth looked down at Jo. "And if I do look into this? What's all this to you?" he asked. "You don't care for Granby's opinion. What does it matter to you who's behind all of this?"

"There's my good name to clear, for one, and my name reflects on my candidate. Not to mention there's the benefit of peekin' into my adversaries' schemes. Someone is behind all this, and it ain't no Whig."

"No Whig that you know of."

"All right," Jo nodded laconically, "what I know of. And there's other reasons, too. Personal."

"What personal stake do you have here?"

"Well," Smalley demurred, "personal is personal. I'll just tell you, there's more eyes than you know on Bellminster at the moment, and on me."

"What does that mean?" Tuckworth pursued, then he retreated for a moment into his thoughts, putting himself in Jo Smalley's place, a worldly man, a shrewd and cunning man, a man with some influence in the Whig party, a hard-won influence, a man they relied on to smooth their way, to ensure results, an orchestrator of outcomes. Such a man might have done this, the riot and the

paint. It would be his job to do such things. He might have worked
to sabotage Bick's reputation, to make Bick and Granby seem powerless to control even their own supporters. He might have done it.

All of this occurred to the dean in a moment, passing through
him like a feeling, not a thought, something elemental and right.
Tuckworth's eyes gleamed with all the possibilities of the situation
as he looked at Jo Smalley, the man smiling blithely up at him,
opening himself to the dean's perusal like a book, compact and
tidy. And the dean suddenly saw something else there, a man who
had made his way through obstacles no other man could ever
fathom, made his way to a place he had no right to be, not as the
world judges such things, a place of position and authority and respect, a place he was not about to lose.

"It's all too bold," he commented at last. "The riot and the blue
paint, it's not subtle enough for you. It's the work of provincial talents and strong-arm ruffians, not a political thinker, not a shrewd
schemer like yourself. If word gets back to your superiors, if they
suspect that you had a hand in this—"

Jo laughed a high-pitched, hearty laugh. "God, but you're
quicker than I thought you'd ever be. Now you know all of it. This
is coarse work, slipshod and sloppy, and less likely of success than
you'd imagine, though like enough. It's a desperate gamble, not my
sort of thing at all, but if any hint of it attaches to me, I'll smell of
it all the same."

Tuckworth nodded slowly and they continued on their way, arm
in arm.

"You're a clever man," the dean observed as they walked. "You
obviously have some connections in Bellminster, the local Whigs.
You've got people assisting you. Why not get their help in discover-
ing who's behind this?"

"Honestly? Because we've got our hands full of too many other
things right now, and this I consider more in the way of being a
personal matter than professional. Sloppy as these outbreaks are,

they're still doin' my side some bit o' good, and that's a fair share of my dilemma. Besides which, like I told you, it's a personal matter for me. This might give your Whigs the result they need, but at what cost to my reputation, eh?"

They passed along for a time in silence, and as they passed, their passing was noted. Eyes looked out from shops and doorways. Heads turned up and down the pavement where they walked. Lips murmured and tongues gossiped, and of those who knew what was what in Bellminster, and who was who, and who this odd little man might be limping along briskly beside the dean, three times that many knew who he was by the time the pair reached the steps of the Town Hall to part.

Tuckworth looked down once more at his companion. "I'll follow my own course in this," he said at last.

"I wouldn't ask nothin' else."

"No," the dean corrected him. "Don't say that. Say what you mean. You want me to work your work for you to clear your name. You want me to uncover who's doing all of this, who's planning and maneuvering just below the surface. I daresay you have your own ideas about it, but you haven't got the time or the connections in Bellminster, and so you're leaving it up to me."

Jo nodded his head slowly, his eyes at last sober and humorless.

"You want to know who concocted these demonstrations," the dean asserted. "I want to know who beat that poor man back there."

Jo squinted searchingly. "Why?"

Tuckworth paused. McAllister was no particular friend of his, only the barest acquaintance. He knew the coffin maker to be a good man, well liked. Still, that was no recommendation to act as his avenger. "Violence I can understand in this world," he replied finally. "Like it or not, it's as much what we are as love or hunger. But that? There was something wanton in that, something terrible. There was no cause for it, no reason. It didn't serve the boys who did this any purpose. That kind of violence frightens me."

"How d'you expect to learn who did it?"

"The most direct way is best, at least to start. I'll ask all the interested parties to get word to me of what they know."

Jo chuckled. "And you think they're like to give it up so easy, and to you?"

Tuckworth considered the point. "No, I don't, but like I say, I have to start somewhere. It will have to be anonymous. Just a note jotted on a piece of paper. I don't want to implicate anyone. I only want to discover the cause of this violence."

Jo nodded again. "You go your way, Tuckworth," he said. "Maybe, when you get your answer, you'll stumble on one for me, too. It's as like that you will. All I ask is the knowin' of it, who's workin' his own game in this."

"I'll inform you *and* Lord Granby."

Jo smiled. "All right, then. Me and his lordship. If there's a third party at play here, we both deserve to know."

"If I learn anything, and I'm free to tell it, I'll leave word at the Arms." And with only a nod between them, they parted.

Tuckworth wound his way once more into the maze of the Town Hall, passing through polished and paneled hallways, past oblivious faces, sallow and lightless eyes, men intent on the arcane practices of their faith. He came at last to Danny Trees, sitting hunched at his desk, scribbling the same figures in the same ledger.

"Is he in?" the dean asked, pausing in the outer office.

Danny reached up with his pen and tapped the face of the softly ticking clock. "Half past eleven," he said.

"I see that, Danny."

"You was on the books for ten. You missed your chance."

Tuckworth drew in a sharp breath and let it out again. "Can't you ask him if he'll spare a moment for me? It's rather urgent."

The boy leaned back in his chair, balancing on it, creaking its back legs, and surveyed the dean with a critical eye. "What's it in regards to, then?"

"It's about the election."

"What about it?"

"I want to talk to him about the riot, and about last night's vandalism."

Danny Trees thought this over for a moment, before settling back down with a thud and rising lazily from his desk. "All right," he said with a weary condescension, "only he won't want to." Danny moved to the door of the inner office, knocked lightly, and went in.

Of all the insupportable things in the insupportable world, Tuckworth found the arrogance of youth most insupportable of all. Danny had always been a rambunctious lad who had known his share of trouble, a boy's share. Yet he was also amiable, eager to please, to do almost anything that might win a bit of praise from his elders. Now he seemed to have turned, not surly, but self-important, playing some role for the dean's benefit, a boy acting the part of a man, filled with that ravenous sense of himself that devours greener memories. Tuckworth had no illusions about childhood. He knew the savagery of the young, unable as they were to guard right and wrong against the pull of desire. But he saw no great improvement when youth was replaced with the put-on airs of adulthood, like trying on a coat of paint to fix a crumbling wall. He knew enough men, and women, too, he thought darkly, children hiding in the guise of maturity, people who masked their vicious, play-yard ethics behind the powder of respectability.

Then he thought of Lucy, and his heart lightened a bit.

The door to the mayor's office opened and Danny Trees emerged.

"Hizzoner'll see you tomorrow at four."

"*Tomorr—*"

"And you're lucky for that," Danny added, sitting back at his desk and marking the appointment in the ledger. "Now I've got to shift around three other chaps just to 'commerdate you."

The dean thought he might inform Danny just how accommodating his attentions felt, but he held his tongue and left without a further word, notwithstanding. He saw no sense in aggravating a situation that had already passed from annoying to ridiculous. Instead, he determined to try other means to his end.

CHAPTER XII

THE DEAN ASKS MORE QUESTIONS

The first of these means led through the growing crowds of the streets of Bellminster, under the spreading sunlight of a cheery day, to the bright, airy office of Wilfred Cade, Esquire. The attorney sat before a bank of sun-bathed windows, behind the shimmering mahogany of his desk, a vast battlefield kept swept and polished and neat for future wars. Rich appointments adorned the desktop like ornaments—a letter opener, a pad, a pencil box— all gilt and sparkling, each perfectly placed and unassailable. Cade's office showed no sign of clutter, no vestige of a misplaced page or blot of errant ink. The walls stood invisible behind a leathery sheen of books, each one of which gave Tuckworth the keen impression that, had he pulled it from the shelf, it would have opened as crisp and clean as when it was first put up, its pages uncut and its chapters unthumbed. The only hint of certain business about the room was an elaborate oriental screen carved with dragons and impish apes, behind which sat a clerk scribbling at papers, his invisible presence strangely oppressive.

Cade had attained that degree of success that precludes all effort to maintain itself. Had he worked more, his purse would have suffered for it. The man's chief occupation appeared to lie in augmenting his reputation as he augmented his girth, through doing as little as possible.

"My dear—I may say 'dear'?—Dean Tuckworth," the great man intoned, as the clerk scratched audibly away. "What brings you before me? I'm afraid that, if you have some professional engagement to proffer, my docket is as full as it will allow of being."

"Nothing like that, Mr. Cade," the dean explained from the stiff luxury of a green leather chair. "I only have a few questions about these disturbances that have so shocked the town."

"Shocked, Mr. Tuckworth? That's a powerful expression, and one that wants of a precise definition if we are to use it with any delicacy."

"Well, let's just say disturbances, then."

"Ah, but there we flout precision once more. Disturbed? Who is disturbed? How disturbed?"

Tuckworth sighed. "The episodes of the blue cockades, Mr. Cade, and of the blue paint from last night."

Cade grinned broadly. "Admirable, Dean Tuckworth. Precise and unaffected. What of these two episodes?"

"I'm trying to determine the cause, or causes, behind them." The dean found himself measuring each word as he spoke it, creating a halting cadence that made him sound an imbecile.

"Causes, Mr. Tuckworth? Look about you. The mill failing, jobs gone a-begging, corn dear and bread dearer. Can any man not see the causes of such things? It appears that political reform has succeeded only in reforming prosperity into something else."

Politics, the dean thought to himself. It always comes back to politics. "I was hoping to get at more immediate causes," he said. The attorney only looked at him, a bland grin of unconcerned ease gracing his large face. The clerk behind the screen paused in his scribbling, clearly awaiting the dean's next utterance that he might continue his official record of their conversation, and Tuckworth suddenly realized that he had no idea how he should proceed. After all, Cade was as much a suspect in all of this as anyone else. He had been a leading contender for Granby's patronage, or had certainly acted as such. The attorney's hopes were now vanquished. But were they? Did some smoldering coal of ambition allow his hopes to glow within, unseen, ready to flare again? Was he arranging these events to diminish Bick's stature in the community? Was he secretly preparing to step forward into the vacuum of leadership, to accept the acclamation of his fellow citizens, to mount the stage of the great national drama for Bellminster? And if so, what could be gained by asking him if he were?

Tuckworth hesitated for one moment more before beginning.

"These episodes, these events are nothing to me in themselves."

"Nor to me, either."

"But now a man has been hurt, might possibly die. You've heard what happened to McAllister, the coffin maker?"

"I have been informed."

"Well, that *does* concern me. It concerns me deeply."

"That's more than I know, Dean Tuckworth. Your legal standing within the parish *is* dean, I believe, and as such, ministering to the congregation is not within your purlieu. Forgive me for speaking with a precision that might seem unfeeling to one in your profession, but my profession is the law, and law is words." Cade grinned unapologetically. "Of course, a vicar's duties are *somewhat* more directly involved with the general populace. Perhaps, since many of the town continue to call you by your *former* title, you are experiencing difficulty in maintaining your new position as *precisely* as you might like. The hard death of an old habit. But," he concluded, magnanimously, "I'm willing to acknowledge your feelings in this matter as your own, though owing to no *official* standing."

Tuckworth took a moment to extract his mind from this tangle of precise language. "As to the events themselves," he started anew, "I leave their consideration to the authorities of the town. My immediate concern is with this attack upon McAllister. I want to know who did this thing, and I want to know why."

The clerk scratched down the dean's desire from his place behind the screen.

"So you wish to know who, among all the despairing, frustrated, disillusioned men of Bellminster, might have laid hands upon the coffin maker."

The dean sighed. "I take your point, Cade, believe me."

"And how, in a town seething with unspoken anger, do you hope to discover the one man who might have let his passions overflow at last?"

"I hope to follow him through his employer."

Cade paused, and an inquisitive eyebrow flinched on his broad forehead. "His *employer*?"

Tuckworth was gratified to have arrived at the crux at last, and to such effect. "Mr. Cade," he pressed, "you were eager to garner Lord Granby's favor for your own candidacy."

"Was I?"

Tuckworth frowned at the evasion. "Please, Cade. Can we approach this matter on a more open footing? You know you were a candidate."

Cade considered something for a moment, retreating within the deep folds of fat about his eyes. "Voles!" he called at last, and the sound of the clerk scratching away from behind the screen ceased. The attorney nodded at Tuckworth. "Very well, I was happy to think myself not ill-suited for the office. Of course, I support his lordship implicitly in his selection. Young Mr. Bick will make an admirable Member and will serve, I have no doubt, to Bellminster's great credit."

"Thank you," Tuckworth said, honestly relieved to have worked his way through Cade's legalistic defenses. "Now, as a past contender for the office, wouldn't you say that these demonstrations are more detrimental to Bick's chances than otherwise? That they are in fact harming his candidacy?"

"Mere gates to be jumped over. They can hardly affect the outcome in a one-horse race," Cade answered, shrugging. "They might slow, they might retard, but they can never defeat his lordship's aims."

"So you don't believe Granby would be inclined to toss off Bick under the present circumstances?"

"No."

"And if circumstances grew worse, if these demonstrations continued?"

Cade shook his head so that his jowls shivered. "Lord Granby has been made to look foolish already in this election, playing off man against man and getting caught." Was Tuckworth mistaken, or had the lawyer just winked at him? "Any appearance of retrenchment at this late date would only add to his embarrassment. I daresay his lordship will be able to push Mr. Bick through, regardless of these episodes. One thing you could learn about politics, Mr. Tuckworth. It's not necessary to have the good opinion of the general population. All you need is the electorate, and only a half-plus-one of them. Votes, Mr. Tuckworth. All that matter are votes."

"Of course," the dean answered. "Of course. But, if the circumstances were to change, if another horse were to enter the race, how would that alter Granby's strategy?"

"Another candidate?" Cade said calmly, casually, but his eyes were alight with a sudden energy.

Tuckworth leaned forward. "The Whigs are bringing in their own man," he confided, feeling the thrill of divulging a great secret.

Cade leaned back in silence, and once more his eyes darted about within the shadows of their fat folds. "Voles!" he called again at last, and in perfect concert to the call, Tuckworth heard a door open and close behind the screen, and they were alone in earnest. "Are you sure?"

"Perfectly. I think by now the information will be generally known. Lord Granby has just been introduced to the fellow managing the Whig interests."

"And that man . . . ?"

"A dwarf named Jo Smalley."

Cade produced a small notebook from the inner pocket of his coat and took up a pencil from a box on his desk. "Smalley," he repeated as he scribbled the name, then sat back, reflecting, tapping the paper with the tip of his pencil.

Tuckworth coughed.

"Ah, Dean Tuckworth," the attorney said, brought back to the discussion at hand. "As you have surmised, this revelation—may I call it a revelation?—materially alters the landscape."

"Yes, I thought it did."

"Were I you, which I am not, I would address my inquiries regarding these episodes to Mr. Smalley. He certainly would have the most to gain."

"He would have something to gain," Tuckworth replied, nodding. "And I've already spoken with him. But I feel that you would have something to gain, as well."

Cade's eyes sparked at the accusation, and he looked wistfully at the screen.

"I'm not accusing you of anything, Cade," the dean was quick to add. "I only point out what should be obvious. Several men toyed with the nomination, but you, Ian Fellowes, and Winston Padgett were the most forthright about it. You three openly pursued Granby's support."

"A support which he had already manifested upon Mr. Bick."

"Precisely. If Bick can be undermined, if he can be blown up,

Granby would be forced to turn elsewhere. He couldn't risk the seat on an ineffectual candidate."

"My dear Dean Tuckworth," Cade said, once again the broadly magnanimous man, "I confess, I do not understand your method of interrogation. No, sir, I do not understand it at all." He laughed good-naturedly. "You are too bold, too—may I use the word?—too honest. A man has only to lie as boldly and you are thwarted. You baffle me, sir."

"I must admit, I have no method," Tuckworth replied, unable to suppress a smile. "And this is no proper interrogation. I don't want to find out which of you is behind these demonstrations. So long as no one is hurt, it doesn't interest me."

"Yet someone has been hurt. We return at last to the start of all this."

The dean nodded. "Someone put those boys up to it last night."

"Boys?"

"Yes, boys. I don't believe the responsible party foresaw what would happen. I don't think he had any cause to want it all to end the way it did. But that's how it ended. I only want to do what I can to make certain such violence doesn't erupt again. And I want to talk to the boy who did that thing, who beat poor McAllister."

"An act of redemption, Mr. Tuckworth?"

The dean only sat and looked at the attorney.

Cade leaned back in his chair and laced his stout fingers across his waistcoat. For a long moment he stared at the dean, and Tuckworth allowed himself to be stared at. He did not look away, but met the attorney's gaze openly, letting the man derive whatever he could from the inspection. At last, Cade spoke. "It will not do, Mr. Tuckworth. No, sir, I'm afraid it will not do."

"What will not do?"

"This, sir. An act of redemption? But whom will you redeem? If the identity of this person—this young person, as you believe—can be discovered, and if this same young person can be reached—reached through the maddening maze of politics, you understand, reached through the intervention of one most particularly disinclined to allow such an interview—how will you do it? How will you redeem this rogue? It is a matter of law, sir. Let the law work its work. Time enough for redemption behind bars, eh?"

Still, Tuckworth was silent, though whether from petulance or ignorance, even he could not have said.

Cade spread his hands wide, by which he meant that he had done all that he might for the time being, and somewhat more besides, and had absolved his conscience of all responsibility. "Very well. Your purpose, as I understand it, is served. If I am in fact the responsible party—I will not insult you by avowing to the truth that I am not—if I am, I say, then I have been rightly warned. And if I know the identity of this young person?"

Tuckworth rose. "You know where I can be reached. A note left at my door is all that's required. You needn't sign your name. No other identities need be compromised."

Cade leaned forward across the desk, extending his large, soft hand. "Good day, sir."

Tuckworth left, not very pleased with himself, his spirit dampened and discontented, feeling as though he had shown himself a naïve fool, a babe. He stepped back out into the bright midday. A small herd of boys darted madly past, raising a devilish ruckus. The full business of the afternoon was bustling about him, men and women hurrying their independent ways, wagons rattling behind dusty, sway-backed horses, voices calling names he could not catch. Even in Bellminster, he considered, even in these depressed days it was possible to call the town crowded. At times, he realized balefully, even Bellminster seemed a very big city indeed. Maybe Cade was right and he was playing a fool's part, relying on the conscience of one already proven to be a schemer, hoping to unearth a name from the depths of men's darkest dreams, their fiercest desires. Politics, it was all politics, the quintessence of ambition, the longing for power as power alone. How could he hope to appeal to human feeling against that?

He sighed, and ducked his eyes against the sun's glare, and made his way through the crowd.

CHAPTER XIII
AT HOME

Tuckworth stepped through the door of the vicarage, and at once the stillness in the entry told him that something was wrong. The light streaming into the hallway from unseen windows appeared out of place and intrusive, as in an abandoned house, its sprinkle of flying dust only a troupe of wayward fairies passing through, specks lost in that somber space. The thin, tasteless air had a charged feel to it, like lightning just before it strikes, stirring the hairs on his neck without moving them. He strained to listen, to hear the sound of muffled sobs. A man living among women, a foreigner in his own home, he had learned to dread this signal of disquiet. Yet all he heard was a silence that troubled him more deeply than tears might have done.

He moved forward and peered into the parlor. Raphael stood before the neglected embers left smoldering in the hearth, his back to where Lucy sat stiffly in her chair, hands crossed in her lap, a basket of sewing at her feet, discarded, forgotten. The picture they created was formal and homely, a domestic vision devoid of genuine feeling, or too full of it, perhaps. Tuckworth said nothing, simply stood there waiting for the lightning to strike.

Without looking at either the dean or his daughter, as a man discharged of a mission, Raphael turned from the hearth and swept past Tuckworth. "Good day, sir," he stated flatly and left, the door crashing closed in his wake.

Lucy twisted her head away for a moment, caught sight through the open window of Raphael retreating across Cathedral Square, and turned back again, not looking at her father. "Mrs. Cutler has gone out with Bit for . . ." Her voice trailed off.

"Lucy—"

"For the marketing. They've gone to do the marketing."

"He's leaving again?"

Lucy nodded. She would not cry. She would force herself not to cry. She had cried for him too often before this. She would not do it again.

"He's only confused and frustrated with life. It's natural at his age, so young. He's not ready for the compromises life is forcing on him. I'll speak to Raphael, my dear."

"You'll do no—" Her voice caught on a swallowed sob. "No such thing. He's able to decide for himself what's best for him."

"Yes. Well, I might have a talk with him regardless. Just say my own goodbyes. He's my friend, too, you know." He saw her shiver as at a nibbling breeze. "When is he thinking of leaving?"

She shrugged. "He's on no schedule that he let me know of. It might be tonight and it might be next . . . next month and it might be after the first of the year." Lucy took up her sewing, tending to a rip in one of Bit's petticoats, and her fingers worked of their own mind, following their accustomed practice. As she sewed, her father watched her, the sunlight weaving through her raven hair, making the subtler tones, the crimson and auburn threads hiding there, shimmer like a treasure to be sought and won. Her face was in shadow, the furrowed brow and the dark, purposeful eyes a mere charcoal rendering of herself, a faint reproduction of her beauty. She brought the petticoat up to her face, peering closely at the fine work, and her lips parted so that her teeth glistened in a grimace of profound study while she forced her attention into its proper place, to the reality of the task before her.

Tuckworth spoke. "Should we move your chair around to the light?" he asked.

She looked up and in that instant her fingers betrayed her. The needle struck through the cloth and bit into her thumb. With a kittenish mew Lucy jerked her hand away, but not before a single red drop fell upon the immaculate petticoat. She pinched her wounded thumb, brought it up to her lips to suck the sweet misery clean, and stared down at the ruined garment.

"Now—" was all she managed to say before tears flooded over the tops of her defenses, falling beside the red stain, dropping to the petticoat like rain on a snow-smothered field. She did not sob. She only cried silently, hopelessly.

Her father stepped up and placed a gentle arm about her shoulders. She buried her face against his plump waistcoat and wept more silently still.

By the time Mrs. Cutler returned with Bit in tow, quiet behind her, Lucy's eyes were dried, though laced with webs of red. "How *can* they hope to build a nation of men with beef as dear as it is?" the housekeeper declared as she darted through the hall and into the kitchen beyond, her bags full and swaying with every step. "We'll all be living off salt pork and cabbage and the odd turnip and naught else come spring at such a rate," she called out. "Salt pork thins the blood and weakens the heart. Any doctor'd tell you the same. Thins the blood like vinegar. Can't keep strength in the body on salt pork." Her mindless chatter sounded like the blessed balm of normalcy, and the rest of their afternoon passed in relative calm, with Lucy intent upon her sewing, Bit playing softly with her dolls or helping Mrs. Cutler with supper, and Tuckworth, too worried to abandon them for the peace and solitude of his study, sitting in the parlor reading, and not reading, his mind reaching out to each of them in turn between the paragraphs of his book, like a delicate stroll over the smoothness of a frozen lake, secure and uneasy at once. At half past seven they settled in for their evening meal, just Tuckworth, Lucy, and Bit at the table, with Mrs. Cutler serving and then retiring to the pantry.

Bit. Tuckworth watched her now as they supped. She had been with them, living under their protection, in their family, for months now, and he still felt as though she were merely visiting, not really a part of the household. Surely he was the only one who felt this way. She was so quiet around him, possessed of herself the way no child should be. He did not even know how old she was, not exactly. Six, maybe. She had come to them out of Bellminster's darkness like a changeling, had been bought in a pub, paid for and given as an offering to a tortured soul, a man wealthy, weak, and corrupt, and pitiful, too. She had not escaped untouched. But she had escaped, he assured himself. She had.

Bit looked up at him quickly, her wide, dark eyes framed by the wayward gold of her hair. Her eyes were empty and deep, a hole dug out and left unfilled. She held some mystery there that frightened him, that he hoped she might someday forget. And yet—how strange—he felt it must be protected, too, guarded against discovery, or release. He knew of secrets, knew the cruel chains with which they bound the soul. He tried to smile at her, kindly, but she only turned away again to her meal.

Immediately after supper, and as the dishes were still being cleared away, Tuckworth announced that he would be going out.

"So late?" asked Lucy.

Mrs. Cutler huffed as she took up the plates and stacked them noisily at one end of the table. "Fine night to be traipsing about, with a cold wind blowing up all sick and wet from the Medwin. Catch your death." And, in fact, a brisk breeze set up a low howl through the chinks in the casement.

"I'll wear a scarf," the dean assured them all, though he insisted that his mission could not be put off, and so, wrapping his woolen muffler about his throat and letting Lucy tuck in the corners under his coat and peck his cheek, the dean went out again into Bellminster. He was determined to see the mayor, and since it was impossible to get past Danny Trees during working hours, he decided to pay a social call upon the Padgetts.

Unfortunately, the mayor employed a butler who was nearly Danny's equal in obstinacy and obedience.

"Neither his honor nor Mrs. Padgett is receiving this evening," the bald-headed sentry intoned, his voice an oily and lugubrious obstacle.

"Yes, but if you'd just tell him I want only ten minutes from his evening, that's all."

The fellow seemed quite unmoved, however, a stolid presence planted in the middle of the doorway, until Mrs. Padgett materialized behind him, her own formidable figure causing that other to dissolve into comparative inconsequence. "Hayslip, what on earth are you about, letting the dean shiver himself to death on our doorstep?"

The sentry offered no excuse, merely bowed and stepped aside.

Grateful at last to be freed from the grip of clerks and servants, butlers and secretaries, Tuckworth entered the mayor's house, as grand and imposing a residence as stood within the confines of the city. Winston Padgett had made his money slowly, laboriously, as a dealer in anything that might be gathered and shipped with ease— cloth and wool, corn and seed, tea, coffee, and spice—shipped to warehouses filled with the materials of civilized life, to be traded into and out of the country, first boxloads, then cartloads, then bargeloads. In consequence he had made his wealth fast to himself, tied it firmly in golden cords of ownership that not even these hard times could easily loosen. His house was decorated in the finest, most expensive style that fashion allowed, dripping with damasks and silks and satins, gold and silver and ivory and rarest ebony. "The best" was Winston Padgett's sole standard, his household god. It had not been so before his marriage, perhaps, but all it takes is a wise match to make a man.

Tuckworth was escorted by Mrs. Padgett to the parlor, into the presence at last of the mayor. Padgett appeared startled to see the dean come wandering by for a visit, but there was nothing remarkable in his surprise, so remarkable was the visit itself and the cause that made it necessary.

The dean, true to his word, settled into a lavishly comfortable chair and spent only ten minutes conveying the gist of his message, his suspicions and determination, his assurances and resolve. He held back nothing, except perhaps the most livid details of the coffin maker's injuries. Tuckworth spoke of Jo Smalley and Lord Granby, of Evan McAllister and Wilfred Cade, of votes and voices, boys and blue paint. He told again the whole story as if he were being fiercely interrogated himself, though if he were, it was a one-sided business, for neither Padgett nor his wife uttered a word during the entire dissertation, notwithstanding the mayor's blustering harrumphs and coughs of indignation.

"A name is all I require," Tuckworth concluded, "just a few lines left at my door. No one else need be implicated at all. I only want a chance to speak with this boy."

A short silence followed, before the mayor erupted.

"And . . . and . . . and . . ."

"Winston." Mrs. Padgett looked sharply at her husband.

The mayor threw himself back in his chair.

"My husband knows nothing of these things, Mr. Tuckworth," the lady reported.

"I'm not asserting that he does. I've already spoken to Wilfred Cade. And I'll visit Ian Fellowes tomorrow. I hope to have reached the right party by the time I'm done."

"And what do you hope to do with this information once you discover which party is the right one?"

"Believe me, I don't much care who started this awful business, since I don't think anyone meant for things to go this far. But there's a dangerous boy out on those streets, and I want to find him."

"There are many dangerous boys on our streets," Mrs. Padgett pointed out, shaking her head and grinning indulgently. "Our dear Mr. Hopgood has his hands full with them, boys and men together."

"There's none who has shown such reckless violence, not that I know of." With as much discretion as he could, Tuckworth then told them of Dr. Warrick's report, that the coffin maker's hand had been ground into the pavement like a man would step on an insect, that he had been beaten into unconsciousness and even past it, beaten where he lay insensible in the street. He described the man's face as he had seen it himself, discolored and broken, eyes swollen, lips split and bloody, nose twisted. The mayor seemed physically moved by the image Tuckworth called up, as the dean hoped he would be. Padgett passed a hand over his moist forehead and blinked spasmodically, but his wife looked on with a mother's concern in her eyes, or rather, the concern of someone else's mother, her attitude polite, attentive, yet mildly detached.

"I feel certain no one ordered such a senseless attack made on poor McAllister," Tuckworth concluded. "Yet I think someone knows who did it, or suspects who did it at least."

"Mr. Tuckworth." Padgett seemed calmer once the dean had finished, less flustered if still unsettled. "I am sur . . . surprised to come under such an accusation."

"I'm not making an accusation."

"I'd like . . . like to know what else . . . else—"

"Winston, stop stammering so. The dean has accused us of nothing, nothing of which he hasn't already accused the others. We should feel flattered to find ourselves in such select company."

"Still, it's un . . . un . . . ." The mayor sat back once more, looking pettish.

"My thanks for your understanding," Tuckworth told Mrs. Padgett, with a conciliatory nod at the mayor. "It's been a trial broaching this topic without losing every powerful acquaintance I have in Bellminster."

"Now, Mr. Tuckworth," the lady chided mildly, "I trust you see us as more than acquaintances. Winston and I mark you as a friend, one of our dearest. Don't we, Winston?"

"Well, naturally." Though the mayor sounded far from friendly admitting it.

"I'm grateful to you both," said Tuckworth, taking only another minute to detail how the culprit's name might be sent to him in an anonymous note, before he rose to leave.

"I cannot help wondering," Mrs. Padgett said as she ushered the dean to the door, "if this sort of business is more in Chief Constable Hopgood's line. Finding this young person, I mean. The law is, after all, the law, and such a brutal attack." She clucked her tongue in a style that could be regarded only as melodramatic. "There'll be time enough to save that poor boy's soul after he's in jail, won't there be?"

"Of course, Hopgood is pursuing the matter."

"And he's requested your assistance, has he?"

"Well, no, not actually. Not in so many words."

"Wordlessly? How curious. What a remarkable rapport the two of you must share."

The dean was beginning to feel uncomfortable at these remarks, expressed so much more pointedly than Cade had been able to do. "Do you think I'm overstepping my authority?"

Mrs. Padgett chuckled easily. "I must admit, I can't for the life of me recall what authority you possess in this that might be overstepped. But that's no serious consideration when good works are in order, is it? Still," she stopped and turned to face the dean, a distressing openness to her glance, her eyes shaded by a sincere concern, "I would feel more at ease if you promised to proceed cautiously in this matter."

Tuckworth was astonished, though he tried not to show it. "I hope I always do move with caution," he said.

The lady shook her head. "Your history is too infamous, Mr. Tuckworth. You are a rash fellow in search of adventure to color your waning years. I'm sorry to have to state the matter so bluntly, cruelly perhaps, but there it is." She smiled at him, a warm and winning smile. "You're a meddler, dear man. A worrisome meddler, but then, aren't we all? Anyone who hopes to do good in this world must meddle in other people's affairs. Now, I like you. I confess I do. And I would not see you meddle your way into something you can't get out of again, not unsullied."

"Are you speaking of politics, Mrs. Padgett?"

"There you are," she said, laughing. "Quick as a wink. Yes, politics. You know what it is from the outside, Mr. Tuckworth, and it's ugly enough from where you stand. But within, it's worse still. Believe me, far worse. Filthy, wretched business, rotten to the very pit. Governed exclusively by results, you understand. Not ethics or morality, just results. It is itself the great end, for which all means are justified. No man comes near it who isn't spoiled by its contagion."

"If the business is so distasteful, why does your husband pursue it?"

"Because it must be pursued by someone. Given the need for the thing, I think Winston would rather take it on himself, than leave it to others. It's a sort of moral sacrifice, and vaguely noble, don't you think?" She smiled a remarkably endearing smile.

"I suppose a man with his position, a successful man, must either govern or be governed."

Mrs. Padgett smiled again, less familiarly. "There you have it! How astute you are, and clever. Now, please don't allow that cleverness to draw you into any difficulties. My advice to you, if you will take it from a woman, is to leave all of this to Mr. Hopgood. It's his job, after all, isn't it? Each man to his proper sphere, eh, Dean Tuckworth?"

His proper sphere. The words stuck in Tuckworth's mind as he walked through the gathering chill and damp of the Bellminster autumn, passing from the light of one streetlamp to the next, a dull ache seeping into his bones, his hands clutching stiffly at the folds of the woolen scarf about his collar. What was his proper sphere? He had known it once, or thought he had—the world of a country vicar. The town was smaller then, grateful to have grown beyond even the memory of its medieval grandeur, with only the cathedral as a token of that time. There was no mill in those days to define Bellminster's place in the world. He sighed. For so much to have changed so quickly, in the town, in his life. Why was he doing this, taking up a cause not his own? Was he truly so concerned for this boy, or was there something else, something in what Mrs. Padgett had intimated? Was he simply an old man in search of more life, forcing himself into the thick of affairs, making himself out to be more important than he truly was? Was he just meddling?

Tuckworth stopped. Was he a fool, he thought, only an old fool? It was a question for which no answer existed. No oracle could divine it for him. Yes, it seemed he might be. Cade had told him so, and Mortimer, and Mrs. Padgett. He certainly looked that way to everyone about him, chasing will-o'-the-wisps, ghostly gleams in the dark. What right had he, a man with no faith, no God, to seek redemption for another, even earthly redemption, redemption from violence and despair? What was he really seeking? Was it this boy he was trying to save, or himself?

He glanced ahead at the streetlamps, a line of bright spots fading in the distant fog, circled round by darkness, islands adrift in a sea of the unknown, the unknowable. Nothing to do, he realized, but move on through that sea and grasp hard at whatever islands presented themselves. A thought dawned on him as he proceeded, a sudden revelation that struck at his heart and rang with something like the certainty of truth. Only questions are real, he considered. Only doubt is true. All answers, all of them, are a matter of faith.

CHAPTER XIV

BATES TAKES A STAND

I've tried talking to them," Bates insisted, more to himself than to Danny, sulking in the dusty shadows of his flat. "I've tried reasoning with them. But there's no talking to people who won't listen."

"Squeamish, is what it is," Danny offered.

Bates shot Danny a glare as if to ask what right he had to speak. In truth, he was tired of talk. He had just spent an hour trying to talk something—pride or courage or common sense—into the mayor, but even the man's wife had been unable to move him, not that she made much of an effort. Mrs. Padgett seemed almost as willing as her husband to give the whole thing up.

"Such violence is outrageous," she had declared.

"Far beyond . . . beyond anything—"

"But none of it can come back to you," Bates tried to assure them. "It's all laid at Bick's feet. Even the lads think Lord Granby is behind it all."

"Too risky," Padgett managed to say.

"How? Where is the risk? You have no idea where I've gathered the boys from or how I'm commanding them. They wouldn't know me from Adam, much less you. No one in this whole business holds all the information. You wouldn't even know it was boys if it weren't for the dean, so where is the risk?"

"The risk lies in your overconfidence," Mrs. Padgett said, somewhat testily. "Any plan might fail. Any secret might be discovered, especially when it calls attention to itself. Your secret was safe as long as no one knew there *was* a secret, but not now." She leaned back in her chair and forced herself to breathe evenly, to think things through. "No one faults you, Bates," she insisted, calmer now. "And no one wishes more than I that we might continue. You know that. But your entire plan was predicated on the certainty that you could control these boys. Lose that, and we're just a rudderless bark tossing about on the tide of events."

Bates winced at the memory, so that Danny almost asked what pained him. For all her excellences, Bates thought, that woman had a poetical streak that annoyed him. It was her one flaw, or one of the few. Now that Mrs. Padgett was drawing her formidable stature up against his plans, he noticed tiny cracks in the image he held of her, and he wondered why he had never noted them before. No, even she had faults, could be timid when daring was needed, overcautious and short-sighted. And poetical. They must give up their plans, he was told, and with those plans he must give up his dreams, his career, every hope for advancement and power, the very road to London must be tossed away and forgotten.

Bates was desperate, and out of his desperation he had schemed, and schemed quickly. "It's only one boy who's caused all this trouble," he told them. "Why not let the dean have him?"

"Why, that's ridic-ridiculous."

"The danger of exposure is too great."

"Is it? The dean promised to end the matter there, not to delve deeper. This boy knows nothing. He can't lay the finger to any of us. He'll assert that Lord Granby is giving the orders. I've told you as much."

Mrs. Padgett shook her head. "No one will believe that."

"No one believes it now, anyway. No one thinks Granby is behind this, so they'll be no closer to the truth than they are at present."

The lady paused and seemed to consider the chance, just the remotest chance, that such would be the case. "But Granby will know the truth, won't he?" she asked.

"He'll *suspect* the truth. He might even suspect us specifically. But he'll be incapable of proving anything."

All three were silent for a time, examining this new landscape before them, each considering how it might yet be made to serve their joint ends. At the last, however, every avenue proved too dangerous.

"Break it up, Bates," Mrs. Padgett had commanded. "It was a fine plan, only ill-timed. Too much anger in the streets just yet, too much emotion to be controlled. Break it up now, before we get in so far we can't get out again."

"So it's to be a breakup, Danny," he muttered, disgust wringing his voice.

"Lads won't like that. They been havin' a time of it."

"Oh, for God's sake, toss each a shilling and be done."

Bates's wife chirped up from where she sat in the little alcove, knitting. "It seems such a shame after all Danny's work."

"What do you know of Danny's work?" Bates shot at her.

She glanced nervously at her brother, and again at her husband. "Nothin', Charley. I don't know nothin' particular."

"*Anything!* And see it stays that way." The room fell into an uncomfortable silence. Bates never wanted to be short with his wife, never meant to raise his voice to her, but lately his temper could find no check, and he lashed out as a man kicking a helpless pup, the guilt he felt only fueling his anger. "Go make us some tea," he ordered, and she fluttered out of the room.

Alone now with Danny, Bates desired nothing more than to finish with this business that he might bury his ambitions for good and all. "Call your boys together tonight. Toss them a coin apiece and tell them to scatter. I don't want to hear about another disturbance after this."

Danny hesitated.

"What is it?"

"Well, it's just that it might not all go off so easy as you'd like."

"How do you mean?"

"I might not be able to get to 'em all tonight. Might take a day or two. And even then, even with the shillin', they might not want to stop right off like that."

"Not *want* to?"

"Some of 'em, with their blood up, you know, they won't just call it quits like that." Danny snapped his fingers. "Give it a week and it'll all die down, I'd say."

"A week?"

"Or thereabouts. Lads get a taste in their mouths, it makes 'em hungry, as you might say. The odd bit o' mischief is all to be expected. Nothin' serious like."

But Bates was no longer listening. He was busy, stirring the dying coals of his dreams. A week! Who knew what might happen in a week. A week might allow him to call up some pride in Padgett, some manly conviction, might bring the mayor's wife back around. A week! Bates's mind flew furiously over the chance he was about to take, the chance he had to take.

"Find them out, Danny. Take your time but find them out. One day, two days, it doesn't matter. Give them the shilling for a job done well—use those funds I gave you—and tell them to take their own lead a bit." Bates leaned forward, eager to be planning now. "Keep the pressure on. *Bick* is the watchword. I want to see it. I want to hear it stuffed down every man's throat. I want the town draped in blue. You keep them at it in a casual way, but persistent, and I'll work on the mayor."

"Nothin' too violent, right? No repeat o' last night's amusements."

A cloud swept over Bates's brow. "That's right," he considered aloud. "We can't have that. Danny, do you know who was responsible for it?"

Danny Trees nodded darkly. "I can guess at it."

"Do you have a name?"

"Nah, no name. But I know the feller."

"Well, get me a name. No." Bates pondered. "No, don't bring it to me. I don't want to know. Only find it out for yourself. And when you've done, I want you to take that name and jot it on a piece of paper. Tonight, Danny. Do it tonight. Take that paper tonight and stick it by the vicar's door."

"Vicar?"

"Yes, the vicar! Now go! Get it done. And not a word of this to the mayor, right?"

Danny nodded vigorously as he leaped from his chair and bolted out of the flat. Bates heard his pounding footsteps as he flew out of the building, out into the street.

Mrs. Bates poked her head out from their little kitchen, the sugar bowl in her hand. "Danny's off?" she asked.

"Yes," her husband answered. "He remembered something."

"What could it be, so late?"

Bates reached for a book lying on a side table and opened it randomly, his eyes hardly focusing on the words. "Nothing. Nothing in particular."

Danny first stopped at home, at the flat where he had done little more than sleep these months past, three squalid rooms where his father sank into drunken slumber and his mother cooked all day for his three brothers and young sister. She squealed at him as he dashed through, grabbing a potato out of the ashes and juggling it in his hands until it cooled, then throwing his brothers out of the sleeping room that he might close and bolt the door.

Danny took a moment to enjoy the luxury of solitude, taking a lazy bite of the potato. He had been giving them all money lately, just enough to keep them out of his affairs and into a loin of pork and a few pints of beer a week, so now, when he needed his privacy, when he was about his business, there was none there to stand up to him. He finished his supper in three more bites and scrambled to a corner of the room, digging up a loose board down low on the wall. He had known of it since he was a child and used it as his personal bank, keeping string and wafers of sealing wax in a box. The box was there, just where he had left it, the slip of paper still resting delicately atop, a surety that no one had tampered with it. He pulled the box out of its nest and lifted the lid. Amid the rotting, rusted tokens of his boyhood, a leather bag nestled, lumpy and hard. He pulled it out with a clinking rattle, then put everything back, not forgetting to place the slip of paper in its proper place. He hefted the bag once, heard its soft clink again, then buried it in a deep pocket of his coat. Charley had given this bag to him, "just in case." Emergency funds for the campaign, he had called them, and an emergency this was. Three dozen shillings passed out as required, it was a small fortune to be wandering around with, rattling in his pocket, tugging hard at his coat.

Danny grinned. Now *this* was work, real work, not cheap labor, scrabbling away with your hands all day. Charley trusted him, and that alone made him a better agent than he might have been, better than his old man could ever have been. It made him dutiful and cunning, made him a player in the grand game, the machinery of Bellminster that set their world running and wheezing. What was Lord Granby now but more than him, not different? They both worked at the machine, one at the top and one at the bottom, with Charley in the middle. Danny grinned again. Then, with one last clink of the coins in his pocket, he was off.

He had his system, Danny did, places where a word might be dropped and heard and repeated, to spread and grow. He paid a call at three or four such places, then Davey Rose put himself in his usual corner in his usual gin house and waited. Before midnight, four boys had come trotting at him like dogs after a bone, hungry for their shilling. Each one he had asked, "Where's he as caused that dust-up with the old feller?" But each one had shrugged stupidly and raced off with his profits, under Danny's orders. "Keep it up, lads. Nice and easy now, but keep it up."

As the chimes of the town rang half past one, Danny huddled in the shadows of his corner with a lanky boy just turned twelve. "You tell young rascal as did that business last night, if you see him, that I got somethin' particular in recognition of such fine, ambitious work, right? You tell them others you might see to let him know that."

The boy nodded mutely, but was interrupted before he could speak.

"Whatsis? Handin' out sweets to schoolboys?" Danny spun about and looked up into the leering face of young Lucifer. With a sharp jerk of his head, Danny sent the other boy scurrying off with his shilling.

Lucifer settled in easily across the table, rapping the scarred top with a dirty, red knuckle. Danny tossed a shilling down between them and both watched it spin for an instant before rolling flat with a soft, pleasant clink.

"Y'see, I heard you last night, about profits," Danny announced, leaning back casually, "and I can be a reasonable man. There's profit to be had in this after all, ain't there."

Lucifer chuckled soundlessly. "Yeah, I'll rush out and buy myself a coach-an'-four. Only toss another'n up there and I'll be goin'."

"Why should you get twice the others?"

"'Cause I done twice as much."

Danny sat up slowly. "Yeah, you did, didn't you."

Lucifer only stared back with dark eyes that dared a general challenge to the world.

"Why'd you do it?" Danny asked.

"I was bored with paintin'."

"Yeah, but why him? Whatcha got against the old feller?"

Lucifer only sniffed.

Danny squinted. He could not make this one out. The others he understood, why they came to him, what they wanted. Just a bit of excitement, a bit of fun. But this one?

"What's your name?"

Lucifer paused before answering. "Why d'ya ask?"

Danny shrugged, looking tired and disinterested. "Dunno. Might be a bit of extra work to be done, special work, and a chap like you might be up to it. But I got to know who I'm dealin' with, don't I?"

Lucifer's eyes darted about nervously, and the dare they had reflected a moment before changed to something less sure of itself, something defiant but anxious, almost frightened.

"C'mon," Danny urged. "You're the one for profit, ain't you? Well, there's more in this than you think. But I need to know who I'm bringin' into the business."

"I ain't nobody."

Danny leaned across the table. "Gimme your name," he whispered, "or take your bloody shillin' and get out and don't never come to me again."

Lucifer stared at Danny, a hot, angry stare, the anger born of fear and mistrust.

"Kathleen. Kitty. Kitty Wren. My name's Kitty Wren."

It took Danny a moment, the name played so against everything he knew to be true. Then his eyes went wide and he looked Kitty Wren up and down in disbelief. She was mannish, no doubt of that, hard and dark with a lowering glare and thick, black eyebrows and her matted hair straggling out from under a cap. Her nose had been broken, more than once, so that it seemed to flare out at one side, and her jaw was thick, too big for her face. His eyes dipped down, but her clothes were too baggy to tell of her figure. *Ugly,* that was the only word for her, yet something else, too, something that might, with time and more gentle circumstances, grow into a shape, a picture, not pretty exactly, but strange and prepossessing. Yes, this was a girl. Older than he had thought, too. Almost a woman. Danny said nothing, tried to look worldly and bored, but he was surprised, and his surprise showed.

Kitty only stared at him, boldly, fiercely, injury seething within her, her soul cornered, tottering on the edge of rebellion. Beneath the table, a dirty hand stretched down toward her boot.

"All right, Kit," Danny said at last. "Now I know your name." He tossed the second shilling up onto the table, and her hand crept back upward, reaching out to gather in her gain. "You keep a sharp ear out on the street. When I need you, I'll get word out and then you come runnin', right?"

The glint of suspicion gone from her eyes, Kitty nodded slowly. Then, without a wasted word, she rose and slipped away.

Danny Trees sat where he was for several minutes, still and thoughtful until, calling over a serving lad, he ordered a steaming gin and water along with a paper and a pencil. When these arrived, he tossed off the scalding drink, jotted a few brief lines, folded the paper up, addressed it, and left.

A quarter of an hour later, Danny Trees stood in the rising fog on the edge of Cathedral Square. Before him, the topless towers of Bellminster Cathedral were topless indeed, invisible in the luminous shroud of mist and incipient frost. Danny shivered. He liked the gloom as it drifted up from the ford, a cloaking cloud that seemed to stamp his work with its eerie authority. With a stuttering step, as one too aware of the quiet around him, he moved across the face of the cathedral and came to the little walk that led to the vicarage door. One moment passed, and he was on the doorstep.

Danny stooped to lay his letter by the door, the single word *Vicar* scrawled in thick black pencil across the front. Then, thinking of the breeze that furled the fog into a myriad of ghastly shapes, he looked about and found a stone. This he placed atop the note. Danny turned and for a moment thought he heard something move. A sound—a cough, a crow—had caught his ear. He paused. Nothing more. Satisfied, he slunk off into the mist.

The night's vapor continued to swirl and whirl about Bellminster, hiding and revealing crazed phantoms, fantastic creatures that congealed for an instant and then dissolved again into air. Soon, the fog was thick enough to hide the world behind a milky cowl, a cloak rent with holes through which here a tree, there a lamppost, there a something no man could tell passed in and out of substance. Odd sounds, like a scattering of pebbles or the soft sweep of the fog against the walls and windows, fluttered on the edge of hearing. But was anyone by to hear them?

Come dawn, the fog had lifted to an obscuring haze. By the vicarage door, a solitary stone sat mysteriously upon the doorstep, looking lonely and lost, as though placed there by an invisible hand for no apparent reason.

CHAPTER XV

IMPROVISATION

Tuckworth was late returning from his interview with Ian Fellowes. The morning fog delayed his departure until almost ten, and when he arrived at last, Fellowes was so honored by the visit that he held on to the dean like a prize ram, leading him on a tour of his fields and showing him off to all his tenants and neighbors. As for the election, it had flown from the farmer's mind the moment he heard that Granby's favor was sure to fall somewhere else.

"Only did it for the sport, Mr. Tuckworth," he declared without the least embarrassment or compunction, stepping boldly through an especially rustic pasture. "Bit of a lark, eh? Thought if it should fall in my path I'd take the thing up—goin' to Parliament, I mean. And if it don't—which it didn't—none's the harm." The man knew nothing of the violence that had occurred, nothing of blue cockades or boys with paint. Hearing of Evan McAllister, he clucked his tongue and shook his head in dismay, warranting that "it's strange days we find ourselves in, Mr. Tuckworth. Strange days, indeed." By the time the dean was able to escape from the man's simple hospitality, it was as certain that Ian Fellowes knew nothing about recent events as it was clear that Tuckworth had discovered nothing these past two days, with only a pair of more than usually soiled walking shoes for his pains (and he could already hear Mrs. Cutler's views on such an aromatic success).

Which is not the same as to say that the dean had learned nothing at all. On the contrary, as he trudged the long road back to Bellminster in the sloping rays of a setting sun, kicking at the dust of the road to dislodge some of the pasture's muck from his heels, he was inclined to think that he had learned something very valuable. He was beginning to suspect that Mrs. Padgett was right, that he was simply tired and old, the remnants of a dull young man grasping at the last bit of excitement that he could expect to come his way in this life.

With autumn sweeping through the countryside in full splendor now, leaves firing gold and red before fading to the colors of the earth with which they were soon to mingle, breezes blowing a snappish chill that smelled of apples and corn, smoke and cinders, Tuckworth felt free to do that which he had not allowed himself for many months. He reminisced. For an hour and more his stroll home was a journey backward, a retreat to times and memories too long kept locked in his soul. The dean recalled the way his life had been in days not so very distant really, Eleanor at his side, little Lucy running about his shins, her skinny arms upraised to heaven and to him, a world of habit and good use, of love and the comfort that love brings. His thoughts leaped forward, unstoppably, achingly, to those first months following Eleanor's passing— no, her death, her murder at his hands—when the guilt he felt had swallowed him whole, dredging him to the farthest edge of a ragged despair where he had waited, tottering, almost eager to pitch headlong into that place where anguish and grief allowed no foothold, where not even a man's best character was sufficient to carry him along and over and through.

He had not fallen, somehow, and even now the memory seemed less clear, more shadowy with every day, bitter still but with the bitterness of dust and cobwebs, not blood. Two things had pulled him back to life. One was Lucy, not the child he remembered but the woman she had become, free-spirited and true, respectful and, yes, even reverent, yet filled with an independence and resource-fulness that might have made any father proud to find in a son, and that he could not fault in a daughter. Others might fault it, call her headstrong and willful, but he would not.

She had given him a new life, and so had this other thing—how could he name it?—his new role in the town, his Delphic reputa-tion, a man with the vision to see what others could not, or dared not. He had been called out of himself at last to sit at life's gaming table, studying his fellow creatures as he would pieces on a chess-board, noting their moves to himself and keeping three turns ahead. In the past year he had worked for justice—so he had told himself—trying to right the imbalance evil brought into the world. His mind stumbled over that thought now. Evil? No, not that. He knew, more certainly than he had ever known, that no man know-ingly works evil in the world. Every crime derives from a just cause to some man's thinking. *Justice* itself was too slippery a word, too filled with its own meaning. What, then? Was it what he suspected, a newfound love of danger, the chance at this late hour to be what he had never dreamed to be before, to be daring? Were his motives so selfish, so vain? Was that it?

"Now, here's the very picture of a thoughtful man."

Tuckworth stopped and looked about. Without being aware, he had wandered back into Bellminster, his feet moving for him while his mind journeyed elsewhere. From just beside his elbow, the merry face of Jo Smalley leered up at him, grinning with that bold, pasteboard grin. "I've been walking here aside of you these two blocks now, and you wrapped tight in your own world. What *can* you be thinking on so hard, Mr. Tuckworth?"

The dean shook his head, feeling inexplicably guilty. "Nothing of consequence," he replied.

"Nothing?"

"Personal matters."

Jo nodded with a worldly wink, as though he shared Tuck-worth's secret and would hold it to the grave. Linking his arm up and through the dean's, he proceeded to drag him along the road as though they had some joint appointment to keep. "So," Jo continued, "you weren't thinking on that other matter, the one we discussed yesterday?"

"No, not directly."

"Indirectly?"

"I've made some inquiries. So far they've proved fruitless."

"But you couldn't have spoken with all the interested parties already? Not yet? Not with everyone who's got a stake in this?"

"I think I have." Tuckworth was about to run down the short list of subjects he had questioned these past days, but something told him to keep the names to himself for now, and he only repeated, "I think I have."

"Even his lordship and that lot?"

Tuckworth paused, merely looking down at his companion in silence.

Jo grinned and nodded slowly. "Close, close. I've said it of you afore and I'll say it of you again. You're close." He dug a sharp finger into the dean's ribs. "So you've got no answer yet? No name?"

"I don't think anyone's had the chance to communicate with me as yet. But I hope to hear something soon." Tuckworth buried a pang of conscience as he said this, for it sounded to him more like a hopeful dodge than the truth. He was beginning to believe that his chances of hearing anything at all were slimmer than he had imagined.

"And as for my interest, the question of who's behind this? After all that work, no hints? No suspicions?"

"No," the dean answered, and he cast a curiously shamefaced

eye on his companion. "Actually, you recall, I promised anonymity to whoever was involved in this."

Jo looked up with a furrowed brow. "That you did," he remarked slowly.

"It was the only way," explained Tuckworth. "No one could be expected to assist me if they were themselves in danger of exposure. And I'm certain no one meant for things to get this far, so I can't imagine I'm protecting a criminal."

Jo stared up, but said nothing.

"I had no choice," the dean went on, "and I'm afraid that promise might keep me from revealing anything of consequence to you. I told you from the outset, my one goal is to discover who beat that poor man so mercilessly."

"That's right, clear enough. But I don't suppose you'd change your mind later and decide to run to Lord Granby with the news and leave poor Jo in the dark?"

Tuckworth felt the accusation rankle, but he knew how matters must appear. "I can't help your suspicions," he insisted. "I can only assure you, I've no abiding interest in this election beyond my one vote."

"And where do you believe you'll cast it?"

"I don't know."

"You don't?"

"I don't see how I can. You haven't announced a candidate yet."

Jo paused, then laughed. "That's an honest answer," he said. "All right. So long as we're all in the dark, I don't expect as I can complain overmuch. And to show you there's no hard feelings, I'll teach *you* something."

The dean glanced down. "What's that?"

"A name. I'll teach you a name is all. A name you might take to Lord Granby if you've a mind." Jo stopped and, pulling Tuckworth down close that he might lean up to his ear, whispered, "Quentin Draper."

Tuckworth heard the name, noted it to himself, but that was all.

"You get it?" Jo asked, anxious that he had not made a greater impression.

"I have it," the dean answered. "Can I assume that this is the name of your mysterious candidate?"

"You've heard of the man!" the dwarf declared, beaming.

Tuckworth shook his head. "Never."

Jo only heaved his crooked shoulders resignedly. "You'll hear of him soon, though. Hear nothing but glowing reports and dreadful, scurrilous lies. He's destined to be your next Member."

The dean smiled obligingly, and they walked on. "Is this news common knowledge?"

"Not as such. Not yet."

"And I'm free to take this name, this Draper, to his lordship?"

"That you are."

Tuckworth shook his head and smiled a subtle smile. "Thanks all the same, I don't think I will."

Jo looked surprised and a bit put out. "Why wouldn't you?"

Tuckworth did not reply but only stared ruefully at his companion.

A quick, shallow smile rippled across Jo's lips. "You don't trust me. But why not? You think I'd hand you a false name to trip your friends on?"

"Quite the contrary," the dean explained. "I think you've told me nothing that's not true. This Draper fellow is your man, no doubt. But Lord Granby already suspects me of being too familiar with you. If I go to him now, as you want me to do, and tell him how I have your confidence, how you've let me in on your secret, he'll distrust me further still. Or, what's worse, he'll think I only want to curry his favor, and then I might lose both his trust *and* his respect."

"And why should I want to do such a thing?" Jo demanded, acting so outrageously offended that Tuckworth knew he must be near the truth.

"To throw suspicion among your adversaries. To spread dissent. To agitate the waters generally. You don't need a definite strategy to keep your opponents off balance."

"And are you my opponent, Tuckworth?"

"No," the dean gladly admitted. "I'm not. But I'm not exactly an ally, either. And I might make a likely tool for your aims, a bomb with which to undermine your enemy's defenses."

Jo looked askance at the dean, his face a puzzle between sincere injury and calculation. "I never," he muttered. "I truly never. I suppose it just comes of being a political creature to start with. Always suspect, never trusted. Well," he said with a melodramatic sigh, "you've got the name as an act of trust and friendship. You may take it and tell it, or leave it be, just as suits you."

Tuckworth strolled along, his arm wrapped in his companion's own, somewhat better pleased with himself than he had been. He considered that, at worst, he had escaped a subtle trap, and at least he had demonstrated his independence in this affair. Either way, he was pleased. He would not be Jo Smalley's man, or Lord Granby's, and that thought left him satisfied. In a world where every man was running to one side or the other, where one is told to be either this thing or that thing, either left or right, new or true, ancient or modern, he was quite contented to be still, to settle nowhere but within himself.

"Tell me, Jo," he asked by way of mild conciliation, "do you ever tire of your scheming?"

"How's that?" Jo replied, still sounding pettish.

"Oh, I'm not faulting you. It's your duty, I understand that, but all these plots and stratagems, do they ever wear you down? Always grinning at the world, always sharp, always clever, doesn't it get tiresome?"

Jo was silently thoughtful. Tuckworth looked down at him, though all he saw was the top of the dwarf's hat bobbing from side to side as he hobbled along. The dean worried that perhaps he had overstepped himself, but a moment later Jo was grinning up at him as fiercely as ever.

"I'll tell you what, Tuckworth. There's a place in my trade for them that plots and schemes all day long, and it's second place. I hardly ever laid out a plan that didn't go bust afore long. That's not how you win in my game."

"Well, how do you win, then?"

Jo winked. "Improvisation, that's the word for it. Schemes weigh a fellow down. Try to map out your moves too careful, and soon the map becomes more important than the destination. Got to keep light on your feet, ready for anything from quoits to cricket. 'Improvise,' I'm always telling my hounds—my candidates, that is. 'Improvise. Master that trick, and you'll be a match for anyone.' Trouble is, so few of them's got the knack for it."

"And that's why they require your services?"

Jo offered the dean a cryptic leer. "That, and other reasons."

Tuckworth would have followed this question with another, so curious was he about Jo's surprising trade, so like it was to a game of chess. But their discussion was interrupted by a plaintive voice calling in the near distance.

"Vicar! Dean Tuckworth! Mr. Tuckworth, sir!"

They peered down the street to see young Constable Wiley come running toward them, weaving in and about the traffic. He came up at last, breathless, heaving, his brow dampened with sweat even in the approaching chill of evening. "Mr. Tuckworth, sir, thank heavens I've found you. Chief constable's been wanting you these past three hours, and you was expected back long before now or we'd have sent—"

"What is it, Wiley?"

The man stood before them both looking suddenly confounded, as though the question were somehow unaccountable.

"Why, it's Evan McAllister, sir," Wiley explained. "The coffin maker."

"What of him?"

"He's died, sir."

CHAPTER XVI

AGENT OF THE FORCE

eanin' it's murder now," Hopgood declared, making himself sound important and official within the close, dank walls of his office in the Constabulary House.

"Yes," Tuckworth answered. "Of course." It had all seemed so different before this. A beating—savage, brutal—but still, the word had sounded like the thing itself, only a beating. *Only* a beating. And Tuckworth felt the small, angry ember within him glow red once more, smoldering in his heart, anger at himself, at the others, anger at Cade and Padgett with their political dodges and diversions, and even at Ian Fellowes for wasting his time all morning. But mostly anger at himself. "It's just so sudden. Why was it sudden?" The dean appealed to Dr. Warrick, who shrugged.

"Sometimes it's sudden, that's all. McAllister was an old man. There must've been injuries to the internal organs. No doubt of it now, in any case. I don't say this sort of a turn is regular," Warrick sniffed, "but it's not unheard of."

The chief constable's door rattled open and Lord Granby came stooping in, with Reverend Mortimer behind. Bick was not with them. Granby darted a glance about the room, his gaze lingering on Tuckworth a bit longer than was comfortable, stoking the dean's anger further.

Hopgood noticed the glance as well. "Vicar's here at my request," he explained, his voice quavering between assertion and appeal.

"Yes," Mortimer said from the door, closing it behind him. "The constable outside informed us of the dean's inclusion in these proceedings."

An uneasy silence settled over the now-crowded room. Constabulary House was in truth a series of buildings, a block of old dwellings patchworked together with brick and mortar and iron, converted into wardrooms and chambers, cells and a common yard. The chief constable's office was small and homely, formerly the bleakest corner of a musty parlor before thin walls went up to divide it. A few red coals glowed in the brazier of a sooty stove and a smattering of notices and handbills were tacked about to hide the cracking plaster. The room was dark and drear, and seemed to Tuckworth's mind well suited for such work as it witnessed.

Granby continued to stare at the dean, who stood his ground with an independent air that bordered on defiance. Mortimer watched close-by, studying these two, his eyes working from one man to the other, while Hopgood shuffled nervously about and Dr. Warrick appeared merely worn and impatient to leave.

"Well," the chief constable said at last, taking command of the proceedings, "I think the question is, what do we do now?"

"We find who did this," Granby asserted in a croaking voice laden with age and emotion.

"And who is behind this execrable crime," Mortimer added.

"Yes," observed Tuckworth archly, "that's what I've been about these past two days."

Hopgood cleared his throat. "Vicar here has been makin' inquiries into this business already, as he done said, the which I'd ask him to relate now." He nodded at the dean.

Tuckworth looked back at the chief constable, a boyish guilt stealing over his face. "I've learned nothing," he confessed.

"Nothin'?" Hopgood repeated in dismay.

"Nothing."

"And if one may ask," Mortimer pursued, "whom did you interrogate? I believe that is the proper term, *interrogate*. Please correct me if I am mistaken, Mr. Tuckworth. You clearly have the precedence of experience over us in these matters." He smiled a remarkably noxious smile.

"I interviewed Wilfred Cade, Mayor Padgett, and Ian Fellowes," the dean answered. "They were the main contenders for the candidacy, as I recall."

"What?" Granby demanded. "Not your little imp friend?"

Tuckworth paused, surprised, nearly shocked. It was the first genuinely unkind thing he had ever heard Granby utter. His lordship might be unthinking at times, brusque and tactless, but he was never purposely mean, never cruel, and in the face of such bare hostility the dean's own anger shriveled, though just a bit.

"I questioned Jo . . . Mr. Smalley, after a fashion."

"And what fashion was that?" inquired Mortimer.

"My own." All eyes turned to the dean, silently demanding more. "It wasn't a formal interview, but I learned what I wanted to learn."

"And you're satisfied that he's completely innocent of this?" Granby pressed.

Tuckworth shook his head. "Jo Smalley didn't beat Evan McAllister to death. Nor did Cade, Padgett, or Fellowes. Or Mr. Bick, if it comes to that. Besides, I'm not interested in who set all these political schemes in motion."

"Well, perhaps you ought to be," his lordship observed acidly. "You know, inciting to riot is still a crime in England, and disturbing the peace."

"And so is murder," Tuckworth snapped, his anger beginning to peek through his calm command once more. "That's what this has become. Not just inciting to riot or disturbing the peace, and not just assault, not any longer. It's murder. Any inquiries I make—"

"And exactly why are you making inquiries, if I may ask?" Mortimer interrupted, his voice carrying that soft, ponderous weight that he used to such guilt-inducing effect in the pulpit. "It would appear that I am always brought back to the same question and am never to receive a satisfactory reply. Why, Dean Tuckworth, are you involved in this matter at all? Why are you not busy about the resurrection of Bellminster Cathedral? That is your proper sphere, if you've forgotten." He turned to the chief constable. "Mr. Hopgood, what is the dean's official position in this?"

Hopgood hemmed from behind the clutter of his desk before answering. "Well, as a matter of fact, the vicar ain't got no official position, as such."

"No," the rector said, his eyes glinting, "I know he has not."

"But *un*officially, now, he's what you might call a civilian agent of the force."

"A what?"

"What am I?"

"A private operative," Hopgood explained, reciting the term as though it had come from one of his professional circulars. "A sort of consulting investigator. At least, that's how I come to think of him." Hopgood looked at Tuckworth as he said this, a shy smile gracing his rough stubble, and the dean felt a warmth and gratitude for the chief constable that he had not been aware of before.

"And why would you wish to consult with Mr. Tuckworth?" Mortimer continued, unappeased. "Why would you abrogate your own duty, your *sworn* duty to protect Bellminster, for the advice of a country parson?"

"Because he's good at it," Hopgood answered simply.

"Good at it?" the rector scoffed. "*Good* at it? I am gratified to hear that Mr. Tuckworth might be—"

"I don't care who consults whom in this," Granby croaked, "so long as someone catches that twisted little bastard at his game! The Whigs are behind all of this, it's obvious. You watch. That dwarf is an agitator, a Whig agitator stirring things up, setting neighbors at each other. Comes in from London and he thinks he can own these streets with his slanders and disturbances."

Tuckworth saw it again, that startling streak of meanness, and something else as well, a hunched, haggard, world-weary air that startled him. The dean had always known how old Granby was. That is, he was aware of the number of Granby's years, but he had never thought of him as an aged man until now. For the first time, Tuckworth noted how his skin was lank and sallow, his eyes rheumy, his hair wispy and brittle. Over the course of the past few days, over the cares and worries of an election called suddenly into doubt, Lord Granby had acquired the look of a man one step nearer to death than to life, and the sight struck Tuckworth forcibly, struck him to the heart.

"I'm sorry, Lord Granby," the dean said as kindly as he could, "but I can't see that Jo Smalley is more suspect than anyone else in this. I've spoken to him twice now—"

"Three times!"

Tuckworth hesitated, his eyes narrowing as he looked about, and again he felt the spark of anger within him flare. "Excuse me?"

"You've been seen with him three times, three discussions or interviews or however you care to call it. Three times in three days. You've just this hour come away from talking with the man!" Granby stood, stooped yet tall, a slight tremor shaking him, causing the clothes on his gaunt frame to shiver so that he looked older still, and weaker, and Tuckworth's sympathies were touched once more in spite of his anger.

"Your lordship—"

"No, Mr. Tuckworth," Mortimer intervened, taking a step forward. "Do not compound your culpability with a vain denial. We know you have been in regular, one is tempted to say constant, communication with this deformed person." The rector paused dramatically. "We have received reports."

This was all the tending Tuckworth's anger needed to burst into flame at last. "You've had me watched!"

"Your actions, sir, have been so blatant, so flagrant that there was hardly a need—"

"You've had me watched! While I've been busy tiptoeing about your political garden for you, trying to get to the bottom of this, you've had me followed and watched!"

Granby stared down at the dean, his eyes watery with pain and disappointment. "You don't understand," he muttered. "This is politics. You're playing a game you can't comprehend."

"I'm playing at nothing!" Tuckworth declared, humiliation and compassion battling within him. "Though I'm beginning to see how I've been played. Nearly everywhere I've turned, I've faced half-truths and mistrust. From you, from them," with a bold sweep of his hand encompassing all of Bellminster's political population. "This whole wretched business, this election is a taint against the spirit of this town, don't you see that? Jo isn't turning us against each other. We're doing that ourselves, without his help."

"Now, now," Granby responded, lifting a vein-carved hand, trying to soothe the dean's feelings now that the guilty ebb of his accusation began to flow back against his conscience.

"Clearly our suspicions have been warranted to this extent," Mortimer doggedly persisted. "You have become a particular favorite of this Smalley. Tell us, Mr. Tuckworth, on what topic were you discoursing this afternoon? Three separate meetings, and all on the most innocent of pretexts? Chitchat about the weather, Mr. Tuckworth? Even a babe would find it ludicrous, sir. Ludicrous and insupportable, such betrayal—"

"It's none of your business whom I talk to or what about."

"No." The rector laughed. "I think it's none of *our* business, certainly."

Tuckworth clenched his jaw tightly for an instant, as though to hold back the words, and then he spoke with a resigned calm that was terrible to watch. "We talked," he said, "about the investigation. We talked about the same matters I have talked with everyone about, the same matters I have been talking with you about. I have had no secrets with Jo Smalley, no talk of politics. That is—" the dean stumbled suddenly over a remembered detail, "I've instigated no talk of politics." He could see Mortimer's eyes squint in ravenous anticipation, but there was nothing for it. He could not hide what he knew, the name that Smalley had planted in him. For the briefest moment, Tuckworth weighed his integrity against the wisdom of caution. As always, caution took second place. "He did tell me one thing this last time. The name of the candidate. The Whig candidate, I mean. His name's Quentin Draper."

Mortimer glowed with triumph, yet he was satisfied now to stay silent and only stood meaningfully beside Lord Granby.

There are times when facts are the greatest enemy of truth. The two men looked at each other, their affection foundering between them for all they might do. Tuckworth knew that no explanation could redeem himself in Granby's eyes, just as surely as he knew that his lordship would pretend to accept any desperate lie he might concoct in his defense, knowing it for a lie. Tuckworth could not do that, cheapen their years of respect, years of warm regard and honor and friendship—yes, even friendship between a poor vicar and a wealthy peer—he could not cheapen them with a lie.

Granby waited a moment, then lowered his head and shook it in palsied convulsions. "I never would have dreamed—"

"I never—"

"Lord Granby," Mortimer said, intercepting the dean's plaintive words, "this Whig, this Draper?" The rector allowed the question to hang unacknowledged in the air until Granby raised his head, aware that he was being addressed. "Quentin Draper, your lordship," Mortimer prodded. "Who is he?"

"Draper? Son of Lord Arthur Draper, Viscount Something-or-other. Sixth son or seventh."

Mortimer nodded. "Yes, rather far removed from the title, I imagine. The fate of an extra son, wouldn't you say, your lordship?"

Granby looked about, his eyes struggling to focus for a moment. Mortimer stepped forward to draw his attention. "Draper?" Mortimer asked again.

"Draper. Yes, I met the lad once, when he was four or five. Perfect little beast."

"What of the father, the viscount?"

Granby waved his hand in the air dismissively. "Liberal-minded chap. Not a bad sort, but not quite right. Too many sons and not enough places in the military or the church to hold them all. I believe this one took after the law."

"The apple has not fallen far from the tree, then?"

"It would appear not," said Lord Granby, who was once more at work on political matters, his mind, if not quite clear, at least quickening.

"So," the rector continued, taking the older man's arm to lead him away, "now that we know our man, what shall we do next?"

Granby hesitated, however. He cast a furtive, uncertain glance at the dean, a look filled with things left unresolved, then turned to Hopgood.

"This other business," he said, "this murder. Do what you must, Hopgood. Anything you need, just get word to me and you'll have it."

The chief constable nodded wordlessly.

Granby looked around the room once more, his eyes falling on and passing over the dean. "I'm taking the carriage home," he told Mortimer as he left. "I'm tired. You go find Bick and come right away. We'll teach these upstarts who controls the streets of Bellminster." But the threat had no fire in it.

The door rattled shut behind them.

"Well, then, if that's all . . ." Dr. Warrick rose and left as well.

The room was still for a moment.

Hopgood coughed. "So, about this murder now."

"Yes, murder," Tuckworth replied, looking at the door as though some answer lay behind it or beyond it. "Yes." He was silent for just one sad moment longer, then he spun about with manic energy. "I've been going at this all wrong, Hopgood," he declared, a sudden ferocity in his eyes, his voice, every emotion surging now to engulf this one clear purpose. "I've been trying to work through the political end as the surest means. But it's a morass that way, and since I can't get through it, I'll just have to take the long road around. It'll be quicker and surer in the end."

"How's that?" the chief constable asked, his brow furrowed in confusion.

"The streets, Hopgood. I've got to take to the streets."

At that instant, another man was exhorting his companion with the opposite advice: "Keep off the streets. That's the most important thing. If you remember nothing else, remember that. Keep off the streets."

Danny Trees looked at Bates, his eyes damp with agitation and fear. "But I didn't do nothin'," he insisted weakly.

"Not even for food or drink, understand? I'll send up everything you need. Lay it out for you on the landing. I'll knock three times, then you knock twice, and I'll knock twice more. Then you unlock the door and step back. Or if you lack anything you want, write it out on a piece of paper and slide it under the door after I knock the second time."

"Second time," Danny repeated, his face an image of worry and bewilderment. "But I didn't do nothin'."

"Dammit, Danny, it's murder now!" Bates hissed under his

breath, afraid to raise his voice even in the privacy of his rooms. His wife had been exiled to the back of the flat, to their bedroom, out of sight and hearing. "Do you comprehend what that means? You're the only one who can connect the mayor to any of this. You're the keystone, and until we're through this I want you out of sight. Now don't even stop home on your way. You just fly to that address I gave you." Danny clutched the slip of paper, crumpling it in his fist. "You sit tight, you keep quiet, and we'll get through this clean as anything."

"How long?"

Bates shrugged. "I can't say. Just a few days, most likely."

"But won't it look queer, kind've? Me runnin' off to nowhere? Shouldn't I just hang about like all's normal and right?"

Bates shot a glance at Danny, saw the sweat beading on the end of his nose, the twitch at the corner of his eye, the dryness of his lips as he vainly licked them. "They'd have the whole story from you in a heartbeat," he said, contempt lacing his words. "They wouldn't even have to ask you."

"But if they get to Kit, won't she tell 'em about me?"

"Don't tell me her name! You've told me too much already." This was all falling apart too suddenly, Bates realized. Maybe he could get to the girl first. Or maybe he should go to Lord Granby, solicit aid in the name of the party. Or still, he might be able to wash his own hands clean of it all, set up a plausible string from Padgett right to Danny. Bates needed time to think, time to plan. So he needed Danny out of the way, someplace safe and convenient. "They can only reach her through you, right? So if you're not around, how can they find her? And if by some unaccountable chance they do get to her, she'll only tell them that ridiculous name you gave yourself. Just keep low and all will come out. It'll just be a few days, Danny," he repeated. "I promise you that."

"But I didn't—"

"Danny!" Bates stilled his temper in slow, measured breaths.

"Danny, you're worrying about nothing. This isn't about murder, can you understand that? You're in no danger from the law, because you didn't kill anybody. It's about the election. It's about getting our man to London. We didn't set that girl to kill McAllister, but she did, so it involves us. But only as far as the election is concerned! If we still hope to win, then we *can't* be involved until afterwards. By then, everything will be easy. We'll just hand her over then." Bates was so fervent in his explanation that he almost succeeded in convincing himself.

Haltingly, stupidly, Danny nodded his head.

"All right. Go straight to the flat. I'll be by tomorrow with some food. You'll just have to be hungry 'til then. Do you have any money?"

Danny nodded again.

Bates held out his hand. "Give it here. It'll just tempt you to go out and spend it."

Danny dug into his pocket and took out the purse with his emergency funds, the packet of shillings. It clinked softly as it landed in Bates's palm.

"Remember, three knocks, then two from you, then two more. Got it? Now go."

Danny ran from the room. Bates rose and stepped to the window, peering out to the street, watching as Danny bolted out and away. Then, taking his hat and coat from their place by the door, he left, hungry for fresh air and the space to think.

Only after he was gone, only after he had left the room deserted, could the sound of sobs be heard reaching out from the back of the flat, from the bedroom, reaching out through thin walls to the emptiness of the front parlor.

CHAPTER XVII
THE STREETS OF BELLMINSTER

The girl limped over in her smeared, ill-fitting frock and refilled the pint in front of Raphael, removing the meatless bones scattered like fallen comrades before him. She hesitated to leave, looking for one moment longer at the handsome gentleman, so brooding and melancholy and blond, his box of paints and crayons, his easel and his pad piled across from him signifying his wonderful difference from anyone she had ever known before. Something about great sadness was very pretty, she thought, and then limped off again.

Raphael sat oblivious to this attention, nor did he hear the slovenly merriment of the pub—the smattering of song, the shuffling of weary feet in a stumbling reel, the slurred overtures of romance—as one day slunk into the next. He did not look about him to note the faces swimming in smoke, men and women and the odd child, each wearing a mask of grins or tears, or both, hiding some secret pain or dying hope. At such an hour on such a night, drink was not the accompaniment to life, but its goal.

Sensible souls were long since in bed, and yet, for all the hour's lateness, there was activity up and down the lane, the intermittent skulking of shades in the night, the boisterous heroics of drunken men. This was not the easy, well-ordered life of Cathedral Square and the Granby Arms. This was a low dive in a filthy corner of Bellminster, more a den than a public house, where the gas sputtered obscurely as if to hide what went on under its failing light, and the unmoving air stank of sick and sawdust, vinegar and sweat. Raphael sat close to the window, staring out into the dark with dull, unobservant eyes. He had spent all day watching, wandering the streets with his pack and easel slung to his back, waiting for the sublime moment, trying to force his eyes to see what his mind thirsted to see, the truth beneath the skin of things. Countless times he had set up his easel to stab and slash at the paper with color and charcoal, only to toss aside his work after an hour, a bland picture with nothing real about it, as flat and dead as the paper and the paints. He drank again, deeply, and let his eyes sweep the world before him, watching everything, seeing no one, just figures gliding by on the other side of the waving ripples of glass.

Wait! Raphael's mind jumped unexpectedly to life, as when a cog catches its teeth in a gear and moves some distant, sympathetic piston. He leaped from his seat and rushed toward the door. Before he could reach it, however, the barman called out, "Hey! Slow there!" and lunged forward, grabbing Raphael's collar with a rough hand. "That's sixpence you owe!" the man said with a jerk that recalled Raphael to his obligation. The young painter only motioned impatiently at his paraphernalia in the window seat, an earnest of his return. "And if you don't come back? I ain't no artist!" the barman insisted with another shake. Irritably, Raphael groped into his pocket, snatched at some coins, and tossed them onto the bar. Free again, he darted out into the street.

"Dean Tuckworth!"

The dean turned about along the ambling path he had been trudging. "Raphael?"

"Mr. Tuckworth, what on earth—" As if to complete the question, from a score of church steeples and clock towers the bells of Bellminster chimed midnight at last, dark trough of the day.

Tuckworth pulled his watch out by the chain and opened it, gently adjusting the dial to match the chimes. "Late for you, isn't it?" he asked, placing the watch back in his waistcoat pocket.

Raphael smiled, despite his recent temper. "I was about to say the same of you," he observed.

"Me? Oh, not so late," confessed the dean as his jaw stiffened in a stifled yawn. "No, not so late, really. I don't sleep well. You know that."

"But why are you wandering about so far from home? And in such a neighborhood as this?"

The dean glanced around him. "I haven't come that far, have I?" he wondered aloud.

A band of boys scuttled out of the darkness on the far side of the lane, emerging from the shadows in raucous disorder and scurrying back again like a small army of rats, and the dean instantly and quite inexplicably bounded after them, waving his arms like a lunatic, calling and making an absurd and futile spectacle. He got only two dozen yards before he gave up with a disgusted sigh at his failure.

"Cursed wind," he puffed, just as Raphael shot past him at a dead run, quickly overtaking the slowest of the boys beneath a streetlamp, grappling two of them under his arms so that the rest stopped just out of the light, curious to know the upshot of this pursuit. Tuckworth came trotting up behind, wheezing so that he could not answer Raphael's quizzical stare, or the jeers of the gang surrounding them, not quite out of sight. Finding his voice at last, he addressed the two captured lads. "Now, now," he said reassuringly, "no need to struggle. I'm not the magistrate."

"As if we thunk you was, y'old grampus," a derisive voice called from the half-light encircling them.

"All I want's a word, boys, you should know that," Tuckworth insisted, motioning at the pair still struggling in his friend's grasp. "Raphael, let them go."

Not clear why he was holding them in the first place, Raphael shrugged and freed his charges. One of the boys managed a single, ferocious kick at his captor's shin before darting off into oblivion, but the other brushed himself off with mock grandeur, aware of how his companions were watching him.

"Well, my fine fellow," Tuckworth began, his attempt at a winning manner sounding terribly condescending and paternal (or perhaps grandpaternal). "You know what I'm after, I suppose?"

"Yah," the boy acknowledged contemptuously. He shook his thick, reddish mop and passed a dirty hand over a dirtier face. If he was more than nine or ten, then he was notably puny for his age, but his brash manner gave him an older air, more worldly and knowing of life's underbelly.

"Good," the dean continued. "So, do you have anything to tell me?"

The lad thrust his thumb up his nose. "Piss off!"

Raphael cuffed him sharply, but the boy shook off the blow and danced away. "Me mum hits harder'n you!" he called as he disappeared into the night, cackling with his friends.

Raphael cast a puzzled look upon the dean, who only turned aside and retraced his steps. "I've been three nights about it," he said absentmindedly. "Three nights and I think I'm getting slower every night."

"What is it you're after?"

"I'm trying to get a name, to find someone who knows about this murder."

"The coffin maker?"

Tuckworth nodded. "I know boys had a hand in it that night, boys like these, lost and all but homeless. And they've been at it since." He motioned toward a blue BIK slopped across a brick wall. "I don't really think any of them remembers what the word means anymore. It's just a game to them. They're putting it up every night, on every corner. Scrape it off by day and it just shows up again by morning."

"But isn't there some . . . I don't know, a smarter way to find out what you want to know?"

Tuckworth managed a weak grin. "It's a harsh lesson that intelligence will carry you only so far into some things. I tried all the smart ways. Now I'm trying the stupid ones. Slow and stupid."

A voice called out to them as they passed by the pub again. "Here, you!" the barman bellowed. "I ain't no boardin'house! You come pick up them paints or I'll charge you for use o' the table!"

Raphael's brow darkened at the rebuke, evidence that his mood had not lightened appreciably, but he hurried back inside nonetheless, emerging again shortly with his easel slung on his back and the pad and box of colors tucked under an arm.

"I've offered everything I can think of," the dean went on as they walked. "Sweets, toys, cakes, even money. But I can't get one of them to trust me. Three nights." He stopped under a streetlamp and looked into the black about them. "They all know what I'm after by now. It's amazing, how fast news travels on the street. They all know but not a one will talk to me."

Raphael shifted the weight of his paint box to his other arm. "When I was doing portraits in London I had the same difficulty," he confided. "With the children, I mean. Trust is the only thing we ever want from them, really, so of course it's the one thing they're least likely to give up. Holding it back is the only power they can wield."

Tuckworth walked on, the hour and his recent exertion having worn away the last ounce of hope he held to, at least for that night. "I remember children being less of a bother when I was young," he observed. "Is that true, I wonder, or do I just forget the hard times?"

The two men rounded a corner and before Raphael might answer, they came up against another band of nocturnal travelers, only these were not boys.

"Lookee here," a small, wiry man in front said, flourishing a coachman's long whip in one hand, waving it before him like a blade with which to slice through the dark.

"Who's 'at, Ringle?" a gruff voice called from the back. There must have been eight or ten of them, a few with lanterns in their fists, rough young men arrayed in a crude wedge with the thin Mr. Ringle as the point.

"Couple o' suspicious characters, eh, lads?" Ringle announced, giving the two a harshly critical glare.

Raphael was not in a mood to be accosted. "Don't be stupid," he said. "This is Dean Tuckworth of the cathedral."

Ringle squinted. "'At's more'n I know. And who might you be?" he asked, tapping Raphael's chest with his whip.

Raphael brushed it aside. "First, you'll tell me your business."

"*My* business?" Ringle cast a look backward at his comrades, who spread out and around the dean and Raphael, encircling them quickly like a pack of wolves. "My business is askin' you *your* business," Ringle asserted, confident in his superiority of numbers and position.

Tuckworth could see where this was heading. He knew Raphael too well to think his patience could be counted on. So he stepped forward, placing himself between his friend and their inquisitor. "Mr. Ringle," he said with a genial nod, "may I introduce Mr. Raphael Amaldi. He is a painter by training and practice, an artist. Raphael, Mr. Ringle here is apprenticed at the livery, if I recognize him. Isn't that so, Mr. Ringle?"

"'Ey!" a surprised voice cried from somewhere beside them. "It's vicar!"

Ringle leaned forward sharply to examine his catch, so that Tuckworth could see his mottled face and smell his stale, beery breath. The apprentice pulled back again after a moment, disappointed. "A'right," he acknowledged. "So it's vicar. But what's this other chap. We're lookin' for painters, ain't we?" And he swung his whip about in general address to his companions. They laughed in dull appreciation, and Ringle returned his attention to Raphael with a smirk. "You been out paintin' this night, painter?"

Raphael took a step forward, so that Tuckworth had to move sidewise to intercept his rash anger. "I see, I see," the dean said. "You're out to clear the streets of mischief, that's it? Did the chief constable send you out, Mr. Ringle? Very cautious of him. Very forward-thinking, I daresay."

Ringle pulled himself up proudly. "Weren't no constable. Lord Granby hisself called us out. Called out all the 'prentices. Help keep order durin' the election."

"Granby?" Tuckworth repeated, genuinely surprised. "He called out *all* the apprentices?"

"All as is right for the Tory cause, yeah. Some four gangs out to-night alone."

"The Tory cause?" The dean took a closer look at the men surrounding him, noticed now the clubs and cudgels they carried with their lanterns, the bloody purpose behind their dark eyes, their twitching muscles, the nervous shifting of their feet from side to side, men waiting for something to happen, anything, and eager for it to come. "Not *all* the apprentices?"

Ringle spat. "Nah, some fools held back, bloody Whigs. We run into a couple o' them a while back, right, lads?" A gruff laugh circled about Tuckworth. "We taught 'em the wisdom o' Tory politics."

"Dear God, no," Tuckworth muttered.

Suddenly, from between two close buildings halfway down the lane, a band of chattering boys, or something more than boys, emerged into the light of the streetlamps carrying buckets and brushes, dripping blue along their path, pants and shirts and a few bare chests dappled in blue, blue in their hair and painted across their faces in savage streaks.

" 'Prentices!" Ringle cried to his troops, pointing the charge with his whip, and at once the whole band set off with a murderous whoop, scattering boys about the lane, blue lads dodging and ducking, paint buckets flying like sodden missiles through the air or held on to and swung with vicious effect, blue spreading down the street like blood. Boys ran in all directions, chased by the fury of the apprentices with their clubs and knouts sweeping wildly before them, crushing the air, with Ringle standing in the middle brandishing his whip and flicking it here and there to command his forces. The battle dissipated quickly enough, dissolving up alleys and down holes and through open doors and windows. A few pale lights shone briefly from upper stories and a few curious heads poked out of casements, but soon Tuckworth and Raphael were the only ones left in the lane. It all proved to be a great victory for noise and disorder, but not much of a one for the Tory cause.

Following the effects of his initial outrage, Raphael was hard put not to laugh openly at these antics, but one glance at Tuckworth smothered his mirth entirely. The dean stared after the retreating battle, despair spread across his face, planted in the deep furrows of his brow, shading his eyes in anguish.

"It's nothing, sir, I'm certain of it," Raphael tried to assure him. "It's just a bit of roughhouse. No real harm."

"Harm enough, Raphael," Tuckworth muttered. "Harm enough to Bellminster. Bands of armed men patrolling the streets. Armies set to clash by night under our windows. How long, do you think, before the Whigs send their own out, looking for mischief like these, ready for anything like these. What was Granby thinking?" He shook his head and looked away. "What are we coming to, Raphael? What is Bellminster coming to?"

They proceeded on their way, but had gotten only a few paces before a noise behind stopped them and they turned about again. A boy, tall and thin, perhaps just gone thirteen, stood in the shadows of the streetlamp. He stood as if waiting to keep an appointment he was eager not to miss. His eyes darted about, searching for someone or something, though only Tuckworth and Raphael were in the lane and nothing else could have moved without attracting their attention. Furtively, guiltily, the boy motioned for the men to approach and then vanished with two backward steps into the darkness.

They followed, retreating into the night from the comparative security of the streetlamps. Tuckworth found the boy again, a mere shade in the blackness about them, featureless, almost shapeless, standing in the open mouth of a narrow alley.

"I been watchin'. You after some'at?" His voice came like a faint breeze and it was clear that he held himself in some peril, as though he were violating a sacred trust.

"I'm after information, yes," the dean whispered, not quietly enough.

"Hsst!" the boy commanded. "I sees you well enough, both o' you. You just nod or shake and shut up, ol' grampus."

Tuckworth nodded.

"Right, then. You want some'at, and I want some'at. Clear?"

Tuckworth nodded.

"You want a name. Feller as set all this a-goin', these gammons, spreadin' that word 'cross the town." The lad waited. "Right?" he asked urgently.

Tuckworth nodded.

"Right. Now, so much for what you want. Now for me." The boy pointed behind the dean at Raphael. "I want that." The two men looked at each other in confusion, then Tuckworth turned back and shrugged.

"The box! I want them paints an' such."

Instinctively, Raphael raised a guarded hand to the latch of his paint box.

"It's them paints or sod off, right?" the boy hissed.

Tuckworth turned and looked at Raphael. There was nothing he could say, no appeal he could make that would seem right. He only looked, as slowly, and with far less introspection than he might have ever thought possible, Raphael pulled the box from under his arm and gave it over. The dean took it in his hands and held it out to the boy, who snatched at it greedily, but Tuckworth did not let go at once.

"The name," he whispered.

The lad looked about for an instant, then spoke. "Granny. It's ol' Granny done it."

The dean held on as the lad tried to jerk the box free. "Who is this granny? Whose granny?"

The boy seemed frantic now to get away. "Christ, grampus!" he declared. "His high and mighty lordship! Who else?"

"Granby? Are you telling me Lord Granby set you boys to this?"

"We's doin' it for his chap, ain't we? It's all Bick, Bick, Bick!"

"But . . ." This made no sense, the dean realized. All of this was working against Granby, not for him. Certainly to these lads it might seem as though Granby was behind it, might even appear obvious that he was. Yet they were wrong, and he would not allow Raphael to make such a sacrifice for this. The boy tried to wrench the box from Tuckworth's grip, but the dean held on ferociously.

"Leave off, grampus!"

"How do you know?" the dean pursued. "You're just guessing, aren't you! How do you know it's Lord Granby?"

"Davey said so."

With a great yank Tuckworth pulled the paint box back to himself and stood there in the dark, facing the boy. "Davey?" he wheezed.

"Davey Rose. He set us on it, but he let us know who was behind it all. We's all workin' for his lordship, right enough."

"What's this Davey look like? Describe him!"

"'Bout tall as me, and skinny, but older. Pocky face and an ol' lady's whiskers. Acts like more a man than what he is."

Danny Trees. The dean stood motionless for a moment as the name fell into its proper place, suddenly making the muddle of the past days seem a bit clearer, a shade brighter. Then, he held out the box once more. The lad snatched it away and turned to dart off into the night.

"Boy." It was Raphael, taking a step forward with his hands outstretched, holding his sketch pad. "You'll need paper."

The lad hesitated for just an instant before taking this, too, and disappearing.

"Danny Trees, Raphael," the dean began, turning about again.

"The mayor's lad?"

Tuckworth nodded. "I'm getting somewhere at last."

"Tell me about it as we walk. Maybe you can find some use for me in all this. God knows, I've been little use to myself."

"I'll make it up to you, Raphael," the dean insisted as they set off. "I'll buy you another box, more paints—"

"Fine."

That was all, just the one word. Tuckworth looked deeply at his friend, wondering what was happening within him, what mysteries he was holding on to. Wherever the dean turned these days, he found mysteries. "Lucy tells me you're leaving."

"Do you believe Padgett could have devised such a scheme on his own?"

All right, Tuckworth considered. Very well, it can wait. Let him work it out in his own time. "I don't believe Winston Padgett ever devised anything on his own, but first we've got to speak to Danny."

Away they moved, talking softly back and forth, both men deeply involved in their business, yet each equally detached from it, too, separated by a gulf, narrow but as deep as the earth. Behind them, they left only the darkness of an uneasy night.

CHAPTER XVIII

WHERE IS DANNY?

N ever!"

The word rang across the square, rebounding from the distant walls of the Arms to echo faintly back on the cathedral steps, where a large, huddled mob had assembled in the chilling cold, a dark puddle of hats with the steam of fifty breaths hovering above it. Reverend Mortimer looked down upon the faces beneath him, tired faces and curious faces, dirty and impeccable, unkempt and neatly trimmed, faces of the powerful and the powerless, of old and young, and very young. He smiled to see such faces turned toward him, eager to appreciate his gifts, ears open for his resounding call, his trumpeting influence. Mortimer drew a deep and satisfying breath.

"When have we ever known such a dutiful servant of Britain?" he asked. "Never! When such energy? When such vitality? When such vision put to the good use of his fellows?"

A few well-placed and well-rehearsed voices called out "Never!" from the crowd, and the rector smiled again. "When has the sun shone on such a son of Bellminster as this?" He raised a hand to indicate the slight frame of Mr. Bick, standing behind him with Lord Granby. "When have we been possessed of such an opportunity to place Bellminster at the forefront of national affairs, at the seat of progress? When has Grace shined so lovingly upon our collective futures as she now shines upon the noble form, the sagacious eye, the Roman brow of Bick?"

"Never!" a few more hearty souls cried, willing to join the fun.

"Never!" Mortimer confirmed. "Never, Bellminster, never!" But, as beatifically as Mortimer's expression had gleamed before, a shadow now passed across his face as a providential cloud drifted overhead, masking the sun. He turned mournfully to one side and dropped his gaze, a gesture he had often employed from the pulpit to indicate the need, the dire yet regrettable need for censure. He looked up again, sharply. "And when, stout hearts of Bellminster, when shall we allow the scant powers of division to separate us from our own best interest? When shall we let the selfish nature, the worldly nature, the radical nature of Whiggery to win a slanderous victory among us?"

"Never!"

"When shall we welcome the serpent to our table, the adder to our hearth?"

"Never!"

"When shall we surrender, purposely surrender, perfidiously surrender our best hopes, our best virtues, our best selves to this Whig invasion?"

"Never!"

"Never, I say! Never!"

Mortimer eyed the mob below him and was willing to be satisfied that he had done his duty, and that it was the best that might be done, certainly better than anyone else might do. He turned around with a dim, smug smile for Lord Granby, who nodded his careless approval.

Tuckworth also found much in this performance to recommend it, though not in the same way perhaps as Mortimer did. Standing at the vicarage gate with Raphael, buried in the warmth of his woolen scarf and watching this display of patriotic Tory spirit from a distance, the dean had a professional's appreciation for the talent, though he was gradually becoming aware of a deep contempt for the cause in which such talent was engaged.

"Reverend Mortimer speaks as highly of Mr. Bick today as he speaks of God on Sundays," the dean observed.

"Is that much of a surprise, sir?" asked Raphael, his voice unable to veil the distaste he felt whenever he considered the rector.

"Not especially, I suppose, but I'll tell you something that is a bit surprising."

"What's that?"

"Look up there, on the steps with Granby and Bick."

Raphael squinted to see better, and he noted aloud a few minor dignitaries of the town, Sir Anthony Heald and Horace Hardesty and Pleasance the excise man, along with some others moving from foot to foot to stay warm. Wilfred Cade sat off to one side on his camp stool, rubbing his fleshy palms together, but there was no one else of any consequence. "Who am I supposed—"

"Winston Padgett. The mayor is not present, nor is Mr. Bates."

"Would you expect Lord Granby to want them here?"

"Not particularly, but I'd expect the mayor would want to be here. His absence strikes me as significant."

"Of what?"

"Of I don't know what, not yet," the dean replied, turning away from politics and wandering across Cathedral Square with Raphael in tow. "Maybe he's embarrassed, or disgruntled, or feels himself threatened by the turn of circumstances. Or maybe he just has a stomachache. Shall we ask Danny about that when we see him?"

Before they had traveled more than halfway across the square, however, they were arrested by an amazing commotion erupting from a side street. A small band made up of three horns, a tuba, a bass drum, and two banners came rollicking around the corner, playing an unidentifiable air in a variety of keys while the drum-

mer and the four marchers with banner poles aloft shouted incoherently. Their message might have been lost were the banners
less eloquent, but they made up in bold red letters what the band
lacked in sense. QUENTIN DRAPER FOR BELLMINSTER! announced the
one, and FREE BEER! heralded the other.

This raucous tribe made a long, looping arc in the direction of
the cathedral before veering off at the last to set up beside the gate-
way of the Arms, trailing behind them the scurrying Whig rats
from the Tory ship. The rest was all confusion and damnation, as
Mortimer tried to salvage the rally with the threat of a celestial
prerogative against his enemies. The several dignitaries arrayed
along the steps laughed behind their gloved hands, and Granby
simply stood where he was, a monument to another time, as unmoved by this desertion as he had been by Mortimer's harangue. It
saddened Tuckworth to see him so, and yet he had no time at present to contemplate his lordship's sudden decline.

"It would appear they've begun in earnest at last," observed
the dean.

"It does. It should be a remarkable contest."

Tuckworth only nodded as he took Raphael's arm and together
they continued on their way to the Town Hall. They walked in silence through the late-morning streets, which were transformed
from their previous night's thrilling mystery. Where before was
shadow and mist, threat and fear, now all was familiar and comfortable, open, free, and welcoming. Heads nodded in pleasant
succession as the dean made his way along, and eyes smiled and
lips wished "Good morning" to Tuckworth and his young companion, so that the town almost seemed what it always had been.
Children played in the dust of the streets and shopkeepers
hawked their wares and men clutched at their hats in the rising
autumn breeze. Gossips prattled and horses trotted and women
smiled and babies laughed. As much as things can change, the
dean considered as he walked, so much again can stay the same,

must stay the same if life is to know any continuity to it, not dissolve into chaos.

Yet men *must* change, something told him as he recalled the aged figure of Lord Granby, and life *is* chaos. Order is the illusion, he realized, the thin varnish brushed over life to keep all smooth and presentable. All must change, that's the only real law of nature.

"You're leaving us, Raphael," he stated as he walked, the truth of it rising from the depths of his thoughts.

"I've decided to, yes, sir."

"Why?"

"I can't paint here anymore."

"No? Nor in London, I recall. Where can you paint, do you suppose?"

Raphael hesitated before answering. "I don't know. I just don't think I can paint in Bellminster."

"Oh, you don't *think* you can paint here."

"I haven't been able to. Everything I try comes out flat. There's no art in me anymore." He breathed deeply, not sighing. "It's all gone out."

"Do you think you can run it down? Chase after it and find it again?" They both sidestepped out into the street to avoid walking under a ladder. "Can you wrestle it back to you, my boy?"

"Please don't quiz me this way," Raphael pleaded. "I haven't got all the answers."

"I just want to be certain you have any answers at all. Now look," Tuckworth stopped and turned Raphael toward him, "you're a grown man making a decision about the course of your life. Very fine. No one has the right to make that decision for you. But I can't keep silent, either. This course involves me as well. It's causing great pain to someone I care for, someone who matters to me, and I think you should ask yourself some rather harsh questions before you decide on it."

"I know how Lucy is suffering! Don't you think I see it?"

Tuckworth placed a calming hand on Raphael's shoulder. "Yes, she is. But she's not the one I was speaking of."

Raphael looked confused for an instant, and then surprised, and then slightly guilty, though resolved.

"All right," Tuckworth went on, continuing their journey, "I can see you're set. Well, resolution is a fine thing, too. Most people avoid making decisions all through their lives for fear of being wrong, but any decision is almost always superior to no decision."

"Well and good for me, then. I've decided."

They walked on a few more steps in silence.

"When will you leave?"

"Soon."

Tuckworth grinned inwardly at such limp decisiveness. "Raphael, you know I'm not the sort to offer advice where it's not asked for."

"Excuse me," the young painter replied, a note of cool defensiveness in his voice, "but I think you are, sir."

"What?" the dean exclaimed as if stung.

"You are. You're always advising people how to be and what to do. You might not know you do it, but you do."

Tuckworth was silenced by such unexpected honesty. Was it true? First from Granby, then Mrs. Padgett, and now Raphael? Was he a meddler?

"I'm . . . I'm sorry," he faltered.

"It's not your fault, sir." Raphael shrugged as though it meant nothing to him, nothing at all. "It's just how you are."

"Well," the dean said at last, "if I can't help it then I can't help this. What I mean to tell you is, go off if you've a mind to. Make your decision and follow it through. Just be certain that you know where you're going. If you truly believe there's someplace, someone out there who can restore what you think you've lost, then that's fine. But if your art is only slumbering within you, only resting after years of labor before striking forth again refreshed to explore something new, something you can't even imagine, then maybe you should rest with it, and not chase it about the country-side. Time enough for that later."

Raphael was silent after this, and Tuckworth could not be certain whether the advice he had offered was being valued or ignored. They only moved along, side by side, careful of their friendship as it strained against the truth as a dog at a leash.

When they arrived at the Town Hall at last and had descended into that beehive of ambition and stunted dreams, they learned that Danny's place was occupied by a wizened old clerk biding his days in the dark, awaiting his pension. No, he hadn't any idea where Danny could be found. No, he hadn't seen him for at least some days. No, he couldn't recall how many days that was. And most emphatically no, the mayor was not to be disturbed. He had a headache. The dean and his young friend might return on Monday at eleven o'clock.

So, for the third time, Tuckworth was to be put off from seeing Mayor Padgett in his office. For the third time he was forced to make an appointment for a later date, another time. Yet, for the first time, the dean would have none of that. In three steps he was at the mayor's door, with Raphael by his side. He knocked twice, for he would not be any ruder than he must, and strode boldly into the office.

"Wha . . . wha'?"

"Mayor Padgett," Tuckworth announced, turning to where the mayor sat behind his desk. "I regret to disturb you like this, but it's about McAllister's death."

"Dean Tuckworth," Mr. Bates said, rising from his usual chair, "his honor is eager to assist you in any way that he might. Unfortunately, he is a very busy man."

"We won't take long. I'm looking for Danny Trees."

"Danny?" his honor blurted. "Danny?"

Bates coughed mildly. "Is Danny embroiled in this ugly business?"

"I think he is. At least, I want to talk to him about it."

"Well, when you find him, please tender our regards."

"You don't know where he is?"

"We do not."

"When did you see him last?"

"Oh, good heavens, when was it?" Bates turned to the mayor. "Three days ago? Four?"

Padgett shrugged, a pained look on his sweating face.

Bates grinned his apology. "It's so difficult to recall with any certainty, Dean Tuckworth. You see, Danny was never terribly attentive to his duties. Not the most regular fellow, regrettably."

"I see." Tuckworth looked from the mayor to Bates and back again. "Mayor Padgett, may I have a word with you in private?"

"I'm afraid his honor is not well enough to entertain your questions just now," Bates said, intervening. "As you can see, he is afflicted with a most lamentable headache."

All eyes turned to the mayor, who raised a moist hand to his brow, dropped his head, and groaned pathetically.

The dean nodded. "Forgive us," he whispered. "We had no desire to intrude upon your suffering. Some other time, perhaps?"

"Of course," murmured Bates, leading the dean and Raphael away from the now perpetual moans of Mayor Padgett. "We'll just make an appointment with Collins on your way out. So many calls upon the mayor's schedule, you understand. The demands of office." Bates accompanied them back to the antechamber, where the ancient clerk scratched away at his ledgers. "Collins," Bates said, "please make an appointment for the dean and his friend. The soonest available, Collins."

"Already told 'em Monday at eleven," the man muttered, closing one ledger and opening another.

"Monday, Collins?" Bates remarked, sounding surprised and slightly embarrassed. "No, no. Monday is quite full up. In fact, all the next week is just one interview after another. No, I'm afraid it shall have to be the week after. Shall we call it Tuesday a week, say two o'clock?"

The dean nodded with a close-lipped smile, which was answered in kind by Bates. "Until then," Tuckworth said, and taking Raphael's elbow, the two left to make their way back up the darkling maze.

Bates returned to the mayor, closing the door behind him with a firm click. "There, now was that so difficult?" he asked, his voice calm and comforting.

Padgett moaned in earnest now. "He'll just come to my house. He won't stop."

"Then you be sure to keep him out. Plead health or fatigue. You certainly look the worse for all this excitement. Keep him away from you and let Mrs. Padgett handle him."

"But he knows!"

"We don't care what he knows, if he can prove nothing."

"But . . . but—"

"No!" Bates snapped, then recovered his composure. "No, sir. There is no 'but.' We must be strong. We must be a stone wall, and then there is no way for him to get around us and no place else he can go. Agreed?"

Padgett only turned his head away.

Bates stepped up to the mayor's desk, stood there implacably, forcing his presence upon Padgett's notice. "Are we agreed, sir?" he said, uttering each syllable like a slap to the face, hard and sharp.

The mayor nodded without looking up.

"Very well." Bates smiled easily and went back to his chair. "You'll see. By two weeks' time this will all have blown over and we'll be able to bring Danny back, or send him off completely, whichever suits our needs. It's only the death of an old man, after all. And we had no hand in it. Remember that when you feel squeamish," he admonished with a finger raised in the air. "We had no hand in it at all."

Back on the street, Raphael turned to Tuckworth and was startled to see the dean's eyes dancing with excitement. "Sir?" he asked.

The dean measured his words carefully, calling his enthusiasm to heel. "I believe, Raphael, I believe that we have our responsible party at last. They were both lying to us, lying clumsily."

"Why?"

"They've been behind these disturbances all along, trying to force Granby to give up Bick."

"And the murder?"

"Not part of their plan, I daresay. They set it all in motion and then failed to control it. We still have a murderer at large, but we're beginning to find a path through all this muddle. At least," the dean took a deep breath, "it appears that way. We mustn't leap ahead too far. Right now, we have to find Danny."

"Where do we go to find him?"

Tuckworth set off at once, forcing Raphael to trot up behind. "Where he is most likely to be missed," he said, and dragged his friend briskly along the pavement, into the clear light of noon.

CHAPTER XIX
"NOBODY'S FAULT!"

Men of wealth and preeminent station are sometimes, though not often, heard to express a modest appreciation for the way Fortune has smiled on them. Fortune, a lady of high standing and therefore apt to associate with those of position and power, fashions her dress along various styles for her different suitors. With some, she resembles hard work coupled to opportunity. For others, she comes dark and cloaked to the bedside of a dying relative. At times she will forward the investments of one over the failure of thousands, sending her loyal acolyte to the opera and the club while countless families are left to beg in the streets for bread. In rare instances she seems to lead the inept or incompetent by the hand, guiding their path and guarding their progress like a sponsoring angel. She is courted by great and meek alike, though hers is a fickle affection, fickle and capricious, as they will tell you who have been abandoned by her in some needful hour.

And yet, how much more fickle are her suitors? Having once tasted her favors, how many men adjure all knowledge of her acquaintance? How many acts bearing her unmistakable mark are credited to some other, some self-serving oaf's good sense or sagacity? How often is she afforded the courtesy of even a nodding recognition, but goes about the world snubbed, cut, ignored, and abused, actually abused by those most indebted to her patronage? (This, perhaps, explains why she is known for a lady, in that what man alive, having once rumpled his mistress's sheets, will not eventually treat her so?)

Tuckworth, even Tuckworth, was not above such scandalous neglect, and in subsequent days as he recalled the events surrounding Bellminster's infamous by-election, he was given, not so much to embellishing his own accomplishments, as to discrediting subtly the role that Fortune (née Luck) played in what occurred.

And yet there was no mistaking how startled he was to discover Mrs. Charles Bates (née Trees) visiting her mother at the very moment when he arrived with Raphael to pursue his inquiries into Danny's whereabouts. The dean had never given the girl a thought in all of this, despite everything that should have driven him to her from the first. He had been delighted to find Danny in the mayor's employ, an aid and relief to his parents' depressed state. Old Daniel Trees was a respected foreman at the mill before being cast out with some three score others one bleak day, and the blow had sapped the man's will to work, if not to live or to drink. But the dean had inexplicably failed to mark the near relation by marriage that won Danny the position, and he might never have thought to speak to Susannah Bates on this matter had she not been with her mother just then. So much for the dean's outstanding debt to Fortune.

He was let into the flat by a pair of ragged boys who pointed the way in and then darted off to their own adventures. The room he entered with Raphael contained furnishings that had once gleamed and sparkled as new, tables that had once been unscratched, chairs that knew what it was to sit unworn, unrent, unsoiled. The knickknacks cluttering the shelves had once been thought fashionable in certain unremarkable quarters, though now they appeared shabby and quaint. The room seemed to have been abandoned not by care, for all was clean and tidy, but by hope. Sitting among this sad display was a small, slender, pale young creature, more girl than woman, excessively pretty and smartly dressed in pale, pale blue.

"Susannah," Tuckworth said with a nod and a spark of sudden revelation. "I'd forgotten you were married. To Mr. Bates of the mayor's office, isn't it?"

The girl nodded demurely.

"I hope you and Mr. Bates are well. Have you met Mr. Amaldi?" The dean turned to indicate his friend.

Susannah smiled a limp smile that might have succeeded in haughtiness, befitting her new station in Bellminster, had the dean not noted the redness about her eyes and the smeared damp of her cheek. "I have seen Mr. Amaldi painting about the town," she said softly.

Raphael bowed. "Delighted, ma'am."

Mrs. Trees called out from the cupboard, "If that's painter, tell 'im not to touch nothin'! Painters is always wet with their last bit o' work."

Tuckworth glanced sideways at Raphael, who shuffled nervously, and the dean could not suppress a twinkling grin.

Mrs. Bates hemmed delicately. "You've got to . . . must forgive Mother," she said, sounding falsely proud as though she were reciting lessons from a book. "She doesn't understand art and such like."

"No need that she should," Tuckworth assured her, and as if in proof of his point Mrs. Trees came bustling in, carrying a tea tray arranged with a small and homely service and looking as though art were the furthest concern in the world.

"If you'd like a cup just say so and I'll fetch it," she announced, setting the tray down on a side table with a bang and a rattle. "Ain't got much, but what there is is good enough. Susie, you still take sugar, I trust. Always was expensive in your habits." And she laughed a mother's contented laugh to know that one child at least was free from care.

"Two . . . I mean, one sugar, if you please," the girl answered, and the dean followed Susannah's gaze into the nearly depleted sugar bowl.

"Two's what you take and two's what you get," her mother chided kindly, clinking the cubes into the cup and pouring. "Vicar? For you and young painter?"

"No, thank you, Mrs. Trees," Tuckworth replied, debating within himself what to do, how to proceed under these new circumstances. "I don't want to take away from your precious time with your daughter. I was just hoping you'd be able to tell me where I might find Danny."

"That's queer," the woman said, looking at her daughter quickly. "Susie was just askin' after the same thing. Boy seems to have dropped clean from this world." She set her plump body down with a wheezing grunt in a thinly padded chair. "Still," she resumed, reaching forward to prepare her own cup, "that's nothin' peculiar. Lad's a right man now and's got his own concerns."

"Why are you looking for him?" Susannah asked with an unexpected fervency that she failed to mask, and that showed Tuckworth the terrible road he must take. Her voice sounded strained to him, pulled tight like a thread drawn from a spinning wheel, delicate and liable to break. She looked at the dean, stared at his mouth, his ears, the tip of his nose, covered his entire face with her glance but kept well away from his eyes.

"I need to talk to him," the dean replied, calculating as he spoke, weighing the moment carefully, wondering if he dared to do what he had to do. "I'm performing a service for Mr. Hopgood. I need to ask Danny about these disturbances that have been going on, and about Evan McAllister."

Mrs. Trees muttered something unintelligible, shaking her head and clucking her tongue in sympathy for the dead. "Dreadful business. Just awful. I daresay the mayor's got Danny well up on that for you, vicar. That's official town business now, I imagine."

"Mother," Susannah said, setting her cup on the tray and nearly upsetting it, "I'm afraid I must be leaving."

"But you only just arrived, my dear."

"I forgot," she insisted cryptically, rising from her seat.

Tuckworth steeled himself and hated himself, too, for what he was bound to do. "Mrs. Bates," he said softly, his voice gentle and clear and inescapable. "Mrs. Bates, I wish you would stay. Just for a minute or two."

"But I can't," she insisted again, her voice cracking now in agitation, panic showing in her watery gaze. "I can't."

"Susie, dear, what is it?"

"Just a few questions, Mrs. Bates," Tuckworth mercilessly pursued.

Raphael stepped forward, his hand extended in concern. "Mrs. Bates?"

Susannah Bates fell backward into her chair, and then pitched forward, burying her face in her hands, her breath catching in sobs.

"Raphael," Tuckworth said, softly still. "Fetch some water."

"There's a pail in the cupboard," Mrs. Trees told him.

Raphael was gone for less than a moment, returning with a dripping cup that he handed to the mother attending to her child. Soon, sooner than the dean would have thought likely for so susceptible a creature, Susannah had recovered herself enough to talk.

"You mustn't think he's had any hand in this himself," she implored the dean, still sniffling. "You mustn't believe he wanted any of this."

"I don't believe it for a second," Tuckworth reassured her, not entirely convinced who *he* was and not much caring. "I only want the chance to talk to Danny about it all, to find out who did have a hand in it."

"But couldn't all this wait 'til after the election, is all? Won't there be time enough then?"

The dean shook his head sadly.

Susannah sighed. "I don't know where Danny is. Charley never told me nothin'."

"It's true," her mother confirmed. "She come here askin' after him herself."

"But Charley knows, doesn't he."

Susannah shook her head and stared vaguely at the floor. "I'm worried for him, vicar. I'm scared for Danny. I don't know why. He's been gone three days now, no one knows where, except Charley, and I daren't ask him. I know Charley wouldn't let Danny come to no . . . to any harm. But I'm gettin' scared and can't help it."

Tuckworth considered for a moment. He had not been expecting such a windfall, to discover this child, the key to so much he needed to know, and he was not altogether prepared. "Mrs. Bates," he asked at last, "what property does your husband own?"

"Property? You mean like our flat?"

"No, no. Does he own any flats himself, or a house, something that he lets out?"

Susannah shook her head. "He don't make as much as that, not what you'd think, workin' for the mayor like he does. Folks think we do so well, but just enough ain't too much, you understand. Charley's always complainin' about how shabby we live. I don't see as how he could own some other place, and us where we are. Not that it ain't nice," she added with a hurried glance at her mother. "It's lovely, for me. But nothin' suits Charley, he's got such fine tastes. His clothes is always the best. You seen him, vicar, how handsome he is. And he eats out regular, three and four times a week, sometimes." The girl's face glowed as though she were seeing a vision of something holy. "Charley's the best as is ever happened to me, but I ain't been near good enough for him."

"I see," the dean replied, seeing perhaps more than Susannah intended him to see. "And do you ever eat out, Mrs. Bates?"

"Me?" She looked at her mother for a moment, confused. "Why would I ever? Larder's always full. We's never wantin'."

The dean smiled touchingly. "Of course you always have enough. Your husband does quite well by you, I'm sure." But a pang of aching sympathy shot through him as he said the words. "Does he go out often in the evening?"

"Near every night. But that's just his work."

"When would be a good time for me to stop by for a visit? I'd like to have a word with Mr. Bates outside his office."

Susannah looked suddenly frightened. "Oh no," she almost cried. "Charley don't meet no one at home. Except Danny."

Tuckworth raised a calming hand. "Very well, very well. I wouldn't want to cause you alarm for any reason. I'll see him at the mayor's office and maybe I'll invite him to supper. Nothing wrong with that, I'm sure."

Susannah smiled gratefully.

"Now are you quite well? Is there anything we can do for you before we leave?"

"Just please don't mention none o' this to him, vicar. He wouldn't like it, me talkin' to you about Danny and such things."

"Of course not." And with that, Tuckworth and Raphael said their goodbyes and left.

Once outside, they turned back up the street and then cut across the slope of the town, that long rise up from the Medwin to the cathedral. Raphael did not ask where they were going. He simply bounded along like a contented pup, and it was clear that this adventure had for a time erased all memory of his own problems. He slowly became aware, however, that the dean was not so satisfied with how things had gone. "Are you well, sir?" Raphael asked.

Tuckworth glowered out at the world from under a black cloud. "I'm as well as I'm like to be," he murmured, and there was something in his voice that surprised Raphael, a sickness and disgust that seemed to have no cause.

"Where are we going?"

"We're going to Constabulary House to betray that poor child back there."

"What?"

"We're going to do what we have to do," the dean spat out, trying desperately to justify himself to himself, to make it all seem a dreadful necessity, not just an expedient scheme to a dubious end. "We're going to do the one thing that poor creature doesn't want us to do, begged me not to do. We're going to tell Hopgood what we've learned and have him put a man to follow Bates."

"And he'll take us to Danny?"

Tuckworth made no reply. The answer was too obvious to need one, and he was not feeling talkative.

"It's not your fault, sir," Raphael tried to reassure him. "If that girl gets hurt in this, it's Bates' fault, not yours."

"Who says it's my fault? Of course it's not my fault."

"I just—"

"It's nobody's fault. What's Bates done but what Granby would have done if he'd thought of it, what Granby *is* doing now that he has the need? Set a few boys out to make some petty mischief, that's all. Whose fault is that, to scratch a few votes together? And now a man's dead and Danny's in hiding and that girl's just betrayed her worthless husband and she's about to be betrayed by us and whose fault is that? It's nobody's fault!" Tuckworth realized that he was shouting, and he stopped suddenly and wrapped himself in a foul temper.

But as they walked on, the thin varnish of silence crackled between them, and Tuckworth found ample opportunities to place the fault of his current scheme, and always, in defiance of reason and justice, against all good sense, the fault lay squarely with him. Why was he meddling in this? So a man was killed and some unknown, unnamed creature out there was the cause. What of that? he thought as they walked on. Wasn't Hopgood sufficient to make an investigation? And if the chief constable never came to an answer, did that really matter? McAllister was dead and beyond needing an avenger. It was all of less interest in the town's thoughts than this election, anyway. What did it all matter, that this girl should be made to suffer now? So there was another soul wandering about with blood on his hands, blood that could never be washed off. Were Tuckworth's hands clean? Weren't his hands as bloody as this nameless killer's? Weren't murderers left to walk the streets every day?

And on they walked.

CHAPTER XX
JO SMALLEY PAYS A CALL

J o Smalley paused and smelled the midnight air of Bellminster. He liked this town more than he had liked a place in a very long time. He had expected just another provincial nowhere, primitive and backward, always twenty years behind, never able to catch up and falling further back all the time. But things were different here, more well on, more advanced along the proper paths. That mill had something to do with it, and hardship. Hardship was a great advancer of men's talents.

He hobbled on a few more paces and then paused and sniffed the air again. Nice, he thought. Country air, grassy even here, even in the middle of town. You never get that in London. The air smells like air there, thick and greasy, flakes of humanity drifting on the wind, into your lungs, breathing people.

Jo heard a sound ahead and ducked into a dusky corner, out of the lamplight and behind an alley ash can, crouching low until he was only the shadow of a shadow, the darker part of night. A company of half-a-dozen drunkards caroused past, knouts and clubs in their fists, blue ribbons pushed through their lapels and hat bands. Blue for Bick. Jo watched and smiled to himself, and when they had passed he emerged from his hole and scuttled on his way.

Now, there was forward thinking. These roving parties had saved him a mountain of work and left the field of virtue clear. Progressive, even stylish, after a modern style. That was rarely the case in these provincial jobs. Too often the low road opened up and the high road must be left for the local talent, but here, Quentin Draper could be kept above the fray, spotless and bright. Yes, he liked Bellminster, as well as he liked anyplace, except London. But how could they even compare? London was London, after all. He must be fair about such things.

A few more blocks, over the river, and he entered the New Town. He counted to himself, noting the numbers of the bystreets, and glanced at the buildings as he went. They were ugly, depressed blocks of flats, uglier perhaps for being less depressed than they might have been. A thorough sense of dilapidation would have added a certain worldly charm. Few men appreciated beauty in distress the way Jo Smalley did. But these were only the poor homes of poor laborers, all soulless brick and graceless mortar.

He turned down a lane and up another, ticking off the buildings. They looked all the same, these hives of flats. Jo stopped, carefully studied the numbers of the houses across the way, and then settled on one in his mind. Walking across to it, he entered softly. The stairs loomed at once above him. Never on the ground floor, he mused with a woeful shake of the head, then started up, step by step, leaning on his cane, pulling hard on the balustrade, hauling himself ceilingward as a man might hoist a crate. It was a laborious, awkward climb. He went up two flights before pausing to catch his breath, then heaved his way up the last stretch. Stopping at the top, he peered into the darkness above, up the fourth and final flight of stairs.

A figure in the shadows stirred, then descended into the sickly light of the smoldering oil lamp hung on the wall.

Jo jerked his head toward the door beside him, a mute query.

The figure answered by stepping forward and knocking sharply, three short raps. They waited, and two soft knocks came in response. Knocking twice more, the dark figure stepped aside as the lock in the door clicked and Jo Smalley went boldly in.

"Such a great many hurdles to leap over just to see you, Danny," he said as he limped into the room.

"Hey!" Danny Trees shouted in surprise; then, more hushed, "Who the hell're you?"

"Don't worry yourself, Danny," the dwarf replied, grinning. "I think you know who I am right enough. Call me Jo." He moved straight across the bare and dusty floorboards to a stained table with two chairs pushed out and a sputtering candle on top, the only furniture in the room save for a hard iron bed with a night table and washbasin. The crumbs of a cold supper were strewn about, some dry crusts and cheese and a nearly empty pail of beer. Jo hopped up onto one of the chairs and breathed easily now. "Such a long way up. Couldn't Charley have afforded to set you a bit closer to the street? Oh well, all ways is up to me." And he laughed a pleasant laugh.

Danny eyed his visitor with a suspicious squint. "You know Charley?"

"We're all in the same business, Danny. You, me, ol' Granny, Charley Bates. We're all associates, as it were. Come in, child! Don't loiter about the landing!"

The figure from the hallway came shuffling in and closed the door, "Hi, *Danny,*" she muttered, laying emphasis on his right name, anxious with bravado.

"Kit!"

"Kathleen and I are great chums now, Danny," Jo declared, motioning his protégé into a corner near the door. "I want you and me to be chums, too."

"But how'd you—"

"*You* told me. You told me who she was and where I'd find her."

"I done?"

"Have a sit, Danny, and we'll talk it all over. Come to an understanding, as it were." Jo nodded at the empty chair and instinctively Danny took a step toward the table. But he stopped again.

"How do I know Charley sent you?"

"Now, did I say Charley sent me? Is that what I said?" Jo tilted sideways in his chair and winked, then grinned broadly. "No, Charley didn't send me. I appear before you at my own discretion, Danny, to make your acquaintance. Now, if you'd just kindly sit down." He craned his head about. "Lookin' up all the time stiffens my neck."

Out of notice of the two men, Kit began to sidle her way along the wall, about the edges of the room.

Danny sat down at last and leaned forward across the table. "So, when did I tell you about Kit? When'd I ever have a word with you? When'd we ever meet, eh?"

"Right to the point, Danny. Commendable, commendable." Jo reached into his waistcoat pocket and pulled out a piece of torn paper.

"That's the note . . ." Danny's voice trailed off in comprehension.

Jo unfolded the paper, showed it to Danny, and recited what was written there. " 'Kitty Wren, to be found in the neighborhood of the Three Pears. Ask the tapster.' That was a pretty bit there, Danny. Askin' the tapster. He knew our Kathleen right off, and I had no trouble findin' her after that." He stuffed the note back into his pocket, as Kit crept a few steps farther along.

"I left that with vicar. How'd you come across that?"

"I took it from off the dean's doorstep where you left it." Jo chuckled. "I knew someone would come around to peach. It's what I would've done. And damn me if you didn't show up right on schedule. There's no gettin' around me, Danny. I'm too sharp. But you're a sharp one, too. That's why I'm here."

"Yeah, why *are* you here?"

"Like I said, me and Charley are kind of associates in the same business. Competitors, true enough, but just a friendlyish competition. Like gents at the racetrack, each backin' his own entry at the stakes, but with no real animosity betwixt us, right?"

Danny nodded slowly.

"That's good. That's brave, Danny. Not one man in ten would get it right off like that. Not one in twenty." Jo lifted his gold-handled cane onto the table and began rolling it back and forth gently as he talked, so that the gold glistened in the candlelight.

Danny's eyes were drawn greedily to it. "A'right," the boy said after a moment. "You's competitors, the two of you. What's that to me?"

"Why, you're in the same game, aren't you? You're up on all our political arts, and you've impressed me. Now, there it is, Danny. Simple as that. You've impressed me, and I decided, any young man as can manage like Danny Trees has managed, that's a young man I want in *my* stable, helpin' to back *my* horses."

Danny leaned back, his eyes not leaving the gold head of the cane, mesmerized by its glinting light. "Your stable?" he repeated. "You mean the Whigs?"

Jo let go a good-natured laugh. "Whigs and Tories, Danny? Conservatives and liberals? That's just silks for jockeys to wear. We're talkin' politics, not government. The political arts. It's a grand game. Old as the oldest Greeks. Older, even. And as soon as I come to Bellminster, I seen right off there was someone here who knew how to play it. That's you, Danny."

"But Charley made all the plans. I just done what he told me to do."

"Plans," Jo scoffed. "We got planners enough. It's doers I want. You're a doer, Danny, and that's why I'm offerin' you the life's chance, the chance Charley'd give anything for, the chance to play the game in London."

London. The word was a magical incantation, and the boy's eyes grew wide and bright at its sound.

"That's the real game, Danny, the true game. Not this." He waved his hand dismissively about the room, about the town.

"So whatcha want from me to get in your game, then? What's the stakes?"

Jo laughed. "That's it! Right to it! You sees your way through like a lighthouse in a thick fog. Now, I'll wager a sharp chap like you knows right off what I want."

Danny leaned back and squinted, and Kit edged farther about the room. "You want someone inside, like me, someone as has an ear in Charley's plans."

Jo chuckled. "That I do, Danny. That I do. Well reasoned, lad. I want to know what t'other side thinks, what they've got cookin'. Charley comes here regular, don't he?"

Danny nodded.

"Then all I want's for you to talk to him, draw him out, learn his plans."

Kit inched the last few steps about the room, until she stood directly behind Danny Trees. She placed her hand in her pocket and fingered a hard, ivory handle.

Danny leaned back in his chair, far back, delighted with himself and proud. He had always played the game before under Charley's guidance and direction. But now, to be pitted against his teacher! "So," he said, feeling like a great man, an important man, a man at last, "how would we—"

From behind, Kit leaped forward, grasped his hair in her sharp fist, and yanked his head back, bringing a blade swiftly across his bared throat in a red, ragged arc. A spurt of black blood shot across the table, splattering Jo's waistcoat, and the dwarf leaped down from his chair. "The hell!" he screamed softly, his voice dropping through habit to a thick whisper. "Christ, girl! What the hell are you—"

"Ya peached on me, Danny," Kit hissed in Danny's ear as he flailed at his throat, his face twisted, the blood cascading down, covering his shirtfront, flowing dark and heavy, bubbles forming as he tried to gasp, hands smearing his life about. He tried to reach around, to grab Kit, but she pulled back, keeping a firm grip of his hair. Slowly, his arms drooped, then hung limp at his sides.

"Ya shouldn't oughter've peached." Kit let go with a disgusted shove and Danny's body slumped forward and down, sliding from the chair to the floor.

Jo Smalley's mind was working furiously, sizing up the girl, the room, making certain the door was closed, the hallway silent. Instinctively he knew, as he always knew, what the situation required, and he forced himself into a calm, almost friendly tone. He took two deep breaths to allow the shock to pass, and then steeled himself to reality. "Well," he said, his voice heaving with excitement, taking command in an easy fashion, "that was a messy business, Kathleen." He looked down on himself, surveying his soiled clothing. "I liked this waistcoat," he muttered.

Kit stood above Danny, her eyes black and wide, her nostrils flared, each breath coming into her and going out of her like her last. In her hand she still held the knife, the sharpened steel tinted red now with Danny's blood.

Jo motioned at the blade with his cane. "Drop that knife, Kit. You've made a muck of this night, and we've got to start thinkin' how best to get out of it and be on our way."

She only stood there deaf and blind, panting, sweat beading on her brow, her eyes smarting and dry, and she blinked hard to squeeze a drop of moisture out of them.

Jo hobbled around Danny's body. "Now, listen to me, Kit," he said soothingly. "We need to be going, one at a time. First you, and then me. So put the knife on the floor and collect yourself." He reached up and gently touched her arm.

Kit spun about as if roused from a dream and raised the knife in alarm, threatening the empty shadows. The gold-handled cane hissed through the air and cracked her soundly on the wrist. The

knife clattered to the floor and Kit glared down at the dwarf, her
eyes still fired by passion and murder, still red and dry.

His voice rang soft and cold through the haze of her hatred.
"Collect yourself, girl. We're not finished here yet."

Very slowly, the fire went from Kit's eyes. The thought of work
to be done seeped through her anger, cooled her blood. Her teeth
unclenched and she nodded.

Jo grinned. "That's right, Kit. No denyin' you're a hellcat and a
damn foolish thing. That was rashly done." Jo eyed Danny where
he lay, blood pooling about him.

"He peached on me," was all she said by way of explanation.

"I'd say you've evened that score, and come out a deal ahead in
the bargain." Jo was silent for a moment, and slowly a plan knitted
itself together in his mind, something that might turn this
calamity into something worthwhile, something even creditable.
"All right, you've done what you've done," he said, "but perhaps it
ain't all bad. Now, when was he here last, that other one?"

"This morning," Kit murmured glumly, but with a whipped look
of obedience in her sullen eyes as she rubbed her wrist.

"And who's on the top floor, in the garret?"

"Pair o' dandies. Whole damn building o' toffs and dandies."

"They ever see you?"

She sneered. "No one never seen me."

"That's right. Be proud of your gifts. Now, I'll manage this for
you. You get on your way but stay close. I might need you again.
And, Kit—" She turned and saw Jo's eyes go hard and black. "No
more rash acts."

She nodded, and Jo peered into her, the way he had of seeing
into people. She had never killed before, not on purpose, not like
this, and that meant he had a hold over her. She was his now, if he
could use her, but he had to be careful. He had found a way to har-
ness her hatred to his cart, but she must be reined in sharply.

"Off then, and watch you don't get spied."

She took two steps toward the door.

"Kit!"

She stopped. Jo was pointing down at her feet, and she saw that her shoes were tracking blood about the floor.

"You pull 'em off and go and drop 'em downstream in the river. Downstream at least two miles. And fill 'em with stones."

She nodded, tore off the shoes, and then she was gone, as smooth and silent as silk thread over glass. He wondered what she'd look like cleaned and dressed proper. She might be quite presentable, her hair done up. It was only the thought of an instant, however, for Jo Smalley had other work to occupy his talents. He eyed Danny, lying on the floor, crumpled and misshapen, awash in a spreading lake of blood.

Well, Jo considered, the messier the better. Makes a more dramatic picture. Over years of practice at the hands of tormentors, men and even women who delighted in exercising their passions against his weakness, he had trained his feelings to shrivel into a hole in his heart. He was a planner and a plotter, and his emotions were only an inconvenient tie to another life, as useful as an old language vaguely recalled from childhood. He looked down now at the sight before him and coldly, unfeelingly, he knew what to do to exercise his own advantage. He improvised.

Jo reached down and grabbed Danny's collar, dragging him toward the door like a leaky sack. Danny was tall but thin, and the dwarf was strong, deceptively strong. He pulled with no great effort, and as he went, he stopped every few feet and planted Danny's dead palms on the floor, leaving a crisp, bloody print behind. He pulled Danny to within a few feet of the door, then stepped some paces back and looked at what he had accomplished. A black smear trailed across the floor, with Danny stretched out at the end of it, for all the world appearing to have died where he dragged himself. A pretty picture indeed, and Jo seemed happy with it.

He pulled out his watch, gold and ornately fashioned, a true Italian timepiece. He opened it and marked the hour. Two o'clock. Must still be some roving bands about, bloodthirsty apprentices and the like. He snapped the watch shut, made certain that the candle was trimmed and sure to burn, and opened the door at last. He opened it wide, so that anyone passing by must see the dead figure lying within. Satisfied, he hurried out into the night. Hurried, though going down was always slower than coming up.

Once on the street, he hung to the shadows on his way out of the New Town, back to the Granby Arms, under the gloom of the cathedral. He saw it rising above him in the moonlight, its two headless towers stark against the stars. For the briefest moment he paused to appreciate it, the sight of these twin guardians, beaten and unbowed. Now that's an affecting picture, he thought. Desolate and affecting. He spent but a moment in such reverie, however, for his night's work was far from done. He glanced down again at the blood-speckled waistcoat. Improvisation, that's what this called for. He might try to hide the offensive garment, or burn it, but there was a better way. He could disguise it in such a way that no man would know it was even hidden.

He kept to his path in the shadows and dark corners of the pavement, and as he entered the older part of Bellminster, he heard the brazen carousing of a local force of vigilantes, drunk and shambling on their patrol. He sought them out, hung behind them as they wandered aimlessly, singing and calling out to the night, daring the Blues to show their faces, for these were some of Granby's men. Their progress was slow and swaggering, and Jo had no trouble keeping up as they led him a twisted, torturous path through the streets.

Finally, convinced that they were precisely nowhere, lost in the maze of old Bellminster, Jo stepped out into the middle of the lane, into the moonlight, and improvised.

"Here, you!" he called, and they stopped and turned about.

"You lot! Clear the streets of your drunkenness! Clear off before I call the constable!"

"Whazzis?" one of them asked, peering blearily into the night.

Jo advanced into the middle of them, surrounding himself with spite. "Clear off, d'you hear me. You're a disgrace to this fine town with your bullyin' dumb show."

"It's runty chap," another voice said.

" 'Ere now, Runty!"

"This 'un's a right Whig, boys!"

Unseen hands pushed Jo from behind and the dwarf sprawled to the pavement. He was up again quickly, however, and lashed out with his cane, catching the knee of one assailant and thrusting the gold head into the stomach of another. In a moment they were on him, punching and kicking and shoving drunkenly, and for every two blows he dodged, one caught him squarely. But his blows never missed, and his strength took them all by surprise so that they learned caution before long and only waded in at him two or three at once.

One against so many could not stand long, no matter how drunk they might be. Soon, Jo lay in the street, blood streaming from his nose and from a cut on his lip. Pleased with themselves, though nervous, too, the band dispersed into the night. Waiting until he knew he was alone, Jo Smalley pulled himself up and surveyed his success. The waistcoat, only dappled with drops of blood before, was now splattered with it, fresh and dark. Looking down at the gory pattern, he wondered if that innkeeper at the Arms might be able to clean it properly. Country folk do make the best launderers.

He took out a handkerchief and dabbed at the cuts on his face. A thorough job, he thought, wincing. But he'd had worse, much worse, some so bad that he couldn't walk for days after. It was a long time since he'd suffered any man to lay hands on him and get away with it.

He'd have to report this to the constable, he realized. Official corroboration is invaluable in such cases. Jo Smalley reached out for his cane, rose from the filth of the street, and continued on his way. Must keep things official, he thought with a gleeful smirk, moving slowly under the towers of Bellminster Cathedral, lonely and desolate in the night.

CHAPTER XXI
THE MATTER IS RESOLVED

Tuckworth stared in dismay before him, his heart sinking lower with each shallow breath he took. The chill of November was just starting to warm with the rising sun, and the dean's palms felt cool in the morning air, a film of moisture forming in the panic of the moment. He turned and looked beside him, at the proud, beaming face of Abraham Semple. Then he turned back to the floor of the cathedral, to the crisp beveled letters carved white in fresh slabs of granite, names and dates and centuries-old remembrances of those buried beneath, in the crypt.

"Pretty job, eh?" Semple boasted in his subdued fashion, though the man was clearly delighted with this product of his labors. And so, the dean thought, he would be crushed by the truth.

"It's beautifully done," Tuckworth began, with just that hesitant note to his voice that said something was wrong.

The smile faded from Semple's face.

Tuckworth took a deep breath and plunged in. "The markers are upside down."

"The which is what?"

"The grave markers. The words in the floor should be facing the other way."

"Other way what?"

"They need to be taken back out and turned around, Semple."

"Face the words down into the dirt?"

"No, turned *around,* not *over.*"

"But this is how they fit."

"They'll fit the other way as well."

"Not without some bit o' doin'. This ain't like layin' squares for a quilt."

"It will just have to be done. They must read the other way."

The foreman groused in despair. "Take a week at least. More like two. Pryin' up is delicate work. If any of 'em gets cracked—"

"Then they will have to be replaced, but they must all be turned around." Tuckworth removed his spectacles and wiped his eyes blearily. "I wish you had consulted me before laying all these in."

"Wish you'd ha' been here to consult."

This last was said under Semple's breath as the man walked away, but Tuckworth had heard it, and the foreman knew he had heard it.

Tuckworth replaced his spectacles. Dammit, what was he supposed to do! He had no head for such work, no patience, and his time had been required elsewhere these past days. Besides, what man didn't know how to place a grave marker in a cathedral? Everything should be laid with an eastern orientation, of course. Everything! Facing east! Tuckworth glowered at the rising sun peeking through the empty cathedral doors, and his anger flared, taking heat from its fiery glow, then shrank to nothing. He could not be unfair. He was too critical of all he did himself for that. This cathedral, it was his job. His care. His responsibility. He should have been available for Semple, or at least been more praising of the man's efforts. Here was the dean's first duty, not prying into others' affairs, off nosing about, meddling. What good was he doing? Even Chief Constable Hopgood had looked askance at the dean's request to place a shadow on Mr. Bates.

"The mayor's Mr. Bates?"

"Yes. He knows where Danny Trees is hiding, I'm certain of it, and Danny is the key to finding out who killed McAllister."

Hopgood had tried to sound sympathetic, but failed. "Now, vicar, I'd be happy to put a man to it if I had a man to spare, but we've got nightly disturbances o' the peace to contend with, and if one of 'em don't end in murder, it won't be for want o' violent opportunities. I got armed bands o' men troopin' about the town, one-half flint and one-half steel, and both sides sparkin' for a fight. Ain't safe for a man to walk about after dusk no more. This McAllister business will have to wait a bit." He sniffed. "Poor ol' man ain't goin' nowhere, anyway."

And that was where it had to be left. Even Hopgood was weary of the dean's meddling. He looked across the nave to where Semple was gruffly ordering his men to pry up the grave markers, saw the foreman shoot a glance in his direction, an annoyed, angry glance, and suddenly Tuckworth felt very much alone.

"Mr. Tuckworth!"

Raphael came running up from the square and bounded through the gaping threshold. "Any thoughts about Mr. Bates?" he asked when he was close enough for privacy, hardly winded by his run.

"None."

"There's my idea, still. All it takes is a long coat and a wide-brimmed hat."

"No." The two had parted the night before determined to find some way to track Bates themselves, but the dean had refused to resort to disguises. He would walk up to the man and ask him directly where Danny was before he tried such a theatrical course.

Raphael looked down. "Your markers are backwards."

"Yes," Tuckworth answered testily.

"And they're not in their proper spots."

"What?"

Raphael pointed to a stone near his feet. "The first duke, he's supposed to be at the center of the transept where it crosses the nave, the heart of the cathedral."

"Really?"

"And the other dukes splay out from there." His finger arced through the air, drawing a neat hierarchy across the floor. "Second, third over there, fourth, and so on."

"Really?"

"Yes, sir. Get me a paper and pencil and I can draw it out for you."

Strange, Tuckworth thought. He had walked across these names for thirty years and more, and he could not have recalled who went where with any accuracy. Before the dean could reach into his coat pocket for a pencil, however, his eye was attracted by a handkerchief waving conspicuously from a side chapel and the anxious face of Constable Wiley hovering above it.

Tuckworth and Raphael walked over to where Wiley clung to the shadows. "Wiley," the dean said, curious at this clandestine attitude, "what is it?"

Wiley nodded. "I got news, vicar, only I ain't supposed to worry you with it."

"Not worry me?"

"That was Mr. Mortimer's orders. Chief Constable sent word to Lord Granby first, as is right, and rector come straightaway and said this done settled everything and you wasn't to be dragged from your cathedral. But, well . . ." Wiley hemmed, embarrassed. "I just thought you ought to at least know, is all."

"Know what?"

"They found Danny Trees pricked and bled like any hog for roastin'. Throat sliced clean through."

The dean took the news coolly, far more coolly than even he

might have imagined. Something about it seemed grotesque and inevitable, the next ghastly step they were forced to take. He had grown so cold-blooded of late. "Where was it, Wiley?"

"Down in the New Town, a block o' flats as is owned by Mr. Bates."

"Have they found Bates?"

"No need to find him. He was sittin' easy as you please at the mayor's office."

"Where is he now?"

"Got him down to Constabulary House."

"Charged?"

"Held on suspicion, but charges is sure to follow."

Without a further word the dean set his course toward the constabulary.

Wiley trotted up behind and plucked at his sleeve. "Wouldn't do no good, vicar. Ain't no one gettin' in to see Bates."

"But Mortimer is, am I right?"

Wiley didn't answer at once.

"Am I, Wiley?"

"Well, as he's the due representative of Lord Granby, and reportin' all the proceedin's to his lordship directly, it wouldn't be right to keep him out."

Tuckworth passed a meaningful glance at Raphael, and the two turned and continued their march to Constabulary House, the young constable taking up the rear with a woeful expression. Yet, even before they arrived, the dean knew that no persuasion he could offer would prevail.

"This matter is resolved, Mr. Tuckworth," Reverend Mortimer announced with smirking finality. "You may address your attentions to the cathedral, from where, I must say, they should never have wandered."

The interview was brief and decisive, and neither the sympathy of Wiley nor the mute appeal of Hopgood could interfere with a due representative of Lord Granby, especially one as adamant as the rector. Tuckworth did not waste his time.

"Where now, sir?" Raphael asked, back on the street, the bright of the day filling him with a certainty that they were not finished.

"New Town."

They had no trouble finding where the murder had been committed. All of Bellminster was abuzz with the news by now, in spite of Mortimer's vain efforts to stifle gossip, and the first person they asked knew exactly where the crime had occurred. The dean and Raphael caused some stir as they journeyed to the building, and every head turned to follow them, certain of their destination and eager to know what would come of it all. By the time they arrived at the building, still swarming with the tense, pointless activity of a hive of bees, they were leading a small parade of the idle and the unemployed.

"If my friend and I might have the scene to ourselves," Tuckworth pleaded to the crowd, which hung back a few extra paces as he and Raphael climbed the stairs. Once they had entered the room, however, a mass of faces jockeyed and pushed into the open door to see what the dean would find.

Tuckworth made a quick survey, noted the vast, dark stain of blood by the chair, the smeared trail leading toward the door, the footprints that mysteriously stopped halfway across the room, and the crisp, sharp hand prints. The candle was still guttering on the table. He walked over to it and stood behind the chair.

"Raphael, be a good lad and sit here a moment."

The young man did as he was asked, but not without a deep, uneasy qualm. Tuckworth was silent as he observed something beyond Raphael's understanding.

"Who found him?" the dean asked, turning to the crowd in the doorway.

A plump, pale young man stepped forward, or was shoved forward, and stood meekly just within the room.

"I done," he whispered.

"And he was lying here?" The dean pointed to the end of the bloody trail.

He nodded.

"What made you look in? Did you hear something?"

"Door was open."

"How far?"

"All the way, like now."

"I see. And the knife, it was still here, wasn't it?"

"Yeah. Yeah it was," he murmured, "by the chair there. But constable took it. How'd you know?"

"Thank you. Excuse me, please." And with that, the dean forced his way through the crowd and down the stairs, back into the November sun, with Raphael striding dutifully behind.

"Where now?" the young man asked.

"Municipal Hospital," the dean said, and the two shot off, still drawing a slender trail of onlookers behind them, a trail that spread and grew as they proceeded through the bustling streets. As they walked, Raphael looked at the dean from the corner of his eye. He had seen it before, this resolute set of the jaw, the hard, unrelenting glint in the eye, the stride so much lighter and firmer than usual. His painter's insight showed him as clearly as the day's unyielding light that Tuckworth was past it now, past all interference and delay, past the supercilious qualms of men with other aims than truth, other principles than the harsh realities of fact. Now, Raphael thought, there would be something to see, something to do, and for an instant he envied the dean his certainty and purpose.

For Tuckworth's part, he wanted only to lose this embarrassing crowd. Luckily, when they arrived at their destination, the registering nurse refused to admit anyone but the dean and his companion.

Ten minutes later, they stood with Dr. Warrick in the dark, stifling atmosphere of the surgery, where Danny Trees lay spread beneath a dirty sheet.

"Are you certain you want to do this?" Warrick asked. The doctor knew of Tuckworth's squeamish nature, and he looked about the room quickly to locate the bucket.

"Yes," the dean declared, more certain of his desire to view the body than of his ability to do so coolly. The three men stood about the table, though only Raphael appeared moved by that solemnity the moment seemed to require. The doctor merely tore back the sheet like a merchant displaying his wares.

Tuckworth blinked, and he could feel the cold sweat drawing forth on his brow. Danny was pale, waxy, like something carved from soap, the few patches of nascent whisker on his cheek standing out now like dirty streaks. The teeth were pulled back in a death grin, and the eyes peeked white through the narrow slits of the lids. The only real color was the red-black line across the throat, the gash ugly and crusted. He was naked, and his chest appeared shrunken, almost caved, more a boy's figure than a man's. The lad had been so eager for manhood, too, the dean considered. So death makes a liar of life, and exposes more than just our meat and nakedness.

Tuckworth cast a quick eye at the wound. "How was that done?" he asked, gesturing noncommittally in the direction of the examination table.

"I think the murderer came up from behind. The corners of the wound show some signs of distress, as though the head was pulled back forcibly as the cut was made. Nasty job, though."

The dean reached out and took Danny's face in his hand, but recoiled in spite of himself at the cold, taut touch of the flesh. With a deep breath, he managed some control over his nerves and took the boy's chin, twisting the head from side to side. Then he turned to peer intently at Danny's thin hands, white and limp with fingers like candles, the nails tinted red like flames.

"He's been washed," the dean observed.

"He was a fright," Warrick said.

"Where are his clothes? They haven't been washed, I hope."

The doctor reached under the table and brought up a pile of dry, stiff, bloody garments. Tuckworth wretched briefly, but a sharp breath calmed his stomach. He took the clothes and began to lay them out on the floor, each piece in its right place, the tanned hide of a boy. Then he knelt down and ran his face across the length of this macabre display, pausing at times to look more closely still. Raphael glanced at the doctor, who only shrugged.

The dean stood up at last. "I want you two to corroborate my observations, if you please," he announced. "You especially, doctor. I want you to be absolutely convinced that what I see, that what you see, is the truth."

"What do you see?" Raphael asked.

"First, notice Danny's hands. They're relatively unmarked. No splinters."

Warrick and Raphael each took a hand and looked closely at it.

"Very well, no splinters," the doctor agreed.

"But these clothes are covered in splinters," Tuckworth continued. "From the chest down, dozens of them. Yet, look here." He pointed at the shoulders of Danny's shirt. "There are no splinters from the chest *up.*"

The doctor convinced himself of this, then looked up at the dean with a spark of realization. "The boy was dragged along the floor."

"You haven't seen where this crime took place, have you, doctor?"

Warrick shook his head. "They brought him straight here."

"I'd like you to drop by there with me, if you wouldn't mind.

Poor Danny was killed a good twelve feet from the door. I want your opinion as to the amount of blood he lost at that spot, and whether he could have dragged himself more than ten feet along the floor."

The doctor took out his watch and opened it. "I can give you half an hour," he said.

"Fine. And while we do that, Raphael, you go back to Constabulary House and let Wiley know I want to see him. But don't tell anyone else your business, right?"

Raphael nodded. "Do you think he'll get us in?"

Tuckworth's eyes narrowed. He was surprised that Raphael had divined his plan so quickly. Then he smiled. "Wiley's a good sort, and he's freer to act in this than Hopgood is. Yes, I think he'll get us in."

"And then?"

Tuckworth looked at Raphael and shrugged. "And then we find out what Bates knows."

CHAPTER XXII

FACTS

After days of playing at question and answer, sifting through men's hearts, groping for a grain of truth amid the haze of memory and deceit, forgetfulness and falsehood, Tuckworth was relieved to be silent, to stand under the moonless, star-filled sky and simply to think, training his mind upon the incontrovertible beauty of a fact.

He admired facts. They were harsh and hard, like those granite slabs in the cathedral. They might be moved here or there, situated this way or that way in his mind, but there they were nonetheless, chiseled and real, irrevocable if not always irrefutable. Like the snows of an arctic landscape, isolated from man's reach, facts were cold, cruel, formed from the countless possibilities of the past into a shape that could never alter for all time to come, never melt or run off into anything other than itself. A fact might be examined, interpreted, fitted to a purpose, yet it still confronted you, unchanged, as true as the dawn behind the clouds or a chessboard in the final stages of a masterful game, options eliminated, lines of defense cut off, escapes foreseen and forestalled, until the inevitability of fact emerged in a few swift moves and—checkmate!

The doctor had seen everything that Tuckworth had seen. The vast stain of blood under the table, this was a fact. The crisp, unsmeared handprints on the floor, the door swung open, the spot where the body had been dragged within view of anyone passing by, these also were facts, facts that must be accounted for, that must be answered and explained, facts that led to another fact and, just possibly, to a name.

The dean stood now in the shadowy lane opposite Constabulary House, under the fact-filled sky. Raphael had wanted to accompany him on this nocturnal interview, but Tuckworth was convinced that Bates would be more forthcoming with one inquisitor than with two, and the young artist had mastered his youth and retired to the pub in the Granby Arms to await the dean's report.

From the door of the constabulary, a swift, silvery blade of light cut across the darkness of the street. The dean approached, and a moment later he was being led through the halls by Constable Wiley. The two maintained an agreed-upon silence, the hour enforcing a natural hush to their actions. Down ill-lit corridors, out into a star-dark courtyard and up a creaking stairway, past locked doors where violence was left to feed upon its own vitals and through open wards where insolvency slept in fitful beds, the dean slunk behind his impromptu Virgil, and he wondered at the dozens of slumbering souls he passed, that so many might live outside the law in Bellminster. Yet he knew, the law sat like a speck of land in the sweeping river of lawlessness, its shores washed away by tides of human nature and desire.

They came at last to a door, a stout door with a sturdy bolt attached, yet just a door. It might have led the way into any gentleman's study or bedchamber, or into the nursery of some young family. Wiley raised a ring of keys before his eyes in the dim hall and selected one to fit the lock. He turned it, threw the bolt back, and stepped aside for the dean.

Tuckworth entered. The room was modest and bare and terribly small, the sort of plain cell used in better homes to house the underservants. He saw a chair, a rustic cross hung crookedly, a wooden bed with a straw mattress, the stub of a candle burning on the floor in a corner, and sitting against a plastered wall so close that he might have stretched out full length and nearly reached the other side, Charley Bates huddled in isolation, his head bent against his raised knees. He wore a shirt without a collar or buttons, trousers with no belt or braces, no shoes, and his hair was a thin, matted clot upon his sweating brow.

The door closed and the bolt slid home outside with a peremptory click.

"Mr. Bates."

The prisoner did not move, but seemed the black core of dejection.

"Bates, it's Dean Tuckworth."

He did not look up as he said, "The constable told me you'd come."

"I know you had no part in this."

"I played my part," the man muttered, his voice drifting out of the shadows that obscured his face.

"Well, yes, I suppose you did," Tuckworth admitted, embarrassed at the confession. "Many men had a hand in this, but you didn't murder Danny Trees."

"And yet he's d—" Something like a sob choked off the word. Bates raised his head to reveal the dried tracks of tears staining his cheeks and crusting his eyes, and the dean was startled to discover how deeply this man was moved by Danny's death. "He's dead, Mr. Tuckworth," Bates stated with an odd coolness for all his distraught appearance, "and as you say, I had my hand in it."

This was not the man Tuckworth had expected to find. The dean pulled over the lone chair and sat down. "You're lucky to have a candle," he observed.

"Am I?"

"I believe with most, um . . ." He came to an awkward stop. "Most of the men here, I mean. They're considered unreliable."

"You mean they might burn the place down to force an escape?" The dean nodded.

"Well, I can only guess that a man of position has his perquisites, even here."

The conversation fell into an uneasy lull, and the dean felt himself at a loss to continue.

"I mentioned your innocence."

"I heard you."

"Of course, I can't demonstrate it conclusively, but I can show that whoever did this wanted the crime to be discovered, that he deliberately arranged things so the body would be found. That hardly fits with any indictment they might bring against you. If you had killed Danny, it would have been to silence him, not to display him like that."

Bates looked up sharply into Tuckworth's eyes, a dark appeal burning in his gaze. "I know I didn't do it, but can you tell me who did?"

Tuckworth thought for an instant before replying. "No. No, not yet."

The man appeared to collapse under the admission, some support of hope seeping from him, and he let his head fall back upon his knees.

How to proceed?

"If I might ask you a few questions about events these past days?"

Bates groaned his acquiescence.

"I understand that you employed Danny to incite the demonstrations for Mr. Bick. Why?"

Bates threw his head back, invested with a cold sort of command that held his heart at bay, but only just, leaving emotion to play beneath the surface of every utterance, and a tear to swim suspended below his eye. "Certainly you know why, Mr. Tuck-worth," he stated, a note of derision in his voice.

"I want to hear as much as I can from you."

"Sorry to disappoint." Bates fell into a morose and unmanly pout.

Tuckworth sighed. "Very well. If you could just confirm me in my theories?" Silence. "The strategy was to discredit Granby, make him seem ineffectual and out of touch, incapable of control-ling his own party. A violent show of support for Bick might turn the electorate against him. That was the general idea?" Bates did not even raise his head. "It sounds like a desperate scheme," the dean observed.

"When you struggle to advance a man like Winston Padgett, desperation becomes sage advice."

The dean stifled a grin. "You chose boys as your operatives, a small army of boys. Why? Did you really believe they'd be easier to manage?"

Bates sniffed. "A miscalculation."

"You have no children?"

The man grimaced. "I take your point."

Slowly, Tuckworth was drawing the story from him, wearing at the pride Bates still took in a failed plan, allowing the man's van-ity to acquit him of blame. "Weren't you worried that the boys might be taken up in their mischief?" Nothing. "Come now, you must have been concerned that one of them, at least one would be collared."

Tuckworth heard Bates let out a long breath. "That was Danny's part, and it was a clever thing. He convinced the boys that Granby was the one directing him, that they really were working for Bick. We were prepared to get Danny out of the way for a time if things got too hot, leaving only a false path that led back to his lordship."

The dean nodded. It all seemed very reasonable, even elegant. "The mayor approved your strategy, of course," he went on. "But things must have gone wrong when your boy attacked McAllister."

"That boy is a girl."

"What? You know who did this?"

Bates shook his head. "Danny knew, but he never told me. That's how I wanted it."

"A girl?" the dean repeated in disbelief. "How could a girl—"

"Oh, come now, Mr. Tuckworth," Bates scoffed. "She's not a girl as you and I know of girls, surely. More a beast of the streets, an animal." He spoke with a lack of feeling that could not even be called contempt. It was nothing. "A girl beat McAllister. That's all I know."

"Is that when things got hot, the night of the beating?"

Bates stared fixedly at a spiderweb hanging taut in a corner. "Hot? Barely tepid." He tossed his head back against the cool plaster of the wall, keeping his eyes on the web. "That was merely politics. Feelings run high and knuckles get scraped. Padgett wanted to throw it all in after that, give it up. But we'd come too far. Another chance might never appear. Bick is young, might stay in Parliament until he's as old and doddering as Granby. No, this was the time, and we had to risk it. Politics is a merciless business, Mr. Tuckworth. It requires a strong stomach."

"And McAllister?"

Bates shrugged. "Tragic," was all he said.

Tuckworth tried to recoil at such callous disregard, but he found that he could not. Something about this entire business was numbing, as though the normal standards of human conduct had been suspended for the duration of the political contest, as if in politics another part of human nature ruled, another side of ourselves turned outward, a side the dean knew better than he cared to know.

"So things only got too hot for you when McAllister died."

"Murder is more than scraped knuckles," Bates acknowledged.

"You set Danny up in a flat, in a building you own in the New Town."

Bates was silent once more.

"You're a wealthier man than you let on, Mr. Bates," the dean observed.

"Any man's income might be supplemented."

"True, but you appear to live more modestly than your supplemented income would make possible. A tiny flat at a nondescript address. Economy in everything."

A cloud passed across the man's face. "What do you know of how I live?"

"I spoke with your wife."

Bates glowered at the dean for a moment before his frown dissolved into a passionless smirk and he shrugged at some interior question. "She knows nothing of my finances."

"Why keep this income a secret?"

Bates sat upright as though he were shocked suddenly to life. "Will the answer help you find Danny's killer?" he demanded.

Tuckworth paused. Would it? "It will help me understand."

"Is that so important?"

"If I can understand why men do these things, why they plot and what they plot for, what they are willing to kill for and die for, then perhaps it might help me find Danny's killer. If I can understand what it is we're up against, I might . . ." The dean paused. "I might understand a great deal more."

Bates looked indulgently at his interrogator. "Be careful, Mr. Tuckworth. You know what's said of omniscience. To understand all is to despise all."

"Or to forgive all."

The words seemed to offend Bates, and he dropped his head for a moment. When he raised it again, there was a look of hard cruelty about his eyes and in the creased set of his jaw as he spoke. "You want to understand politics? Is that what you're after? Very well, I'll explain. It's power. Power, that's all. Politics is the game of collecting and dispensing power. You know as much, I'm sure."

"Is that all it is?"

"Does it sound so simple to you? I suppose it is simple, to talk of it." Bates fell silent for a moment. "How simple was it, do you suppose, to kill Danny? A quick cut with a knife and his . . . and he . . ." The man gasped, then calmed himself. "The boy was gone. Simple. But who had the nerve to do it?"

"You make politics sound like a criminal act."

"Very well, what of war, then? No crime in war. Yet out of a thousand men, who has the nerve to command tens of thousands to their deaths, send them headlong into massed artillery, watch as they're sliced to pieces by shrapnel and grape? How well do generals sleep at night? I wonder."

Tuckworth offered no answer.

"I'll tell you," Bates went on, "I think they sleep like babes. I think they sleep in Abraham's bosom. Politics is necessary, Mr. Tuckworth, as war is necessary, as the gallows is necessary, and if it requires deceit and lies, if it erases men's scruples and forces them to acts another man might blanch at, then that's the price for our civilized existence. The conscience of a politician is the sacrifice society demands. Thank God there will always be men willing to pay that price, eager to pay it in exchange for the power they can wield. We live and die and eat and breathe under the protection of government, Mr. Tuckworth, and politics is merely the art of sustaining that government through any means necessary. *Any* means." Bates sniffed. "While keeping up appearances of honor and decency, of course."

Tuckworth was not shocked. He had seen enough violence in his life to keep from being shocked ever again, he thought. "Mayor Padgett, he's what you call 'keeping up appearances'?"

"Oh, Padgett *is* appearance, nothing but appearance," Bates spat out, and then chuckled. "There's a sacrifice for you. Winston Padgett. Too scrupulous by half," he observed with disdain. "Find me a rich merchant who's not too sharp and has no scruples, and

I'll make him a cabinet minister inside a year. A prime minister if he's got any sense to him. The power doesn't lie *in* the man, but around him."

"In you."

"In men like me, the schemers and the plotters." A flame of exuberance was burning in Bates now as he warmed to his theme. "Oh, there have been exceptions and might be again. A Pitt or, God help us, a Napoleon can devise plots on his own. But a commonly good man like Bick or Padgett isn't up to it, naturally."

"Naturally."

Bates squinted at the dean. "Naturally." He paused before continuing. "Ethics are a luxury, Mr. Tuckworth. They're what men like me allow to men like you, the luxury of an ethical life, a moral life. A good man can't win the game on his goodness, and he can't govern, not truly govern, except through the schemes that we men in the background employ. Ethics are no defense against cunning. Parliament is filled with good men on the benches. But in the hallways, that's where true power lies, among men wise to the world and its ways, too wise ever to be elected themselves."

"And that's your excuse for your supplemental income. Not for your life in Bellminster, but hoarding for your life in London."

Bates grinned subtly and nodded at the dean's astuteness. "What good is money in Bellminster? London is the goal. London is expensive," he observed. "And money is also power. Not real power, you know. More like massed artillery, to cut your opponent to shreds. That's Granby's way, buying elections whole cloth and then fashioning them the way he wears them."

"After you arrived in London, how soon would you have thrown off Padgett?"

Bates smiled openly, no longer fearful at this discovery of his most secret plans, even eager to share his cunning. "Six months once Parliament was in session. I'm sure I could have found a tidy situation in that time, some influential backbencher, and Padgett would have been none the worse without me. He might even have benefited from my better fortune."

The dean leaned back. "So it would seem that politics is a true marriage of heaven and hell."

"Life is such a marriage," Bates replied. "Politics is only the housekeeping." He slumped back against the wall now and looked deeply at the dean. "You surprise me, Mr. Tuckworth. I should think a man like you would be outraged to hear me go on like this."

Tuckworth considered. "It's not so outrageous. The Bible is filled with greater offenses than you've committed, and for better causes than you aspire to. But you're right about politics being simple. I see that now. You simply want to be God, making the world according to your own laws, benefiting a humanity that can't comprehend the forces at work in your universe."

Bates looked horrified for a moment and then laughed an embarrassed, humorless laugh. "Good Lord, do I sound so depraved? God? No, I will come just short of believing that," he announced.

"Well, perhaps you don't believe it," Tuckworth granted, thinking more deeply yet, "but I imagine there are others who do, others in your profession who see themselves that way."

"Doubtless," admitted Bates.

"Back to Danny's murder." Tuckworth saw Bates flinch. "You never knew who attacked McAllister."

"As I said, that was part of our system. Only Danny knew that. He was the keystone."

"And you didn't have Danny pass that on to me because you thought I'd dig too deep and betray you."

"But Danny did pass it on to you."

"What?"

"He wrote the name down in a note and put it on your doorstep. It was a convenient way to rid us of a dangerous ally. Didn't you get it?"

"No," Tuckworth answered.

Bates rolled his face away from the dean, suddenly uninterested in any more questions. "Unfortunate," he mumbled. "If you had, Danny might be alive now."

"Yes, very unfortunate," Tuckworth assented. He sat silently a moment longer, weighing this information, putting it in its proper place. Then he rose to leave. "One last thing. You said money is power, like ammunition. Isn't money something else?"

"What's that?"

"It's freedom, the power to live one's life as one wishes." The dean paused. "Tell me, this building of yours in New Town. I was there this morning. Do you have any female tenants?"

Bates glared at Tuckworth, carrying all the terror and hatred in his glance that a cornered man might feel. Tuckworth knew that look, those feelings of dread that one's darkest soul might be ripped open to the light. He knew the look and he knew the feelings, and so he had his answer. He had to know all there was to know in this, to fit all the pieces to the puzzle, yet he loathed himself for probing in so personal a place, pricking at the heart of a man who was as much a victim in this as an instigator. The dean turned and knocked at the door, his signal to be let out.

"Do you have any word for your wife?" he asked before he left.

"My wife?" Bates looked confused for a moment, as though he could not connect his situation with her welfare. "My wife," he muttered once more and turned away. "No. No word."

Tuckworth looked at Charley Bates again, lying on the floor of his cell, his soul exposed, his political life in ruin about him. He understood now the kind of nature he was up against, the sort of hubris that would lead a man to such acts for an election, the confusion of public welfare and personal ambition. He looked at Bates, and he thought of Danny, and he understood something else as well. Tuckworth saw that he was not the only man to suffer from secret wounds, to hurt with a pain he dared not acknowledge, to hurt in silence.

CHAPTER XXIII

CONFESSION

A girl.

Tuckworth labored, as he trailed behind Constable Wiley, to place this fact in the picture he had made in his mind, the intricate pattern of these schemes and plots crossing and recrossing one another, ranks and files of facts.

A girl.

It seemed unaccountable somehow. He knew the sins of women, not so different from those of their men. He knew they felt anger and passion alike, were capable of as much sordid depravity, were equally hungry, equally lustful. But such wanton violence, such brutality in a woman, he had never encountered it in all the years he had ministered to the faithful of Bellminster.

And what of the faithless? The question rose within him suddenly, as if asked by another voice that was yet his own. What of those beneath or beyond the notice of the church? What of the drudges and whores, the thieves and cutpurses? What of those, like Bit, who were born to the street? The thought of Bit made it all seem more terrible than ever, and more possible. He thought of what that child had endured, to be sold by her mother to feed the lusts of a wealthy man. If she had been allowed to grow up in such a life as her childhood had promised, what might Bit have become? How might she have exercised her vengeance against a hostile world? Violence. It was the legacy not of man but of mankind, the taint shared by Adam's daughters and Eve's sons.

Wiley stopped. The dean looked about him, uncertain where he had been brought. They had not taken the same way back, that was certain.

"Wiley?"

"He's expectin' you," the constable said, and stepped back from Hopgood's office door.

The dean glanced darkly at his betrayer and instantly forgave him, while Wiley only stared sheepishly at the floor as he opened the door. Tuckworth strode through, wondering how he might explain his skulking behavior, and heard the door shut behind him.

Hopgood sat behind the clutter of his desk looking bleary and confounded. Without a word he motioned toward the one hard chair and stood up as Tuckworth took his seat. The chief constable clasped his hands behind his back and made several turns about the room in silence, going over some idea in his brain, determining a proper course of action for this singular invasion of his precincts. He appeared preoccupied by some misgiving, and the frown on his face fluttered from grim to grimmer. For his part, Tuckworth sat by, deciding on his own course, trying to sail as near the truth as possible without needlessly exposing Wiley to the rocks of official reprimand.

"Vicar," Hopgood said at last, turning to confront his guest, "you've been to see the prisoner, right?"

"Yes," the dean said clearly, innocently.

"Right. What'd he say?"

In as brief a space of time as possible, Tuckworth related the gist of his interview with Bates, only leaving out the seamier aspects of the man's personal life, as well as any mention of Constable Wiley.

"So he didn't do it," Hopgood said when the dean was finished.

"I don't believe so."

The chief constable nodded thoughtfully and leaned against the wall as if some weight were not lifting but only shifting inside him. "Mr. Mortimer seems convinced otherwise."

"I'm not surprised."

"Bird in the hand?"

"Undoubtedly. But that means the real killer is still out there."

"A girl," Hopgood stated flatly, less surprised by the fact than the dean had been, and resumed his pacing. "Any notion who she is?"

The dean shook his head. "No," he answered, his voice trailing off on an undecided note that he swept before him with the force of conviction, "but I think I know who is likeliest to be behind it. It's merely a suspicion, you understand."

"And that would be?"

Tuckworth ran through all the evidence in his mind, ordered it as neatly as he could, glossed over the patchy bits that still marred his reasoning here and there, keeping him from a definite pronouncement. "If I were to lead an investigation into this matter," he mused, "I think I should lead it in the direction of Jo Smalley." This statement had no effect upon the chief constable, either. "I don't say Smalley committed the murder himself, mind you. Whoever killed Danny stood behind him, grabbed him by the hair, and wrenched his head back while delivering the wound. I don't think Smalley is capable of doing that, not physically capable of it. Besides, the footprints aren't his. They're longer, but small and slender."

"The girl?"

"She would have reason enough to kill Danny if he knew what she'd done to McAllister."

"Then why bring Smalley into it at all?" Hopgood asked. "Why're you so convinced he lent a hand to this?"

"If Danny's murder had been discovered by accident I wouldn't be as convinced as I am," the dean mused, speaking to himself as much as to Hopgood, "but he was dragged across the floor and laid very deliberately by that door."

"Couldn't she have thought o' that herself, the girl?"

"I've thought of that," Tuckworth admitted. "But consider how she left McAllister in the street. She wasn't that cunning. She'd have been more likely to close the door, lock it from the outside, and trust to her good luck. And while Bates might have wanted Danny silenced as well, only Smalley would benefit from the discovery of the murder and the arrest of Bates."

Hopgood appeared muddled by it all. "It's a great tangle, that's true," he said, and then seemed to steel himself before asking, "What of Lord Granby?"

Tuckworth shook his head. "These discoveries are simply making him appear less effectual. No, Smalley is the only one who wins if everyone else loses."

Hopgood thought for a moment. "Don't be too certain of what that little fella is capable of," he observed. "Physically, I mean. Got into a scuffle last night and acquitted himself nicely."

"Did he? Last night?"

"Aye."

"The same night Danny was murdered."

"Aye," Hopgood repeated, rolling this fact about in his mind now that the dean had called it to his attention.

"Was Smalley much hurt?"

"Pretty bloodied."

Tuckworth nodded. It was just another fact to consider.

"Well," Hopgood said at last, "it all sounds like a good, healthy suspicion."

"Suspicion, yes," the dean conceded. "For the time being, that's all it is."

Hopgood sat down again behind his desk, not entirely listening any longer, his own cares worrying him. "His lordship'll be glad to know we're after that dwarfy fella," he said. "That'll put an end to the Whigs for this term."

"But Lord Granby can't know," Tuckworth insisted. "Bates has got to stay here, locked up tight. Smalley must be made to feel that his trail is wiped clean."

"For how long?"

"As long as it takes to get at the truth."

"Beyond the election?"

The question irritated the dean. "This isn't about the election, Hopgood," he snapped.

The chief constable appeared strangely hurt by the dean's reprimand, but after a moment of muted pique, he determined that the dean's course was the only right one. "If Smalley gets wind we're on to him, he'll run," Hopgood declared firmly.

"Yes, if he thinks *you're* on to him," Tuckworth added, sorry that he had bruised the chief constable's feelings. "I might have more freedom to act. Besides, this is all just conjecture as yet. Smalley's the likeliest man, but that's all he is."

"All right then, how do we go about makin' him into a proper suspect?"

Tuckworth hesitated. "Hopgood, you don't need to be involved. I have a plan in mind that can go forward on its own." Again, Hopgood had that odd, hurt expression. "Lord Granby doesn't look very favorably on my interest in this affair, at least Mortimer doesn't, and I'm afraid that's come to mean about the same thing. Mortimer might not like your helping me."

Hopgood shuffled some papers on his desk. It was clear that he had considered this point, that it carried a good deal of weight with him, but it was equally clear that some other influence was stirring within him. He was frankly nervous, but every man is nervous before leaping into the abyss. "Am I chief constable here, or ain't I?" he asked, sounding almost abashed to have to say it. "If it comes to that, I ain't helpin' you. It's you as is assistin' the force, and both of us together is aidin' his lordship." He punctuated this admission with a firm nod.

The dean did not care to hide his gratitude. There are times when the greatest need a man has is just to be believed. "Thank you, Hopgood," he said. "Thank you. The truth is, I *could* use your help. The plan I have in mind is rather, um . . . bold." And Tuckworth felt a silent thrill at the thought of being bold.

"So what is it, then?"

"It's just a notion. The idea is, to get to the girl, we need Smalley, and to get to Smalley, we need the girl."

Hopgood looked thoroughly confused now. "I don't . . ." His voice disappeared in a maze of incomprehension.

But it was all so clear to Tuckworth, like looking at a chessboard and seeing how it would appear three moves into the future. "Look, to find Danny, Smalley would need someone who knows the town. He probably just put a shadow on Bates, but still—"

"Like you wanted done."

Tuckworth paused, mindful of a change in the chief constable, a note of regret rustling inside the man. It was a mild sort of confession, yet within it lay all of Hopgood's guilt exposed, the reason for his willingness to help even in defiance of Granby, the certainty in his own mind that, had he listened to the dean before, had he put a man to shadow Bates, Danny Trees might yet be alive.

The dean stared softly at his friend, not daring to speak of forgiveness lest absolution only heighten the man's pain. There was nothing to forgive, anyway. Hopgood had done what he thought was best. Tuckworth had heard so many muted confessions, more lately that he had gained a special reputation for seeing into the darker hearts of men and understanding their sins. His reputation had become a burden to him, every man in Bellminster convinced that only old Vicar Tuckworth could fathom his guilt, every woman certain that he would know how to ease the ache of her repentant soul. And in a way that none of them suspected, they were right. He did understand guilt, a guilt worse than any of them knew, a guilt not unlike Hopgood's now, the guilty weight of a human life.

He saw the pain Hopgood was suffering, the doubts and the uncertainty, but he saw also the man's strength, to move on without forgiveness, to act as best he could now that he felt himself culpable for some part of this crime. The chief constable's eyes glared at the emptiness of space before him, appeared unfeeling and unrelenting, and only Tuckworth knew the cruelty of the penance he inflicted on himself.

"Well," the dean forged on, "if we can get to this girl—"

"She'll give us Smalley. That much I get."

"Yes, a local girl isn't likely to feel much loyalty to an outsider. If we can reach her, we might convince her to turn king's evidence."

"A girl facing the gallows?"

Tuckworth shrugged. "It's the only idea I have, I admit."

Hopgood nodded. "It's possible. But, if we get the girl as done the actual murder, why bother with Smalley?"

This was the question Tuckworth knew he had no answer for, not truly, not that another man would be sure to understand. Why did he want Smalley more than the girl? She was the killer, the bloodthirsty one. What was Smalley?

He was a man willing to use this girl for his political ends, to take her violence, her anger, and make it answer to the nation, make it a tool of the government that touched them all. She was a criminal of the streets. Smalley was a criminal of the world, a world he helped to create and perpetuate, and there was something terrible in that.

The dean's silence made no difference to Hopgood. His allegiance was set in bands of steel and iron. "So," he said, "how do we get at him? And how find the girl?"

"The same way they found Danny. We shadow Jo Smalley. Only

we've got to prod him along, give him a reason to seek this girl out, and soon."

"All right, what's that to be, then?"

"I have a scheme," the dean said. "There's risk to it, but that's unavoidable. Smalley's a sharp fellow. We've got to do everything we can to keep him on his guard but off balance, keep him moving all the time, don't give him a second to plot, make him improvise."

"Hope he makes a mistake?"

"Hope, yes," Tuckworth conceded with a slight, mischievous smile. "But give hope a little prod as well."

CHAPTER XXIV

A DEAL WITH THE DEVIL

The following day the dean was a blur of activity. He was conspicuous about the town, going from cathedral to constabulary, from tavern to coffeehouse, talking up everyone he met, asking after the dwarf. Jo Smalley? The Whig? Had he been seen? Heard from? Where was he last? Where likely to be next? Tuckworth traveled Bellminster sowing Jo's name on the whirlwind of election gossip, yet never seeing the man himself, seeming almost to avoid him. Once, when he was told that the Whigs were standing drinks at a nearby public house, the dean took the opposite way, cutting a wide swath between himself and the object of his inquiries. And again, hearing that Smalley had been seen dining with a dozen good friends in a particular chophouse, Tuckworth made it a point to return home for his meal.

Word of the dean's pursuit gradually drifted to Jo Smalley's attention, like leaves catching one by one on a grate, pushed there by a relentless breeze. At first Jo tried to ignore such comments as drifted his way or to give them only a passing thought. The campaign was well advanced and going strongly. The election was just a few days away, and Quentin Draper was expected in Bellminster the following evening. Each hour Jo was greasing the Whig's path to Parliament with every trick that he knew, with favors and promises, jokes and good-fellowship, roast beef and chickens and ale, and even the odd shilling or half a crown. But slowly, the day's recurring theme—"Vicar's askin' after ya, Jo!"—"Vic's got some'at for ya!"—"Look up vicar when you've a minute. Ol' chap was right anxious to see ya!"—this round of messages, not exactly sent yet all delivered, piqued Jo's curiosity, and with his day's business dragging to a late afternoon lull before its evening's recurrence, he set out to find Dean Tuckworth on his own.

Smalley found him with comparative ease, considering how remarkably their paths had failed to cross all day. Tuckworth was resting in the shade of the cathedral's towering façade, beneath the famous tympanum with its depiction of final justice levied upon the handful of good and the legions of wicked in the world, a merciless verdict passed by a merciful God.

"H'lo, Tuckworth," Jo called as he labored upward from the square.

The dean stood up, startled like a hare caught in the brush, looking as though he might bolt, before sitting down again with his back against a stony doorpost. "Smalley," he said noncommittally.

Jo raised an admonitory finger as he made his way up the last two steps.

"Jo," Tuckworth corrected himself.

"Now," Jo wheezed, "what's you want to see me for? I've heard it all up and down the lane that you've been wantin' to talk, so talk."

"Nothing, really," the dean replied, sounding as though it certainly was something. "Just curious as to how your efforts are progressing."

"My efforts," he repeated flatly.

"For Quentin Draper, of course, that's all. Just your efforts on behalf of Quentin Draper."

Jo eyed the dean cheerily, a broad, knowing smile on his wizened face. "It's goin' as it goes. Well enough. It's a tough row to hoe in this town, that's true. Granby's got his claws in deep every-where, but we're makin' headway." Jo eyed the dean through slit-ted lids. "But I didn't think you was interested in the election?"

"Oh, I'm not," Tuckworth remarked casually, so very casually. "Chief Constable Hopgood tells me you ran into a bit of trouble the other night. Something with these roving bands of men."

Jo shrugged. "Just a little honest canvassin' from t'other side. Nothin' to it. I got bloodied up a good bit, but I been bloodied up afore this, and I hope I gave as good as I got."

"That was the night before last, wasn't it?"

Jo's smile grew broader. "Eh?"

"Your trouble, with the canvassers. That was two nights back, wasn't it?"

"It was the night before they found that poor dead boy."

"That's right, the night of the murder," Tuckworth noted, sounding too surprised to be surprised. "What a terribly bloody night that was, then. Tell me, what hour were you accosted?"

"Late enough to be early." Jo tilted his head sideways and leered at the dean with a suffering grin. "Here now, ol' fella. Are you soundin' me out?"

"Soundin' . . . no, good heavens," Tuckworth blurted. "I'm just . . . I mean, I only want to get to the bottom of this tragedy, and as you were out that night, well, did you notice anything pe-culiar? Anything especially memorable or extraordinary?"

"Aside from a dozen fists thrown in my face with as many boots in my ribs, no. But I thought ol' Granny put you off these inquiries."

"What? Where did you hear that?"

"Just a word I heard in the street."

"The street?" Tuckworth seemed offended by this smirch against his independence. "The street's full of idle gossip," he muttered.

"That it is, that it is. Still, I seem to recall a meeting you was asked to attend at the constabulary, where you run into a bit of rough handlin' from Lord Granby. I heard things got rather warm for you. At least, your rector's nosin' it about the town that way."

Tuckworth appeared to wince at the news. His only response, however, was a disaffected grunt.

"Now, don't take it so to heart," Jo advised. "Besides, I understand they got their chap in chokey right off, so you needn't trouble yourself. Baines or Beales or some such."

"Bates."

Jo slapped his thigh. "That's it. Bates. Workin' for your mayor, but things got too thick for him. Fell too deep into his own schemes and couldn't get out nohow. It's all sewed and seamed up tight as any tailor could make it. Tight, y'know. Bates is for the drop. Leastways, that's what folks is sayin' in the streets." Jo stuck out his tongue and grimaced as if he dangled at the end of a rope.

"Folks have been wrong before."

Jo's antics ceased, and he looked with a cooler eye upon the dean. "You ain't satisfied what Mr. Bates done it?"

Tuckworth shrugged and looked uncomfortably away. "I didn't say that, exactly. He might have done it."

"He might be the King of Sweden, for all o' that." Jo paused. "All right, if not him, who?"

"I don't know. I just find it strange the way that poor boy's body was dragged toward the door."

"Was it so?"

"No doubt of it. The absence of splinters in his palms gave it away. And the handprints on the floor were a clumsy touch. Too theatrical. Clear, well-marked prints, not smeared the way they'd be if he had dragged himself that far. Not that he could with all the blood he lost. No, that body was moved deliberately toward the door. So why would Charley Bates want the body to be discovered? That's what I can't make out. Why? And of course, the answer is he wouldn't." The two men were silent for a long, restless moment. "But you have your own problems," the dean said at last, veering the conversation very noticeably onto a new course. "You've been remarkably busy these past days."

"How d'you mean?"

"Well, I've been asking after you all day, and you'd be amazed at the impression you've made on the town. Everywhere I turn, people have seen you, or heard of you. Your figure's become as well known as Lord Granby's, I daresay. You're something of an unforgettable chap, Jo. Once seen, never forgotten. At the Arms, in every tavern, even in the New Town."

The dwarf stood transfixed, his eyes motionless, intent on the dean, coldly, cruelly measuring the man. Tuckworth stared back, open and defiant, willing to gamble everything on the next few moments.

Jo spoke without moving more than a whisker on his upper lip. "What is this?"

"Tell me, Jo," the dean continued, his voice soft, whispering, "who brought you to Bellminster? The Whigs didn't send you here on a whim. Someone brought you here, someone with money, with backing. But someone afraid of Granby, who didn't want to campaign openly against him. Who was it?"

For just an instant, Tuckworth thought he saw a look in Smalley's eyes that frightened him, a cursed, angry spark, the precursor of a deed, of a rash and irrecoverable deed. Then the look was gone, and Jo grinned his wicked grin.

"You think I done it! You think I done it!" He laughed, slapping his sides merrily and repeating, "You think I done it!"

The dean was startled, and he said, "I haven't accused—"

"Always the same," Jo went on, shaking his head. "Always the strange chap, the new fella, the dwarf. Everywhere they send me, I'm the one as comes under suspicion for everything. I don't blame you, ol' Tuckworth. You're just human, after all. But I ain't never been accused of murder before. That's a new one." He laughed again and shook his head.

This display was so ludicrous and so convincing that the dean felt a sharp pang of doubt stab him from within. Was he on the right track? Could Jo have directed all of this? Tuckworth could not mask the confusion that swept across his face, but he gained control of himself again, realizing that, if he was wrong, he would only pay for it in humiliation.

"Perhaps that's what I think, Jo, that you're behind Danny's death. Being a stranger here doesn't make you a likelier suspect, but it hardly absolves you of suspicion."

Jo's laughter died suddenly in a dry choke. "Then why go through this masquerade?" he spat out sharply. "If you think I done it, come on with you and prove it." The dwarf's eyes shot across the landscape of Cathedral Square quickly, and Tuckworth knew what Jo was doing, searching out his shadow.

"Now, Jo," the dean said, trying to draw Smalley's attention away, "I don't really know you, as you don't really know me. You've been only a few weeks in Bellminster. But I can tell you, this all smacks of something political, something subtle—"

"And there ain't nobody subtler than Jo Smalley, is that your thinkin'?"

"I think you were brought here by someone, Jo, and I want to know who that someone is."

"Why?"

"Because I need to hand him over to Lord Granby."

Jo paused, a hint of confusion in his eyes. He squinted at the dean, tilted his head to the left, tilted it back. "You've lost me there," he admitted, his manner not quite open but honestly perplexed.

"You're a sharp man, Jo," Tuckworth explained. "You understand that yourself. In just a few weeks you've come to know Bellminster, us and our politics, as well as anyone who's lived here his whole life. But there's more than politics that goes on here, and those things you don't know quite as well."

"Name one of 'em."

Tuckworth rose and looked up above their heads, almost to the sky. "There's my cathedral," he said softly. "It's my home, my life, and you're taking it away from me."

"Am I?" Jo asked, his curiosity snared. "How?"

"You've alienated me from Lord Granby," the dean continued. "I'm not sure why you've done it. I might flatter myself to think that you saw me as some threat, someone who might be able to help his lordship see through your schemes. I know I've made a name for myself that way, and you might have been told as much by the people here." Tuckworth felt both proud and sad, a tired, pathetic old man. "You did it deliberately, looking me up on my walks about the town, making certain you were seen with me, and I with you. You threw a wedge between Granby and me, and Reverend Mortimer has stepped in. You don't know about that part of our politics. Mortimer wants me removed from my position as dean, removed from my cathedral, and now he has Granby's ear and I'm out in the cold, left to shiver."

Jo nodded his head sagely and clicked his tongue, the very image of sympathy. "So you want to hand over the Bellminster Whigs to Granby, the whole machinery, and work your way back in," he said.

"It's not politics, Jo, not your sort of politics. I don't care about the election, but I won't be turned out of my home." The dean laid a hand dramatically against the stone doorpost.

"And the murder? You've got no care about that?"

Tuckworth was silent for a very long time, and Jo let him be silent. "I won't lie. I can't. The murder is a concern to me. And if I could find a way to prove who did it, I'd probably take my chances as I might with Granby. But short of that, short of proof, I must weigh the love I have for this place." He paused again, for just a moment. "It's a very grand place, this place, but still very familiar to me, very dear."

Jo glanced up, as if he might see the grandeur Tuckworth spoke of, but all he saw were stone and sky. He looked down again to earth. "I don't know," he said. "It don't seem right. You could go to Granby now with what you know of me and throw a wrench in everything I've got movin'. It don't take proof to make a fella out as guilty these days. Rumor's good enough in my game."

"As you've shown us all, Jo," Tuckworth answered. "All it takes is the accusation to smear a man. But that's your politics, not mine. Not to demean your accomplishments," the dean said, sounding perfectly willing to demean anything of Jo Smalley's, "but you're only the weapon in another man's hand. I want to catch the hand that wields that weapon. I want someone real to give to Granby. It's nothing so terrible. He's done no crime, whoever he is."

"He's just a sacrifice, right?"

The dean nodded, looking sick with himself. "I don't like it, Jo. But I won't be turned out of my home."

The dwarf stared at Tuckworth, trying to sound the man's depths, to delve into his heart. "I don't know," he said again. "I still don't like it. I'll have to ponder on it. And I wouldn't do it 'til after the election noway."

"That suits me."

"All right then," Jo said, turning to go. He turned back, however, from the top of the cathedral stairs. "I suppose we understand one another at last, eh?"

"I suppose we do."

And with a grunt and a wheeze, Jo made his slow way down the stairs, down to the square below. Tuckworth watched him descend, then took several steps backward into the shadows of the doorpost, hiding ineffectually from view. Jo hobbled across the pavement, making his way back to the streets of Bellminster, and as he did so, another figure, cloaked in a large overcoat under a slouching hat, appeared from a dark doorway, stood watching Jo Smalley as he made his laborious way.

Jo turned a corner and vanished from sight, and the figure followed soon after. The dean retreated back into the roofless cathedral, into the side chapel where a door led to his study in the vicarage, and he settled in to wait.

He did not wait long. Before he had a chance even to doze, a knock came from the cathedral door, and the cloaked figure under the slouched hat stole silently inside. Tuckworth sat up as Raphael swept the hat away dramatically, a gleeful smile spread across his boyish features.

"He lost you that easily?" the dean exclaimed.

"Easy enough, but not too easy," Raphael replied, breathless from the excitement of the game he had played. "I kept after him for five blocks before he dove suddenly through a crowd and disappeared down an alley."

"Do you think he saw Wiley?"

Raphael shook his head. "He was too amused with me." The young man removed his ridiculously long coat and slumped down in a chair opposite the dean. "So, do you think he believed you?" he asked.

Tuckworth looked suddenly alarmed, as if this chance had not fully presented itself before, the chance of their failing before things were properly begun. "No," he said, "I don't think he believed me. At least, I hope he didn't."

CHAPTER XXV
FOUND OUT

Wiley stood on the doorstep of an apothecary's shop under a cloud-drenched sky. The shop was closed and dark, so that the liquids on display in the window, blue and amber, green and red, appeared uniformly gray, the semblance of some witch's brew or sinister concoction instead of the sound medicine they pretended to be. A thick spray hung suspended in the air, trapped between rain and sleet, making it nearly impossible for the young constable to keep his pipe lit, and he had retreated to the doorstep for the chance of drying out. Besides, he reasoned, it was smart to move around a bit, not get caught standing too still for too long. He could see the tavern from where he stood, and the sign swinging in the stiffening November breeze, the three yellow pears bobbing up and down. The dwarf could not very well leave without Wiley's noticing.

Jo Smalley had led a chase about every corner of Bellminster, into parts of the town that even Wiley, who had lived there all his life, had never seen before. At times he would stop in some pub and stand drinks, or he would pause among a group of idle men and joke and talk, or he would seem to wander aimlessly, wanting only to be seen, to register on the mind of the town. At last, however, his path had settled here, in the miserable, gin-soaked haunts by the river.

Wiley knocked the bowl of his pipe against his boot heel to dislodge the dampened residue of ash. A boy darted past in the mist, mud spraying from his every hurried footfall. He turned, paused a moment, and Wiley realized that it was a girl, dressed in boyish trousers and shirt, a cap pulled down over her hair. She disappeared into the tavern.

He tried to light his pipe again, but got only a half-dozen good puffs before it went out. Down the way, past the door of the Three Pears, a huddled gathering of loafers had filled an iron brazier with rubbish and lighted it, creating a warm oasis against the encroaching chill. Wiley looked up. He couldn't see the moon through the clouds, but if he could have, there would have been a ring around it, no doubt. Such a frost always puts a ring about the moon, he recalled.

The constable wandered down toward the fire, passing by the window of the tavern. Glancing in with the corner of his eye, he caught a glimpse of Jo Smalley sitting at the bar, balanced atop a stool like a parrot on its perch. Wiley moved on, strolled silently about the brazier with grudging nods at the others and settled himself so as to keep watch on the tavern door.

Inside, Smalley sipped a dark, bitter pint. The hour was late, and the trade of the tavern was beginning to thin. He had been there for two hours waiting for the girl, two hours sipping the same filthy porter, glared at by the tapster for not ordering more, an object of curiosity for every man and woman who entered. Two hours there before she came tumbling in at last, breathless and conspicuous, to sit by the window, her eyes fixed on him like two unflickering lamps calling a wanderer home. Smalley thought of what the dean had said, that he was known in Bellminster now. Once seen, never forgotten. What of that, though? He had courted such renown in the past. He'd invented a name for himself—

Smalley—an absurd, unforgettable name for a chap like him. Made it up from thin air, made sure folks knew it, then never let them forget it. How can you forget what you're told never to use? That's the way to be remembered, he reasoned, by making himself a joke. Just Jo.

He sipped again at the sour porter, then shot a winning grin at the disgruntled barman. The fellow took the smile as a request and drew off a fresh pint before Jo had the chance to refuse.

And I *am* remembered, he thought, and by great men, too. True, he was remembered first for his dwarfish stature, his broken shape, a curiosity, a freak. But later he was remembered for his industry and cleverness, his subtlety and relentless energy. He worked to win their confidence, to show them what he was capable of despite this twisted form his mind was forced to carry, and their confidence lent him their power, the power of the great. Wherever he went for the party he succeeded, or knew why he failed and never failed that way again. That grotesque name had meant something else once, something obvious and common. Now, men in London knew its true meaning, and valued it and whispered it among themselves in Whitehall and even on Downing Street and, who knew, maybe even at St. James's. It meant a man who won and didn't care how he won, for that was the only way to win, and win repeatedly.

He sipped again. Yet things were different here, almost dangerous. He had played a daring hand in a desperate game, more daring than he had ever played before, and now he had to carry it off to the end or get tangled in his own web. A boy was dead. He'd never planned on that, but there it was, and now he had to improvise as best he knew how, improvise a victory out of the chaos.

He looked over at her, not looking. She was already through her first pint. Well, that's all she gets, he thought, and jumped down from his stool to leave, flipping half a crown on the bar as a sop to the grumbling barman, another vote for Quentin Draper. He wandered outside, stopped to light a cigarette, and waited. Kit came out before he had finished his smoke.

"Don't be in such a hurry, Kit," Jo chided as he started walking. "You've got to learn a sense of time. You kept me waiting too long at first, and now you're too quick at second."

"Didn't get your message 'til not half a hour ago," she muttered.

"All right, then," he assured her delicately, catching the defiant irritation in her voice. The young were always so petulant to work with. "Where's a nearby place where we can talk? We've got to settle on something and settle it fast."

She jerked her head about. "Old warehouse down by the river's got a office lets onto a back alley."

"Watchman?"

"Nah. 'Bandoned."

Jo nodded. "You lead on, right? Slow and easy and don't look back. I'll follow."

He let her get perhaps twenty paces in advance. He dared not fall back farther, for the mist was turning into a true fog, lacing the air like frost on a windowpane. They did not have far to go. The tumbling rush of the Medwin reached his ears within five minutes, and the dank vapors surrounding him parted to reveal the shimmering black of the river a moment later. The warehouse sat on the bank. Crumbling docks stretched out into the shallow waters like an old woman's bony fingers, waiting for barges and skiffs to drift within her grasp, commercial trade that might never come again. A locked door at the back had long ago been pried open and left to swing helplessly on its rusted hinges. It led into a small, deserted office, no desk, no chairs, just a few packing crates and a crackling host of forgotten papers blown into the corners. From the walls, empty file drawers and cracked cabinets grinned crookedly. Another door led into the warehouse proper. There were no windows, no light, but neither Jo nor Kit had trouble with the darkness. It was their common element, and they were used to it.

"All right, then," Jo said, and motioned for the girl to sit. She settled awkwardly on the floor, resting against the inner door.

Jo turned over one of the crates and sat down. "What would you say to a little trip, Kit?"

"Trip where?"

"Why, to London, o' course. You've killed a man, killed two, and we can't have you traipsin' about Bellminster anymore."

The girl turned her face away with a sullen frown, and Jo saw what he had expected, what he had feared. Murder had sunk into her heart and poisoned her. She was feeling it in a way that no one could foretell. She might harden herself to it, form a crust about her soul as protection from hurt, from blame. Or she might go mad from guilt and blurt all out at some awkward moment, make a confession to the empty air that was filled with eager ears. Or she might have developed a taste for it. Regardless, she would be better in London. There were people in London he could send her to, people better suited than he was to make use of her talents, or if they found no good use for her, then they were better suited to ensure that her secrets stayed secret. But he did not think too hard on that.

"What d'you say, Kit?" he pursued. "There's a coach in the mornin', and you can sit right on top. Or inside, how's that! Travel like a duchess! You ever go on a coach afore?"

"Don't know as I wants to."

Jo breathed deep and let the breath out easy. "It ain't your decision no more, Kit," he told her, an icy command creeping through his voice.

She glanced back at him, and in the shadows he could not see what that look meant.

"You peach on me, we both swing," she whispered through clenched teeth. "You was in on it."

"I was there, Kit, as you say." His voice lingered on the word *you* with a lilting threat. "But I wouldn't peach on you. Nobody'd have to peach. Bellminster's a small town, and they'll catch you out soon enough if you stay here."

She hunkered shapelessly in the dark. "How'll they know it was me?"

"Well, just look at you! You give it away with your every move and your every breath. You're not used to such rough work, Kit. You're nervous. Look at you, how jumpy you are." She was defensive, he could see it in her, and his lies made her more defensive still until she stiffened and could hardly move at all. "Why, a constable is trained to spot guilty souls like yours. You had your reasons for killin' Danny, right enough, but I don't expect the magistrate to understand 'em."

She leaned forward slightly. "London?"

"Ah, now London's filled with guilty souls. Nobody'd ever notice you in London. And you'd have work. I could set you up with that. Any kind o' work you like. I know folks what could use someone like you, a real doer."

"That's what you called Danny," she said.

"And I meant it. I would've taken Danny on if you hadn't sliced him. But now he's gone, and that position is left open. Still open, Kit."

She considered. She was not one to consider often, or consider well, but she took a moment to think about what Jo was offering her, ordering her.

"Remember," Jo urged, pressing his point relentlessly, "constable takes one look at you, and it's all up. You're a light one and like to dangle a long time on the gallows."

A cat screamed in the alley, shrieking and bouncing about the garbage and crates and ash cans, thudding and crashing and scraping madly. And gasping. Only a cat does not gasp, not like a man, and it was a man's voice they heard cry out in shock and surprise.

Jo's eyes darted to the alley door before he heard a click and looked back toward Kit. She was gone, disappeared into the warehouse. He glanced again at the door. Someone was out there. Had they been followed? He thought about the dean's clumsy ruse of that afternoon, that comical figure with his oversized coat and hat. Had it really been so clumsy? Had that old vicar duped him? A tide of panic swelled and fell back again as he exercised the control he was known so well to possess. He must think, scheme, improvise. Had he been seen with Kit? They had talked for only a few moments together on the street, outside the tavern. Could have been anything. Asking the time. Begging a penny. Anything. A doxy, that's it! A whore! He glanced at where she had just been sitting, by the warehouse door. The girl had run, thank God. First smart thing she'd done since he found her. So she had stopped him, tried to talk him up, get him interested. Nothing more. He'd followed her here, some quiet place, out of the way. Shrunken fellow like me's got to get it when he can get it! That'll do.

Jo Smalley took a deep breath and prepared to step out into the night. Before he could move, however, he heard again the sounds of ash cans and boxes tumbling, crashing, only now there was no cat hissing in angry accompaniment. He ran as fast as he could to the door and peered out.

Kit was standing over a fallen form, dark and motionless. In her hand she held a brick, and she was just raising it above her head.

"Kit!"

She hesitated, lowered her arm.

"None of that!" He hobbled over and looked at the man, senseless in the filth of the street.

"D'you know him?"

She spat on her fallen foe and tossed the brick aside. "Constable."

Jo passed a despairing hand through his hair. "Sweet Jesus," he muttered. For just an instant he stood frozen, his wits failing him, the need to scheme and improvise coming again too soon, too soon. Then, he waved his hand toward the warehouse door. "Drag him inside," he commanded.

Kit pulled the constable along through the offal and garbage of the back alley and into the warehouse, Jo following and watching intently behind him. Once inside, he closed the door and cursed the fool who had broken the lock.

"Did he see you?"

Kit's brow furrowed in confusion. "He musta done, if he followed us."

"I mean just now! Did he see you before you brained him?"

She gave a mute shrug.

"All right," he muttered, "go get some rope."

"Where?"

"It's a bloody warehouse! Get rope!"

Kit scurried out the inner door, leaving Jo alone for a time, able to think, to plot. What now? What must he do now? The same story, just a whore? He might make it work. "Thought the constable was up to no good," he could say. "The girl snuck behind him and we only learned after who it was." But they'd want to talk to Kit. They'd try to track her down. No, Kit was too dangerous now, too volatile. He couldn't trust her. She must be got to London.

Jo looked down at the young man sprawled at his feet. So the dean set him on to shadow me, he thought. Why? What could the old man hope to discover? Tuckworth suspected Jo of being connected to the murder somehow, and the story about saving the old man's cathedral was a lie, but this seemed too chancy, trusting all to luck, just following Jo about hoping to find something.

And then he saw the truth, saw it all laid out before him like a map. They knew about Kit. Or they knew about the fact of her, an accomplice, someone in the town. They'd know it wasn't a whore, he realized. They'd know who it was and they'd find her.

He had to rid himself of Kit—and not just on a coach to London.

A noise below startled him from his thoughts. He glanced down and saw the constable stir, his hand just scraping about the dusty floor. Jo took a step backward, breathless. The figure moved again, an arm crooking, trying to rise. He moaned.

Kit came back into the room. In a moment she saw the case, walked calmly over, and kicked the man in the head—kicked him twice. The constable fell back and did not move.

Jo bent over. For an instant he feared that she had done him for good, but a hand to the man's throat revealed the least beat of life. He glanced back up at Kit, saw her emotionless eyes, uncaring, uninterested. She reached down, coils of dirty rope in her fist.

"Bind him up, Kit," Jo ordered. She knelt and got to her work, while he stepped across the room to think. Some few minutes later, and they both were finished.

Jo came and inspected her knots. "You've a talent, Kit," he said admiringly, "and no doubt. You've trussed him up pretty." He tested the strength of the rope, tugged at the bindings. "Tight. Well done, girl." He rolled the constable's head over. The dark stain of a bruise was forming on his brow. He would be lost to the world for some time to come.

"All right, then," Jo said, rising and turning about. "I've got to go make arrangements, Kit. This sort of thing needs to be cleaned up right quick, and I know just how it's done. You stay here and keep our friend company. But, Kit," he added, with an admonishing tone, "don't mishandle him. No rough treatment, eh?"

She nodded.

"You got a knife on you?"

She stood for a moment, unresponsive, dark.

"Kit, d'you got a blade?" he demanded.

Grudgingly, she pulled out an evil-looking clasp knife. Jo put out his hand. She stood defiant.

"Kit!"

Quickly, as if bitten, she dropped it into his tiny palm. "Good

girl. You've too much temper, Kit. This is by way of a precaution."
He pocketed the knife and turned toward the door. "I'll be back in
a few hours. You just watch young feller there, and keep your
hands off as best you can. Nothin' rough, Kit. Nothin' foolish."

And with that, he strode back out into the night. He had much
to do before he returned, and if things went the way he devised
them to, there would be even more to do when he got back. Damn
the girl, she was forcing him into schemes he never would have
dreamed of attempting before Bellminster.

The clouds had parted, and Jo looked up into the sky, into the
vastness of heaven, the mirror of his own vast ambition. The
power of the great, that's what he was playing for, and that meant
playing all the way, for all the stakes a man could bring to the
table. Hold nothing back, and win it all or lose it all. As he walked,
the towers of Bellminster Cathedral peeked in and out from behind the buildings on his way. Between them, the crescent moon
hung brilliant and pure, a fairy ring encircling it, hemming in its
celestial glow.

CHAPTER XXVI
PLANS LAID

D'you comprehend me, Semple? A regular demonstration."

Abraham Semple nodded his head resolutely, a look of grim obedience reflected on his weatherworn face. He was not a man to whom obedience seemed natural, being more accustomed to giving orders than to getting them. And yet, Jo Smalley was accustomed to giving orders also, giving them to men like Semple, and he knew how to take the rough edge off a command, to make submission appear voluntary, and service sound like freedom.

"I can promise you two dozen men in an hour's time," Semple said. "More by midnight."

"Can you get me fifty? Stout men, too. It could be hard work tonight. The other side is divided, but they're still dangerously strong."

"Fifty o' the best Bellminster knows."

"Good," Jo exclaimed with a reassuring wink. "We'll set the Tories back on their heels for good and all tonight."

Abraham Semple had been Smalley's earliest contact in Bellminster, the one who had paved his way in the town. The builder wrote to London as soon as the election was set to show the Whigs their opportunity and promised his aid in toppling Granby's hold on the political sport. Semple was a determined liberal, a supporter of reform and universal manhood suffrage, an enemy to enclosure and the Corn Laws, and yet he was something else, something few other men knew. He was wealthy. Abraham Semple had built the mill and most of the New Town. He had made his money at the outset and sunk it deep in investments outside Bellminster, in London and even beyond. His fortune had grown unseen, and he had developed without any man's notice into a miser, which is merely to say that he never paid tuppence for a pennyworth of soap. He lived alone. He earned a lot and spent a little, which has always been a formula for wealth. He labored now through habit and principle, not need, and so he was in the best position in all the town to defy Granby. But even he could not afford to do so openly, not yet.

"You're sure this'll look right?" he asked as Jo Smalley prepared to leave, hopping down from the hard chair in Semple's modest parlor and making for the door. "I don't want none of my men . . ." He fumbled for the word.

"Compromised? Their livelihoods imperiled? Set at defiance by his high-and-mighty lordship?" Jo laughed. "Ol' Granny's done himself more harm that way than you realize, Abraham. Your men'll have the mantle of law and order wrapped about them. They'll be reclaiming the streets for the common folk, be the saviors of the town. And tomorrow, when Draper arrives—" Jo clapped his hands together and rubbed them exultantly. "Granby won't tell which way to turn. He'll be done up and done in, and I only hope he's a wise enough old fool to realize it." Abraham Semple laughed in spite of himself. "Now, you know where I'm talkin' of? Down by the river, that whole section of the town. You'll draw the Blues and apprentices to you like flies to honey. Not many real voters there, so if things get rough, no one who matters is likely to get hurt."

"I'll have 'em there and ready for what-have-you." With that assurance following his heels, Jo left, hurrying, hurrying through the streets, bustling to his next destination, laying the pieces in place. Time was everything to him now, and he must hoard every second.

While at the Constabulary House, time was likewise a great concern.

"It's not gone half past ten, sir," Raphael was saying as he put his watch back in his pocket. "It's just too early yet to tell."

"Young man's right," Hopgood agreed from behind his desk. "Wiley's as sharp as they come, sharp as a ha'penny needle. But we got to give him time, is all."

Tuckworth turned another turn about the office. "I know the hour," he grumbled. "I know Wiley and I know the hour. Very well. But I can still worry if I've a mind to worry. I just . . ." His voice trailed off into an ill-conceived and nameless apprehension. As day had worn away into evening, and evening into night with still no word, the dean had dragged Raphael along to Hopgood's office, the natural place for such waiting. "I only worry, that's all. Wiley is sharp, but Smalley's sharp, too. And somewhere in this is someone willing to kill." The dean knew that he sounded like an old woman, fussy and bewildered, but he dared not hide his cares. He would wear his fears for all to see, would admit them openly rather than try to bury them beneath a senseless, insipid bravado.

So he paced, around and through the office, back and forth, stopping and starting off again. He was old enough to know the wisdom of patience, and wise enough to know he did not possess it to any great degree, not when the risks they ran were this dire.

They waited, three impatient men, waited quietly, thoughtfully. The dean, the painter, and the chief constable, they knew one another well enough by now, and through enough adventures, not to waste the minutes away in idle chatter. They could not calmly deal cards or pore over some broadsheet pamphlet. Their minds were too fully occupied with what was missing from the room, the information that was not there for them to work with. Occasionally an officer of the force would come shyly in, aware that whatever business he brought with him was not what was wanted, and would leave again feeling duly whipped for his impertinence, though not a word was spoken.

After a time, Raphael coughed. It was an annoying cough, the sort of cough that is no cough but a way of saying nothing loudly.

"What is it?" replied Tuckworth, not slowing his progress.

"I've been thinking about when I might be ready to leave Bellminster," Raphael said.

The dean grunted an acknowledgment that Raphael had been thinking.

"I thought I might try before the month is out. I thought I might go west, to the lake country."

"Fine country, that," Hopgood observed. "Imagine you'd find good paintin' there." To the chief constable's mind, the search for artistic inspiration was something akin to fishing.

"Of course, then I'd miss Christmas in Bellminster. I'd hate to—"

"One thing at a time, Raphael," advised Tuckworth.

"I just hate putting off a plan—"

"One thing at a time. There's no lack of days to leave on." And so the conversation died, though Raphael was certain that the dean would eventually try to talk him out of leaving, perhaps even hoped that he would.

Ten minutes later, ten more minutes of pacing and sitting and silence, and the door opened to admit the white head of an elderly officer.

Hopgood sat up. "Dawkins?"

"Fellow here says he got urgent business with chief constable," the man announced, and with a nod from the chief constable the white head disappeared to be replaced by the breathless figure of Jo Smalley.

"I've found your killer. She's got your man tied up in a warehouse down by the river. A girl. Street urchin. There's not much time. She thinks I'm arranging her escape."

Hopgood stood up behind his desk. "Wiley's with her?"

"She surprised him. Bashed his head. He might be dying as we stand here."

The chief constable began to fly across the room, to throw his entire force into action, before Tuckworth's upraised hand stopped him.

"How did you find this girl?"

"She found me," the dwarf explained. "To her mind she'd done me a good turn killing Danny, and she wanted my help to get out of Bellminster."

"Why did she kill him?"

"To silence him. He knew about the coffin maker."

"Why did she lay his body out that way, to be found?"

"I don't know."

"Why did she kill McAllister?"

"I don't know."

"What made her come to you?"

"I told you—"

"But why you? What did she know of you to make her trust—"

"I can't say."

"If she killed Danny for what he knew, why confide in a stranger?"

"I don't know! I don't know! She did, that's all! But if we don't act and act fast, you might have another murder on your hands!"

No power could halt Hopgood now, and he dashed into the outer office, tossing off commands and marshaling his men, sending out word to rouse every available officer and volunteer to Wiley's aid. All of Constabulary House was thrown into confusion, and through the chaos Tuckworth tried to keep watch on Jo Smalley, though the dwarf was constantly disappearing and reappearing again in every corner of the place.

The dean pulled Raphael aside. "I don't know where we're headed or what he's got planned, but try to stay close to him," he whispered.

"What can you suspect him of?" the painter asked, genuinely confounded by the request. "He came here freely. He seems to want this girl captured as much as we do."

"Just watch him, Raphael."

The dean could not place a finger on why he felt so uneasy with Smalley's story. The man's "I don't know" stood like a wall between them, an earthen barricade protecting something, but what? The truth? A clever man would devise a clever lie that might be punctured, but a brilliant man understood that ignorance was a natural state and not to be overcome easily. As long as Smalley held to that, Tuckworth could do little to get at him, could not even be certain within himself that there was anything to get at, so convincing these "I don't knows" sounded. He would have to wait a while longer, keep his eyes on Smalley as best he could, and bide the time before he might interrogate this girl.

For his part, Jo was a whirlwind of assistance, helping Hopgood to a plan, striving shoulder-to-shoulder with the force, eager to effect the rescue of Constable Wiley. He was here and there and there and there at once, describing the warehouse, the alley, the room, the girl, working up maps and strategies, encouraging the men and stoking their bravery for the perils ahead, the grim perils, the deadly perils. He was a font of all information, shrewd and resourceful, and the final plan was his to make, for as he reminded them at every opportunity, he knew the danger they were walking into better than any of them. Twenty constables and volunteers would surround the building on all sides, not forgetting a boat on the river (Hopgood's proud contribution). Jo would then go in alone, for he alone had the girl's trust, and it would be up to him to talk her out of the warehouse and into the street where she might be apprehended safely.

"You think you can get her out o' there?" the chief constable asked.

"Simple plans are always best," Smalley said with a serious air. "I'll come up with some excuse for her. It's dangerous, I know. The girl's desperate and ruthless and like to prove violent if she feels cornered. She might do anythin', anythin' at all. But your man Wiley's the one we got to worry about, not me."

Such stoic bravery made a great impression on everyone who heard it, except perhaps on Tuckworth, who found it a bit too earnest to be sincere. So, less than thirty minutes after Jo's breathless arrival, they were prepared to set off through the streets of Bellminster, one more band of armed men to join the other prowling gangs in the night.

Twenty figures marched down to the Medwin, twenty shapes in loose order. Three pairs of arms cradled rifles, three of the steadiest lads on the force, three sharpshooters ready to do the unthinkable. All others gripped truncheons and clubs in their fists, except Smalley, who wielded his cane, and Tuckworth, whose hands stayed empty. They marched through the town, past deserted shops and lightless windows, sending rats and mongrels and tomcats, whores and drunks scurrying to the shadows, and as they walked, the sound of their silence muffled the night's noise. The tramp of their boots and the swish of their shirts and trousers, their heavy breaths and even the pounding of blood in their ears kept them at first from hearing the telltale signs of disturbance ahead in their path.

The ancient shops and markets melted away into newer buildings, offices of commercial trade, storehouses and yards that fed the barges moving up and down the river, not so many now that the mill was dying, a vast hospital of ailing business. They came to a crossroads, and looking down the opposite way saw a melee of bodies in the street, scrambling and fighting, two parties clashing in the dark.

"Granby's men against the Blues," Smalley said at Hopgood's elbow. "Looks like they've started up in earnest now. You'll have a regular riot on your hands."

The chief constable looked about for a moment, uncertain how to respond to this new threat to the peace. "Send a few men after them," Smalley volunteered. "Four fewer hearts won't hinder our work."

With a quick, decisive nod, Hopgood ordered four of his men to break up the disturbance and then follow along as soon as they could. The band proceeded on their way, toward the river, toward Wiley. By now, however, the sound of violence in the streets was growing around them.

"Sounds like they're havin' at it over there," Smalley said, pointing to their left. "And back that way," he added, pointing back whence they had come. "Better deal with it. Four more men won't harm us."

So another four went off to scour the streets and stem the flow of riot in Bellminster. And now only a dozen marched to the warehouse by the river. They had not managed another fifty paces, though, before the sound of a window smashing in the distance called their attention to an orange glow in the sky.

"Fire!" Jo cried, and at once all dozen tried to bolt away to help.

"Stop!" Hopgood recalled them to their goal. "Might be nothin'. You two, go see after that and raise the alarm if you need to. But you rest stay with me. We've got to get Wiley!"

"Wiley," the ten murmured as they proceeded, nodding resolutely. And only Tuckworth noted how carefully Jo Smalley was whittling at their numbers.

"This way," Jo called, and they turned west for a block. "No, wait!" He hesitated, looking about. "No, back there again! The other way!" But now they collided with another band of men hunting for a fight, and after a brief scuffle these turned and fled, taking some three more of Hopgood's men who followed them in heedless pursuit.

"Damn!" the chief constable cursed. "What have we got?"

"Seven," Tuckworth reported.

"We can't surround a warehouse with seven men!"

"No," Jo agreed. "But we don't have to surround it. Leave it to me. I'll bring her out and then you lot can lay her under arrest easy enough."

There was nothing else to be done. Off they went, seven men, just one rifle, amid an air of mayhem. More violence, more riot, two more dispatched to keep the peace, and by the time they got at last to the warehouse they were five, just Smalley, the dean, Raphael, Hopgood, and the white-haired constable Dawkins. They crouched at the mouth of the alley, ignoring the noises about them, the battle passing from street to street.

Hopgood pointed to Raphael and Dawkins. "You two go down there," he hissed. "Get t'other side of that door. But be quiet! Vicar and me'll stay this side."

Tuckworth, Smalley, and the chief constable watched as their companions crept into the black hole of the alley, disappearing as though they had fallen in. The three waited until they were certain the others were in place, and Tuckworth noticed the look on the dwarf's face beside him, the sweat beading on his lip and brow, the tremble of his hand. Jo was afraid, genuinely afraid, and once more the dean considered whether he was mistaken about it all. Was Smalley lying?

The wait was over at last. With a nod from Hopgood, Jo went forward on his terrible mission.

CHAPTER XXVII

TRAPS UNSPRUNG

The night was alive with violence, the general uproar kindled by sparse pockets of bloodshed as three armies warred through the streets by the river, a handful of skirmishes stretching over some dozen lanes and alleys and courtyards, allegiances confused and shifting in the darkness, sometimes allies battling allies or men fighting for no cause at all, only for the release of their aimless anger. The field of conflict spread and moved with the rapacious hunger of a swarm, feeding on chaos and broken windows, bonfires and barricades.

And crouching in the thick of it, Tuckworth sat and thought. What was Smalley up to? How would it serve him to lure this girl out and place her in the hands of justice? Was he truly involved as deeply as Tuckworth suspected, or was he as innocently embroiled as any of them, an innocence that smelled to the dean as much like guilt as guilt itself could smell? He peered at the spectral door through which the dwarf had passed just a moment ago. What was he doing in there, in that warehouse? If he had had a hand in Danny's murder, why compromise himself now? Why call out the constabulary in such force? But what force, five men where twenty were planned for? And why twenty when only five were needed? What was Smalley up to?

The chief constable glanced over in the darkness and saw the look of strained perplexity that clouded the dean's brow. "Not to worry yourself, vicar," he whispered, trying to reassure Tuckworth. "Your friend'll be safe enough."

"Yes," the dean muttered absentmindedly. "I'm sure he will."

"I know it," Hopgood remarked confidently. "I give him my own revolver back at the constabulary. He'll be right enough with that."

A revolver! The girl! The night and the confusion! A riot and more violence! At once Tuckworth had a suspicion, and in the urgency of the moment that suspicion flared to a certainty. He leaped to his feet and dashed for the door, Hopgood calling vainly after him. He burst through into the warehouse and paused to take in the dark scene before him.

Wiley lay in a corner, trussed and insensible, a pile of humanity. Against the far wall a girl stood, her body crouched, arms held out, fingers spread, ready to pounce, to spring at anything, in any direction. Across from her Jo Smalley stood, his back to Tuckworth, but even so the dean could see the man trembling as he held out the revolver, pointing it randomly at the girl, unable to steady his shaking hand.

"Jo!"

Smalley turned and his finger convulsed on the trigger. A shot fired and a bullet flew into the wall. He stared down at the smoking barrel, and then looked up at the dean, a look of failure and revelation, the look of a man who found he could not do what he dared to do, what he had to do. "I didn't know," he murmured.

Hopgood and Raphael came tumbling into the room, and now the girl dived for the far door and disappeared in a wink. Without a word Tuckworth was after her, not waiting for the others, leaping into the dark emptiness of the warehouse.

She was only a ghostly shape ahead of him, moving through the blackness, a sound of running footsteps, sharp and quick and frightened. In that lightless world she could not find the wall as she stumbled over boxes and abandoned crates, so that Tuckworth kept pace with her better than he might have done in daylight. He saw her dimly, a shape darting straight on, certain to run up against something solid and so scramble her way to a door and find her escape. If she made it to the streets she would be lost forever.

"Raphael!" the dean shouted, the only name he could think of. "She's coming out your way! Be ready!"

"My way?" he heard Raphael call behind him, but the ruse worked. He heard the girl hesitate, then make her way back to the center, crossing the floor of the warehouse again.

"Keep your posts! She might come out anywhere now!" He panted and his age began to tell as she pulled ahead into the distance. He lost sight of her altogether and could follow only by the sound of her running.

"You can't get out, girl!" he yelled into the void. "There's no way for you!"

Suddenly a shape loomed before him, a staircase rising to the next floor, and he realized she was making her way up. Behind him he could faintly hear the others trying to follow in the dark. Why had no one thought to bring lanterns? But he remembered, Jo had done their planning for them.

"She's headed up," he called back, and then began to climb. Here he had a chance of gaining on her. Years of life in a cathedral, a towering home of nearly endless staircases in close, stony walls, had taught him how to climb. He moved steadily, rhythmically, neither too slowly nor too fast. At the next floor he paused and listened and caught the sound of her panting breaths above and ahead of him. She was charging straight up to the roof, of course, four flights above the world. Nowhere else to go now, and a certain trap for her. He raced up, not calling to the others, not yet. Let her get there, all the way up where he could block her way back down, and then let them know.

Another flight and he could tell she was slowing. He came out on the next floor and heard a great crash above him, the trapdoor falling open overhead. One more flight. He labored up the final steps, saw the gaping hole of the sky above, the feeble stars framed by the black ceiling. He turned to yell back down.

"She's on the roof! Hurry and we have her!"

Tuckworth emerged into a night that was absurdly calm. The sounds of the riot below did not easily make their ways up so far, and the orange glow of two bonfires in the streets gave a festive aspect to the scene. He turned about.

She stood some thirty paces away from him, at the edge of the roof looking over the river. She was staring down into the great emptiness of water beneath. He saw into her thoughts at once.

"You'll be killed in the fall," he stated calmly, as a matter of fact, though within himself he was not so sure what daring might accomplish yet.

She spun about and in the starlight he could see the unmasked hatred in her eyes, the longing for blood, the eager hope for murder. She walked toward him, and the dean steadied himself, prepared for any reckless act of despair, any rash move she might make to get by him, through him, to topple him to the roof under her feet. She came almost to within his grasp, but she was young and lithe and wild and he dared not try to match her quickness. He only stood and looked into her eyes.

They were green, like Lucy's. But they were filled with such relentless anger, such uncontrolled ferocity aimed at him, directly and unreasonably at him, that he found no word to set her at her ease, no sane advice that might still her brutal spirit. She hated him, and she did not know him or care to know him. She only hated him completely.

Suddenly, the girl turned and dashed for the side of the roof, for the void that hung above the waters.

"No!" he called but she did not stop, did not slow, not until she was within a few spare paces of the edge. And then some inner voice of preservation arrested her, and she skidded and tumbled to a halt, inches from plunging into the night.

She had lost her nerve at the final moment, and this failure fanned the hatred within her, fanned it into a roaring inferno. She rose and turned her fury on the dean, screaming as she ran at him, shrieking like a demon.

Tuckworth steadied himself, planted his legs firmly, and crouched at the knee. For one odd instant he felt like a football goalie protecting the cage that gaped behind him, her freedom. Then she was on him, hurled herself through the air at him, scratching and ripping with her claws and tearing with her teeth. He tried to grasp her wrists and caught one, but the other lashed his face, seeking his eyes. She cut three red lines down his cheek and the pain drew up something animal in him so that he struck her, closed his fist and hit her with every ounce of force he owned. But she had been hit before in her life, hit often, and she hardly noticed.

The girl clung to the dean, shrieking and flailing, and Tuckworth felt her weight begin to pull at his. He tried to shift his feet but tangled them together instead and his balance abandoned him. He fell, but as he fell he twisted in midair and put the girl beneath him, striking at her now with his own weight. He landed, and the shock tore the cries away from her for a moment. She lay stunned, and the dean took advantage of the moment, straddled her and pinned her hands over her head.

The moment passed, and now the girl found herself trapped under the bulk of a fat old man. Where futility might have stilled another soul, however, she doubled and redoubled her violence, screaming and kicking fiercely beneath him, unable to dislodge her captor, fighting against Tuckworth, against his weight, the weight of the world above him, the weight of fate and all society crushing her.

Tuckworth was too tired even to call out for help. He breathed as though there were not enough air in the heavens to fill his lungs. He breathed and he looked down at her, this girl so capable of everything evil, of everything vile and inhuman, this girl.

Gradually, his pounding heart slowed, his breaths came less urgently, and he tried looking into her once more. But only his own ignorance stared back through her hatred.

"Why—"

She made a noise in her throat like a cat's hiss and spat in his face. Tuckworth tried to wipe her spittle off with his shoulder, but as the force of his weight eased on her arm she fought to escape. So he only turned to call behind him, "I've got her! We're on the roof!"

And even now, even now she would exploit this one weakness to hurt him, and she spat and spat in his face again, calling up the bile of her angry heart to rain upon him, a hateful rain, a burning rain falling upward, as rain must fall from hell. And Tuckworth let her do it, for he could do nothing else.

CHAPTER XXVIII
LITTLE SINS

"Why did she come to you?"

"I don't know. Why does she say she came to me?"

"She doesn't," the dean answered. "She says you came to her. Somehow you discovered who she was, how she was involved, and you flushed her out and took her to see Danny."

Jo leaned back in the chair and looked at Hopgood and Raphael for aid in dealing with such a ridiculous assertion. "The girl wants a bit of her own back, some sweet revenge, that's all. She wanted vengeance against the boy for turnin' on her and she wants the same o' me."

"Then why doesn't she accuse you of the murder itself? She admits to all of it, to killing McAllister, to killing Danny, only she says you were there and managed everything for her, got her away, pinned it on Bates. If she's so set on vengeance, why not tell a story more certain to send you to the gallows?"

"I don't know!"

This was the tale he had repeated now a half-dozen times at least. And yet Tuckworth kept at it relentlessly, under the ever-less-hopeful eyes of Raphael and Hopgood in the chief constable's office. The dean had heard the girl's version of events, listened as she unleashed her hatred at everyone and everything about her, told her story of a life of weakness and pain, a victim to every lustful impulse of every villain she had known, until she had the strength herself to turn from victim to villain, and he had been convinced, if only by the passion of her tale, that she was not inventing it, could not invent it. The dean rubbed a hand over his weary brow. So much to keep track of in this, so many ends and tangles to hack through in this knot, so many loops dangling about that seemed to lead nowhere. He needed to see it all laid out straight for him, somehow.

"So your first involvement in this, in all of this, was when the girl sought you out, tried to get your help in getting free of Bellminster?"

"Again, yes," Smalley admitted.

"And when I burst through the warehouse door and saw you with Hopgood's revolver in your hand, what were you doing?"

"I was protectin' myself. The girl guessed what I done and threatened to kill me."

"With what? She was unarmed."

"How am I supposed to know with what?" Jo cried, appealing in his frayed temper to the others, who were growing more uncomfortable with each question.

"And when you turned to me after firing that shot, what did you say?"

"I can't recall," Smalley stated flatly, "but accordin' to you, I said that I didn't know."

"Didn't know what?"

Jo's temper tore itself from its moorings at last. "How can I tell you what I bloody meant when I don't remember sayin' it! This is insane! Chief constable," he continued, turning to Hopgood, "if there's anythin' you want t'accuse me of, would you do it so as I can get to my cell and get some sleep? Otherwise, you can find me at the Granby Arms."

The dean had nothing else to offer, no artillery to force a way beyond that wall of "I don't know," nothing but his own unwavering certainty that Smalley, only Smalley could have wanted Danny discovered, the girl killed, Bates and Granby discredited. The dwarf left, rattling the door behind him, and the three investigators shared a moment of clumsy silence.

The chief constable coughed. "Perhaps—"

"That girl did not do it all herself," Tuckworth insisted. "She did not drag Danny's body toward the door and she did not leave the door open so the body would be found by the next man passing by. She would have slaughtered him as coldly as a butcher slaughters a hog and left him bleeding on the floor and then she would have closed the door behind her! She would have done that much at least!"

The dean glanced about him at the subsequent quiet and noted the horrified looks of his companions. He shook his head, dismayed, and turned away. Had he descended so far in his insensitivity, in his depravity, to compare poor Danny to a slaughtered hog?

"Well," Hopgood ventured to say at last, "without somethin' more certain at least, we'll not be able to prove a thing. But that don't matter so much," he added by way of consolation. "We got the killer. That ain't nothin', to my mind."

But it was less than everything to Tuckworth's mind. In fact, it was less than half, or felt as such. Kitty Wren was the guiltiest party in all of this, as the law measures guilt. But she had been used by others, used as a weapon in an invisible war, used by men who thought nothing of turning their fellows into tools for some nameless greater good that only they could see. What greater good was it to devour the thing your good is set to protect? Or to make free and terrible use of that last, worst element of the world you hope to govern?

He was disgusted, with himself, with his town, with the world. This was politics, he had been told at every turn. This was the world of civilized men, the world of government and good causes. He was sick of that world.

He arrived home to the vicarage and found Mrs. Cutler and Lucy waiting nervously.

"We heard about the riot," his daughter told him, settling him down in his chair in the parlor. "Was it very terrible?"

Tuckworth thought for a moment. "I honestly can't recall. Hopgood and his men seem to have got things under control quick enough. Just some broken windows and broken heads, and some bonfires in the streets. No real damage."

"Who started it?"

"No one can say."

"Was anyone seriously hurt?"

"Seriously?" The dean paused again. "No, no one was hurt, much. Just enough."

"Grown men acting like ill-mannered little ruffians," Mrs. Cutler declared, then added, "I'll fetch you a lamb pasty."

And suddenly, the dean was ferociously hungry.

The next morning he woke late, which was very unusual for him. Age had made him a light sleeper. He dressed himself slowly, deciding whether to carry his black mood of the night before into the daylight. It was one thing after all to despise the world you lived in, and quite another to despise the life you lived. He felt that he had been away from his home, his dear ones, for far too long, and he wanted only to relax in his study, watch Bit play in the parlor, read a book, muse over his chessboard, and bore himself to a dull vacuity.

He descended the stairs, still uncertain which direction his mood would take. A folded square of paper addressed to him sat on the table by the door. The dean picked this up, opened it, and read. He turned it over, looked at the address again with greater interest, and read once more the cryptic message.

"Mrs. Cutler!"

The woman, daubed in wet flour, came out from her kitchen.

He waved the paper in the air. "Who left this?"

"John Taggart brought it over from the Arms not five minutes ago."

Tuckworth nodded vaguely, looked at the paper once more, and then suddenly his eyes grew large and white, his mouth opened and closed and opened again like a trout's, and he made a noise like a soft whoop. Turning quickly, he dashed out the front door.

Some three hours later, other notes began appearing at the doors of Bellminster's leading men. A note was dropped at Lord Granby's door. Another came for Mayor Padgett. Even Charley Bates received one, and few men cared to associate with Charley Bates since his recent disgrace. All the notes were the same, invitations to a special dinner being given at the Granby Arms, all signed by Chief Constable Hopgood, and all couched in terms that not even his lordship could easily ignore.

At the appointed hour, at half past four, they all assembled in the front room around a table spread with cold meat and brown bread and beer. Bates and Padgett, Bick, Mortimer and Granby, Wilfred Cade, Jo Smalley and Hopgood and Constable Wiley, his head swathed in bandages, they were all there. Even Raphael was there. The arrangements were difficult, and every man found himself sitting next to or across from at least one person he despised, or had injured, or both, but such are the vagaries of politics. Tuckworth entered last of all, with John Taggart in tow to attend to the glasses and act the part of a general steward.

"I have to apologize for bringing you all together in this way," the dean began.

"Yes," Mortimer said, "I suspected this was your doing, Mr. Tuckworth. Our chief constable seems to be your personal attendant in such matters."

The dean looked sideways at the rector with a faint smile.

"Odd," he commented. "I don't recall putting your name on the guest list."

"I am here at the express request of Lord Granby." Mortimer glanced at his lordship, who appeared oblivious to his existence.

"Ah, well," the dean acquiesced, "another stomach to fill more or less, eh? I'm sure John Taggart won't run out of beer."

"Not likely," the tavern keeper reported.

Charley Bates hunched over in his chair, looking disheveled and done in. "Could we finish with whatever it is you've brought us here to do?" he insisted. "I find the accommodations stuffy."

A few sharp looks darted in his direction, but no one contradicted him, and so the dean opened the proceedings.

"I want to end this entire business," he announced.

"I thought . . . thought it *was* ended," declared Padgett.

"If you mean we have the murderer," Tuckworth explained, "yes, it is ended. Kitty Wren is in jail and will undoubtedly be hanged for her crimes." He paused and drew a deep breath. "But when all this began I made a promise. To you, Jo. I promised to keep everyone apprised equally of my conclusions. I'd give no man the advantage over another. Isn't that right?"

Smalley shrugged.

"Yes," the dean continued. "So I've brought us all together to go back over events briefly, to make certain that you all enter into the election on a firm footing, knowing your right allegiances, certain of where your trust should lie."

"It shouldn't lie anywhere with this lot, as far as I can see," Charley Bates muttered.

"An interesting observation, Bates," replied Mortimer, "considering you were the wellspring of all this trouble."

"Actually," Tuckworth corrected, "that was Lord Granby's doing."

Mortimer looked outraged. "That is an unconscionable—"

"Quiet, Mortimer." Granby stared at the dean, a doleful look in his eye, dire though not threatening. He looked instead like a man being led to the hangman's noose. With a soft nod, he indicated for Tuckworth to proceed.

"I'm sorry, Granby," the dean said, forgetting formality in his affection for his old friend. "I truly am, but you set the game in motion, playing out your little strategies for no good reason but your own amusement. You wanted Bick all along, but you made a show of your decision, let the others scheme and plot around you, maybe so you might test them, or perhaps because you liked all those men fawning about you. Oh, it's not a crime, what you did. Only a little lie. But this is all a matter of little things, little sins."

"Need I remind you, Mr. Tuckworth, that his lordship's plans would have remained a harmless sport if you had not revealed them to Mayor Padgett." Mortimer sniffed.

"You're quite right, Mortimer," the dean confessed. "And I'll only say this in my defense, though perhaps I oughtn't. I wanted to spare Padgett humiliation. My intentions were well founded. But then all our intentions have been well founded, haven't they? We all mean only the best for Bellminster." A note of disgust began to creep into the dean's voice. "All doing what's best for the town. Right, Bates?"

Charley Bates looked morosely about the table, his eye lingering on Padgett in distaste.

"You were the first to entertain the notion that Lord Granby could be defied, weren't you? Not openly defied, but made to appear foolish. You arranged for the first riot, a little harmless violence to set people talking against Bick. No one to get hurt, of course. At least, not much. What's a broken arm against what's best for the town? And you didn't plot for yourself, of course, but for the mayor."

Padgett glanced about himself nervously, and seemed eager to slip down under the table.

"And you decided to use boys. That was a telling decision. You had Danny collect them from off the streets, ragged boys eager for some violence. Only one wasn't a boy, and she was a bit too eager."

"And McAllister's death is somehow my fault?" Bates groused.

"Of course not! No one is denying that Kitty Wren is the greatest sinner in all of this, and she'll hang for her crimes. Why, by comparison, you're a credit to the town. Yours are only little sins, like Lord Granby's. Instigate a little riot. Vandalize a few shop windows. Just little sins. But once McAllister died, that made your little sins seem bigger somehow. You knew your innocence, but this isn't a game of guilt or innocence, is it? This is politics, as you've all been so kind to remind me at every juncture, where the right is never really quite right and the wrong is never terribly wrong."

"Come . . . come now," Padgett mumbled, trying to sound offended for form's sake.

"So Evan McAllister died. Regrettable, but what could be done? No one wanted Kitty Wren to kill him. No one wanted *that* much violence. So, Bates realized, Danny had to be got out of the way for a time. In a flat he had prepared, a building he owned."

Bates turned a hateful eye upon the dean, hateful and afraid. Tuckworth paused for only half a moment, aware that there was no need to reveal all.

"Danny was the only link to Kitty," he continued, "the link between Kitty and Bates. But not every plan is a good plan. You were stupid, Bates. You might have given up Kitty and you might have hidden Danny, but you were stupid to try both."

"Thank you," Bates answered icily, though sounding oddly relieved as well. "I'll make a note of it."

"A note." Tuckworth looked about him, his glance resting for a moment on each man, and each glance carrying a different message. He came at last to Jo. "And now we get to the Whigs."

"I knew you must," said Smalley.

"You were the outsider in all of this, but you were a professional, too. This is your business, managing such things, and your method is to sit back and watch, and wait."

"What d'you know of my method?" Jo asked, only a bit nervous to start.

"Improvisation, Jo. You told me so yourself. Your way is to see where the enemy is moving and then counter his moves. To act in the thick of action, move with the current of events. Most ships swamp when the wind turns too sharp, but not you. You sail on. You thrive."

Jo did nothing, but only looked at the dean, an empty, calculating look.

"Jo heard that I'd seen through Granby's plans, how I'd warned Padgett that Bick was the chosen one. And so Jo determined that I might be a helpful ally to his cause. He needed someone in the Tory camp. But, failing that, he set about to keep me from helping the other side."

"Oh, really, Mr. Tuckworth," Mortimer scoffed. "So are you now a political prize worth fighting over? Are Whigs and Tories bidding for your counsel? I think your opinion of yourself is a bit overvalued."

The dean turned to Lord Granby. "He made you feel that I was supporting the Whigs, didn't he?"

"Yes," Granby responded softly.

"He worked a wedge between us. I thought no man could have done that, but he did it easily."

Granby only turned away, looking very old indeed.

"And what if I did?" Jo demanded. "This is politics—"

"That's right, it's politics!" Tuckworth seemed to boil over suddenly and then to cool just as quickly. "Politics, where all is fair. Bates, you mentioned a note. Danny Trees wrote me a note, one that identified Kitty Wren as McAllister's killer, which would have put her in my hands and saved Danny's life. What happened to that note, Jo?"

Smalley looked coolly on, but his hand was groping in his waistcoat pocket and his face had gone white as milk.

Tuckworth took a paper out of his own pocket. "Taggart, did you deliver this to me this morning?"

"That I done, so help me," the tavern keeper avowed. "It's addressed to you, ain't it?"

Tuckworth laid it on the table before him, and they could all see the rough word *Vicar* scrawled across it.

"Where did you come by it, Taggart?"

"Come out of Mr. Smalley's fancy waistcoat as he set me to launderin'. Most dreadful bloodstains all over it. Couldn't get 'em out nohow."

The dean opened the note and looked at it again. Then he glanced over the top at Jo Smalley. "Jo, last night you said repeatedly that you'd never met Kitty Wren before, that she sought you out and not the other way around. You said it in front of Chief Constable Hopgood and Mr. Amaldi." Tuckworth folded up the note again, and now they could all see the blood splattered on the back. "Is that what you still say, Jo? Or did you know someone would turn her over, leave a message at my door? Did you wait for Danny to show up and steal the note? You found Kitty through Danny Trees and then, when Danny went into hiding, you used her to follow Bates and find Danny. You took her with you when you tried to lure Danny over to your side, to be your man among the Tories. Only Kitty had her own schemes you weren't in on."

Every head turned to Smalley, who sat there, grinning broadly. "You're a bloody marvel, and no denyin'. Pieced it all together, right as you please." He laughed easily and leaned back in his chair. "So, what've you got me on? Let's say tamperin' with evidence and be done, eh? Little Kitty admits I didn't kill the boy. I just happened to be there. Moved things around a bit to give 'em the proper look. Hell, I been charged with tamperin' before now, and got off. Just one of the risks of the profession."

"Is attempted murder a risk of the profession?"

Jo stopped laughing. "What? Who'd I—"

"Kitty Wren, last night. You made a great deal of noise about arranging things just so, right down to Hopgood's revolver. You meant to kill Kitty and that would be an end of it."

Jo squinted at the dean, sizing up what Tuckworth knew, what he could prove. "And if I set it up so pretty, why didn't I do it?"

"Because you couldn't. Because it's not so easy to kill someone as you thought. It seems so simple to aim a gun and pull a trigger. But actually to do it, to take a life with your own hands . . ." The dean's voice trailed off to somewhere black inside his heart.

For an instant, silence descended on the room, stifling the breath of every man present. Then Jo Smalley said quietly, "I don't think you can prove it."

"I think I can."

"On the word of that girl and a slip of old paper?"

Tuckworth looked slowly about the table. "That girl is the only one in all of this who hasn't lied to me, not once. Besides, I've spoken to Semple."

Jo looked very thoughtful at this.

"What's Semple to do . . . do with it?" Padgett asked.

"The riot, last night," Tuckworth explained. "Jo required a diversion, something that would throw the plans for capturing Kitty into confusion. That way he could seem to be organizing an elaborate rescue for Wiley, when in reality he was plotting a murder."

Hopgood leaned forward. "But how could he—"

"Semple. That was his man in Bellminster. Abraham Semple is the one who introduced me to Jo. I went to him this morning, just to ask what he knew about you, Jo, how you happened to come to Bellminster in the first place. Semple doesn't have your capacity for carrying guilt. He told me everything. He wrote to the Whigs and they sent you in answer. And last night, before you appeared at Hopgood's office, you visited Semple, had him arrange to turn his Whigs out in force, knew that a riot would develop, and that was just what you needed to confound your false rescue and mask your violence in the general mayhem. Or do you have another reason for why a man leading a rescue stops off on the way to arrange a riot?"

Jo sat for a moment, staring at Tuckworth. "Well," he said at last, "is this how you win elections in Bellminster?"

Tuckworth stared back at him and muttered, "Damn the election."

CHAPTER XXIX
THE DEAN OF BELLMINSTER CATHEDRAL

I 'm sorry."

Tuckworth and Granby stood huddled together in the coach yard of the Arms, the first freeze of the coming winter drifting about them. They were old men, and they felt it to their bones.

Tuckworth tried to look as if Lord Granby's apology were unnecessary. "Really," he demurred, "old friends like us—"

"Old friends like us should have known better. I'm sorry."

The dean reached out a hand and lightly tapped Granby's wrist. And that was that.

"Well," Tuckworth went on, "it seems Bick has a clear field at last."

Granby shook his white head. "Bick's damaged goods. Suppose I'll have to go with Wilfred Cade. Only chap left, and he knows it."

"Is he?" But Tuckworth still cared nothing for who might be the next Member for Bellminster, less than nothing now. He only watched as the men he had just entertained filed away in the orange half-light of an autumn afternoon, Bates and Padgett, Bick and Cade going their separate ways, each man alone, parted by a gulf from the others. Raphael trailed forlornly behind, wrapped in his own misery. The only party to leave as a group was that going back to Constabulary House, Hopgood and Wiley, with Jo Smalley between them.

Smalley paused as he crossed the yard and glanced at the dean. He looked, not angry or injured, or even resigned, but hesitant, as though he feared that Tuckworth might be angry, or injured. Then, pulling Hopgood down so that he might whisper in his ear, Smalley led his companions over to where Tuckworth and Granby stood by.

"Well," Jo said, as freely as though they had just met in some park on a Sunday stroll, "I do hope your jail has comfortable accommodations. I've spent the night in some frightful holes." He shuddered.

"I expect Hopgood will see to your needs as admirably as you might wish," the dean replied.

"Will he, now?" Jo looked up at the chief constable, his eyes glinting. "Then I hope he'll take to callin' me Jo. So far, all he's said o' me is 'the prisoner this' and 'the prisoner that.' Makes a man feel peculiar."

Tuckworth felt a smile wriggle at his lips, and he marveled at the composure of the man. But he managed to suppress his smile, and he said nothing.

"Well, I'll be goin', then," Jo announced, as if his coach were waiting for him. "No harsh feelin's, eh?" He stuck his small hand out to Tuckworth. The dean took it without hesitation, almost in spite of a reluctance he thought more proper to the moment. He could not, even now, be wholly unmoved by Jo's good humor.

"That's right," Jo went on with a grin more sincere than he had ever grinned before. "And your lordship," he added, removing his hand from Tuckworth's and stretching it out toward Granby, who took it easily. Then, with a smart bow and a last wink, Jo turned away with Hopgood and Wiley beside him, starting the long walk to Constabulary House.

The dean turned to Lord Granby when they were out of Jo's

hearing. "Do you think anything too bad will happen with him?" he asked.

"That one?" Granby answered. "He'll be back about his business inside a week. Powerful friends, you know."

A week. Kitty Wren would likely hang inside a week, Tuckworth thought, and the thought troubled him as only one last death to end this crescendo of violence.

"Mr. Tuckworth!" Mortimer approached, looking severe and officious. "Mr. Tuckworth, a word. You said in there that Abraham Semple was at the heart of all this."

The dean's expression grew a shade darker. "I don't recall saying anything of the sort."

"He sent for that malicious imp, that Smalley."

Tuckworth shook his head. "Semple only wrote to the Whigs in London. They sent Jo Smalley to us."

"Yes," the rector said with a smile aimed at Lord Granby. "A fit representative of a conniving party. Now, as to the question of Semple's further employment—"

"There is no question about that," the dean said firmly, each clipped word a knife to cut off the rector's objections.

"I quite agree with you. The man must be sacked. Such betrayal—"

"Semple will not be sacked."

Mortimer, curiously satisfied with this response, allowed the dean's statement to hang for a moment in the air for his lordship's benefit. "Are you saying, Mr. Tuckworth, that you will harbor under the aegis of the cathedral an avowed enemy to his lordship?"

"Enemy," the dean repeated with disgust. "The man's a Whig, not an assassin."

"It would appear that there is little to note between the two. I believe you just orchestrated the arrest of a Whig for attempted murder."

"Semple had nothing to do with that, nothing at all. In fact," and the dean pulled himself up to his full, middling height as he spoke, "I've personally assured Semple of his continued employment."

"*You* have done so?"

"As dean of the cathedral, I believe it's my right to hire whom I please."

"And it pleases you to employ a man who defied Lord Granby, defied Mr. Bick and the whole town?"

"The Tories are not the whole town, Mortimer. Nor are you."

"Nor are you perhaps the entirety of the cathedral." The rector glanced tellingly at Lord Granby.

His lordship coughed and turned to the dean. "Semple's a good man, is he?"

"Very."

"Sound builder?"

"Quite sound."

"No bad habits? Doesn't drink too much?"

"I have never seen him drunk."

Granby nodded sagely. "Well, if his only sin is being a Whig, I think we can forgive him that, eh, Mortimer?"

Mortimer was no fool. He glanced at the two men, their easy manner, his lordship's renewed humor, the dean's relaxed confidence, and he saw how things were in an instant. He was sufficiently adept not to show his disappointment. "You must pardon me, Mr. Tuckworth," he went on with a magnanimous bow and a mirthless grin. "If I have offended, it's only in deference to his lordship. His lordship has a too humane and forgiving spirit. Like one of the early church father's."

"I'm not *that* old," grumbled Granby.

The rector chuckled. "It was not my intention to imply so. I only—"

Tuckworth coughed. "We understood you, Mortimer. No need to go on."

"I merely—"

"Listen to the dean, Mortimer," Granby advised. "Always listen to the old men. You'll hear either wisdom or folly, and either one's good for the soul." His lordship laughed drolly at his own rather apt witticism.

Tuckworth did not stay long in the coach yard. Aside from the remarkable chill in the air, he had other business that required his attention, worthwhile business, anxious business. He had what he hoped was good news to impart, but he knew that it must be imparted carefully, in just the right way, or it might turn into bad news quickly enough.

He found Raphael exactly where he expected to find him, milling about the square, and his thoughts were divided between the cathedral and the vicarage, images of his two lost loves.

"You know," the dean said as he came up from behind, "I must admit, in a certain sort of soft, late afternoon light, with the sun shooting up from below, and maybe a few low clouds to deflect the rays, it doesn't look quite so much like a ruined vessel."

"I can see that it's beautiful," Raphael conceded, and in that concession a great deal was left unsaid, that he could not re-create that beauty any longer, that he could only recognize it, feel it, but not make it.

"Beautiful?" Tuckworth made an impatient sound. "Beauty's not even half, not a tenth of what it stirs in you. But, I'm no artist. Come on, let's walk about inside." And the two set off for what the dean persisted in calling the inside of the roofless cathedral. They passed the workmen leaving for the day and strolled for a long time in silence and solitude, each man alone. The dean and the artist had done this many times before when the cathedral was whole and lofty, the light sifting through the colors of the glass, sprinkling life with art, yet they had never shared such a moment since the fire. It was as though they, or Raphael at least, feared to acknowledge the loss of something more than the cathedral, more than just the building.

As they walked, Tuckworth watched his friend closely, and he was encouraged by the little signs he saw. Raphael went up to the columns still standing and laid his fingers against them, searching for cracks, perhaps. His eyes were drawn to the work on the floor, the paving stones and the grave markers, and sometimes he would frown and sometimes he would nudge a leaf or a stone away with his foot, but he seemed to want to examine everything. He had known the cathedral intimately, before the fire, had painted it repeatedly, studied its history and architecture, knew which saints had stood in which niches and which chapels were consecrated to which saints.

"You've been meaning to talk with me about something," Tuckworth said suddenly.

"About my leaving."

"This month."

"Before Christmas."

The dean nodded. "Seems a shame."

Raphael was silent again, and the dean wondered what it was about men, young men or old men hardly mattered, but men as a race of creatures, that kept them from saying with their tongues what their hearts were feverish to speak.

"This is ridiculous," the dean blurted out at last. "Look, lad, you're flailing about because you're afraid you've lost your gift." Raphael only looked down at the markers, kicking the dust about. "You think if you go out there somewhere, you'll find the inspiration that's abandoned you, and you very well might be right. A change of life is a good thing, sometimes. A man needs to shake up his insides a bit and see how things settle. But there are different ways to go about the shaking."

Raphael did not raise his head, but his foot had stilled.

"Here's my offer. You need employment, something to busy yourself with while your insides settle. But it must be something artistic, right? So work for me."

Raphael looked up. "What?"

"Work for me, here in the cathedral. Semple's a good man, but he builds stores and flats and factories. Lots of brick, but not much art. I need someone who can help him, work alongside him, to make sure when this place goes back up again, it won't look like that blasted mill."

Slowly, Raphael's eyes turned upward, to the walls, the columns, the sky.

"I've already talked to Semple. He's willing. The man owes me a good turn, but he's agreeable to it, too. You know this place as well as anyone. So, earn your bread as an artist here. Let this be your canvas. Oh, you can paint as much as you like, when you feel like it. You might even manage some of those illustrations for Leigh Hunt that he wrote about. But this," and the dean's hands spread wide, "this can be your artwork, too."

"This?" The thought was too impossible for Raphael to grasp all at once. "This?"

Tuckworth glanced up. "All my life, I've thought of it as just my home, but mine, you know. Something personal. You can do the same, Raphael. I want you to. We want you to."

Raphael looked at the dean through narrowed eyes. "Does Lucy know?"

Tuckworth shook his head. "This is between you and me. A proposition of business. But I won't interfere between you and Lucy."

"There's not much between us, these days," Raphael groused.

"Well, think of this as another chance."

"I don't know." The young artist looked over toward the chapel that led directly into the vicarage. "I don't know. Things have been . . . well, not good."

Tuckworth sighed. "Raphael, you've been very troubled lately. We've all seen it. But your troubles have become her troubles. That means something, I think."

Raphael was quiet again.

"Look, you needn't decide right away, but go on into the vicarage and talk it over with Lucy. You'll know soon enough if she
likes the idea, and maybe that will help decide you."

Raphael gave the dean one last look, grateful and unsure and almost frightened, and then he turned and walked calmly to the vicarage door.

The dean watched him disappear, heard the door that led into
his study open and close. Then, he turned and wandered back out
to the top of the steps overlooking the spreading twilight of Cathedral Square. The oncoming night was already creeping into the
corners of the town, tossing dried leaves about, stirring up tiny
whirlwinds of dust. Men and women scurried against the promised
cold, retreating to the warmth of their hearths, their families. A
few souls scampered into the Granby Arms for a quick touch of another kind of warmth, and the dean smiled. Were these people
truly rioting in the streets not twenty-four hours ago? Perhaps,
Tuckworth thought. Perhaps they were, but things seemed settled
now. Bellminster felt strangely at peace, and so did he. How suddenly things can return to what they once were, if one only lets it
happen. Indeed, it seems to happen whether one lets it or not. The
world finds its own place and it's up to men to settle into it. That's
likely what *comfort* means.

When had he been in such good spirits before? Not for a long
while, he knew. His thoughts turned back to the vicarage, to those
two young people charting out the course of their lives, and the
idea thrilled him, reminded him of when he sat down with Eleanor
once, two other young people, and they had determined together
that he should accept the post of vicar, to make Bellminster their
home. So many years since.

A solitary star flickered in the soft blue of the sky, silent herald
of a million others soon to be lit. Dean Tuckworth thought of his
wife, and of their home, and he smiled again.